Praise for Lancaster County Secrets

The Choice

"Fisher's writing brings that Amish sense of peace into your own world. *The Choice* brings an entirely new perspective to the Amish way of life. You will love it!"
—Kristin Billerbeck, author of *What a Girl Wants*

"A story of endearing characters. . . . Fisher writes with a fresh mix of humor and depth, splashing raw emotion onto the pages. I guarantee your heart will be touched."
—Ginger Kolbaba, founding editor of Kyria.com, former editor of *Today's Christian Woman*, and author of *Desperate Pastors' Wives*

"Fisher kicks off a refreshing new series, Lancaster County Secrets, with characters that are strong, both in body and spirit."
—Romantic Times

The Waiting

"More than just a story of the Amish, *The Waiting* is the story of a woman, sometimes triumphant, sometimes struggling, carried through turbulent times by a plain faith."
—Lisa Wingate, national bestselling author of *Tending Roses* and *Never Say Never*

"In *The Waiting*, Suzanne Woods Fisher takes the sweet story expected in Amish fiction and adds a kick of realism. I treasured my time with Jorie King and the whole Zook family, sharing their grief and laughter—what a lovely read."
—Sarah Sundin, author of Wings of Glory series

The SEARCH

Books by Suzanne Woods Fisher

Amish Peace: Simple Wisdom for a Complicated World
Amish Proverbs: Words of Wisdom from the Simple Life

ೋ LANCASTER COUNTY SECRETS ೪

The Choice
The Waiting
The Search

❧ LANCASTER COUNTY SECRETS ❧
Book 3

The SEARCH

A NOVEL

Suzanne Woods Fisher

DOUBLEDAY LARGE PRINT HOME LIBRARY EDITION

Revell
a division of *Baker Publishing Group*
Grand Rapids Michigan

© 2011 by Suzanne Woods Fisher

Published by Revell
a division of Baker Publishing Group
P.O. Box 6287, Grand Rapids, MI 49516-6287

Printed in the United States of America

ISBN 978-1-61129-084-4

Scripture used in this book, whether quoted or paraphrased by the characters, is taken from the King James Version of the Bible.

Published in association with Joyce Hart of the Hartline Literary Agency, LLC.

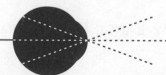

This Large Print Book carries the
Seal of Approval of N.A.V.H.

For Steve,
who has been such a supportive
and kind husband
that nobody would believe it if I were
to write him into a book!
Thank you with all of my heart.

farm needed sprucing up. So sauwer wie gschleckt. *It was as clean as a whistle.* The vegetable garden ran neat and tidy from the kitchen steps down to the greenhouse, beside the yard where she stretched her clothesline. Why, hardly a rose petal dared to wilt without Bertha flying out to the fields with a pair of pruning shears in her big hands. And besides that, folks visited each other all the time. But then Billy remembered that something was not quite right between Bertha and Jonah, her son, Bess's father. He had left years before. Billy didn't know what had caused the rift, but he knew enough not to ask. Bertha could be private like that, keeping her business to herself.

"Could you tell me something about Bess?" Billy had asked Bertha the other day as he helped her turn the mattress in the spare bedroom she was readying for Bess.

Bertha flipped her end of the mattress and let it slip into the wooden bed frame with a soft sough. "Like what?"

"Well, how old is Bess now?" He vaguely remembered a towheaded,

1

It was a June morning, hazy with summer's heat, and Billy Lapp was already bone tired. Only one person on earth could wear out an eighteen-year-old farm boy, and Billy happened to be her hired hand. For over two weeks now, Bertha Riehl had met him at the barn door of Rose Hill Farm with a to-do list that seemed to grow longer with each passing hour. Bertha's granddaughter, Bess, was coming for a summer visit, and Bertha wanted the farm so spic-and-span clean a body could eat off the barn floor. Which, Billy knew, meant he would be the one scrubbing that barn floor until it shone.

He didn't know why Bertha felt her

skinny wisp of a girl coming in from Ohio a few years back when Samuel, Bertha's husband, passed.

Bertha raised an eyebrow at him, as if she thought his motives were highly suspect. "Old enough," she said, lifting her big chin. "But too young for you."

Billy sputtered. "I wasn't asking for that. Besides, me and Betsy—" He stopped abruptly. He knew how Bertha Riehl felt about his Betsy Mast, and he didn't want another lecture about thinking with your head and not your nether regions, a comment at which he took offense. But that was Bertha Riehl for you. She didn't mince words and she didn't hold back her opinions. And she had plenty of both.

On this sunny day, Bertha handed him a broom. "When you're done sweeping out the hay loft, you need to clean out the ashes in the chimbley place." She bent over to pick up her favorite rooster, a fourteen-year-old leghorn named Otto, who followed her around the farm. Bertha tucked Otto under her arm, football-style, and headed up the hill to the farmhouse. Her left side was flanked by Boomer, a big black dog who had appeared one day and never left.

"You gonna finally cook that ol' rooster for dinner, Bertha?" Billy said, grinning.

"Been giving it some serious thought," she called over her shoulder, stroking Otto's feathers like he was a pampered housecat.

Bertha was always threatening Otto was going to end up as Sunday's stew, but Billy knew better. Bertha Riehl was all bluff and bluster. Well, mostly bluff and bluster. He couldn't deny she had a way of intimidating folks that was a wonder to behold. It had happened to Billy only once, when he made the mistake of asking her if she was six feet tall. Bertha planted her fists on her deluxe-sized hips and narrowed her eyes at him. "I am five feet twelve inches." Then she stared him down until he was sure he had shrunk an inch or two, right in front of her.

From the kitchen door of the sprawling brick-and-frame farmhouse, Bertha turned and hollered at Billy. "Es is noch lang net faercih wann's yuscht halwe gedus is!" *Half done is far from done!*

He dashed into the barn and picked up where he left off, sweeping the concrete floor with a dash and a fury. One thing to be grateful for, he thought as hay and dust flew up around him, the day of Bess's arrival had finally come.

Jonah Riehl was seeing his daughter, Bess, off at the bus station in Berlin, Ohio. He handed her a ham sandwich for lunch and bus fare for the return ticket home. Bess would be spending the entire summer at his mother's farm in Stoney Ridge, Pennsylvania. His mother had written recently to say she had suffered through some female surgery and could Bess please come? She was in dire need of someone to help.

Jonah knew it couldn't be true that his mother needed help. Bertha had lived in Stoney Ridge all of her life and had plenty of sisters, cousins, and neighbors she could count on. Wasn't that what being Plain was all about?

And yet he couldn't rest easy telling his mother that Bess wouldn't come this summer. His mother was getting up there in years, and she was the type who had never been young to begin with. A few years back, Jonah's father, Samuel, had an accident while cutting timber. A big tree fell into a smaller tree, and the smaller trunk snapped under the weight, striking Samuel with terrific force in the forehead. He died seven days later. After his father's funeral, Jonah had invited his mother to come live with them in Ohio. She said no, she wanted to stay on the home place. Still, he knew his mother had a difficult time, losing her partner of so many years. Bertha Riehl did like she always did: she dug in her heels and made do with life as it was.

So, in the end, Jonah showed Bess the letter from his mother.

"The whole summer?" Bess shook her head. "I can't leave you, Dad. You need me around here."

He couldn't deny that. It was just

the two of them rattling around in the house. He hadn't wanted to think of summer without his Bess—much less about the fact that she was growing up so quickly. It wouldn't be long before boys would start buzzing around her. Too soon, she would have a life of her own. It was the natural order of things, he knew, the way things were meant to be, but it still grieved him to think of it. So much so that he had written a letter to his mother to say he couldn't spare Bess.

That very afternoon, before he had a chance to mail the letter, Bess came home from school and announced a change of heart. She would go to Stoney Ridge, after all. "It's the right thing to do, and you're always telling me that we need to do the right thing," she said with a dramatic flair.

It still puzzled him why she had flip-flopped on the topic.

Now the loudspeaker was announcing the bus's departure, and Jonah's eyes got blurry. "Be careful, Bess," he said, "because—"

"—because you think I'm five, not fifteen." She smiled at him.

Jonah clamped his mouth shut. Bess teased him that each time he said goodbye to her, even as she left for school each morning, he would add the caution, "Be careful, because . . ." *Because . . . I won't be there to protect you. Because . . . accidents happen.* He knew that to be true. At any given moment, anything at all could happen. He brushed a few stray hairs from her forehead and gave her shoulders a quick squeeze, his way of saying that he loved her and would miss her.

As the bus pulled out of the station and Bess waved goodbye to her father, it was her turn for blurry eyes. She had visited Stoney Ridge only one other time, for her grandfather's funeral. That time, her father was with her. Now, it was just her. At the other end of the trip—Mammi. And no Daadi to soften her grandmother's rough edges. Bess had adored her grandfather. He came to visit them in Ohio every other year—

as often as he could. He was a tenderhearted man, as lean and lanky as
Mammi was wide and round.

As Bess watched the phone lines
swoop up and down to each pole
along the road, she remembered what
wouldn't be there—no phone in the
barn, like at home. No bicycles, only
scooters. And no indoor plumbing.
When she asked her father why her
grandmother still used a privy despite
knowing that their district allowed
plumbing, he told her that his mother
was a woman who held on tight to the
old ways. "If it isn't broke, why fix it?"
was her life motto, he said.

Hours later, when the Greyhound
bus pulled into Stoney Ridge, Bess
climbed down the steps onto the sidewalk. The driver yanked her suitcase
from the belly of the bus and thumped
it down next to her. There Bess stood
at the end of the world with all her
worldly possessions. Her suitcase and
Blackie, her cat.

Blackie had traveled in a picnic hamper and spent most of the trip trying to
claw his way out. As Bess set down

the hamper and looked around, a small knot of fear rose in her throat. She assumed her grandmother would be here waiting for her. What if she had forgotten Bess was coming? What if no one came to meet her? How would she ever find the farmhouse? Maybe her grandmother had gotten even sicker since her female surgery. Maybe Bess had come too late and Mammi had up and died. Bess had to shield her eyes from the late afternoon sun, beating down on her. She was tired from the long, hot ride and briefly thought about getting back on the stuffy bus to head home. Home to her father, Ohio, and all that was familiar.

Bess sat down on top of her suitcase. These were the moments in life when she wondered if her mother was up there in heaven looking down at her now and maybe trying to figure out how to help her. She loved imagining what her mother was like, what she'd say or do. She never tired of hearing stories about her from her father. She hoped that she might be able to find out even more from her grandmother this summer. That is, assuming she could ever locate Mammi. She shaded her eyes to look as far down the street as she could.

Bess let out a sigh of relief when she saw a horse and a gray-topped buggy veering around the corner. The buggy tipped so far to the right, Bess worried it might topple right over. The horse stopped abruptly right next to Bess, and the buggy tipped even more sharply as her grandmother disembarked. Land sakes, but she was enormous. Bess hadn't seen Mammi in three years, and she was even bigger. Taller still with her large black bonnet. She had several chins with wattles like a turkey. She drew nearer to Bess till she blotted out the sun.

"Where's your father?" Mammi asked, looking up and down the platform.

"He didn't come," Bess said. "I'm old enough to travel alone."

For a long moment, Mammi stared at her. Then something passed through those dark brown eyes, something Bess couldn't quite make out. Irritation? Or disappointment, maybe? Whatever it was, she shook it off in a flash.

"Old enough, are you?" Mammi hooked her hands on her hips and looked Bess up and down. "You look like you need a dose of salts and a square meal." The picnic hamper in Bess's hand quivered and Mammi noticed. She pointed to it. "What's that?"

"Blackie," Bess said. "My cat."

"Hoo-boy," Mammi said. "Better be a good mouser."

With a powerful arm, she swung Bess's suitcase aboard the buggy, lifting it high as if it was a feather. "Well, make haste." She climbed into the buggy and Bess hurried to join her. A big black dog with a muzzle of white hair sat in the back and leaned his head forward to sniff Bess. He must have decided Bess passed inspection because he gave her ear a lick. "That's Boomer," Mammi said. "He showed up out of the blue one day after my Samuel passed."

"Boomer?" Bess asked, trying to push the dog back. "Where'd you get a name like Boomer?" The dog sniffed out the hamper with great interest. Blackie let out a hissing sound and Boomer drew back.

Mammi shrugged. "Wait'll you hear his bark. Sounds like a blast of dynamite."

Boomer settled down onto the buggy floor and fell asleep.

"A good guard dog," Bess said, trying to be friendly.

Mammi snorted, but she dropped a big hand to stroke Boomer's head. "The day that dog barks at anything worth barking at is the day there'll be white blackbirds in the sky."

"Mammi, do you want me to drive? You must not be feeling too well after your female surgery and all." Bess hoped she might say yes. She enjoyed driving horses. Some of her fondest memories were sitting with her father on the plow, holding the giant draft horses' reins in her small hands, his big hands covering hers.

"Female surgery?" Mammi gave her a blank look. "Oh. Oh! Had my teeth pulled." She opened her mouth wide and clicked her teeth. "Store-bought choppers. As good as new."

Then what am I doing here? Bess wondered.

Mammi slapped the horse's reins and it took off with a start, as if they were heading to a fire. But instead of turning down the road that would take them to Rose Hill Farm, Mammi steered the horse to a little bakery called The Sweet Tooth. She stopped under a shade tree and wrapped the reins on a low-hanging branch. "Bet you're hungry. Let's go get us something to eat." She turned to Boomer, who had a hope to go in with her. She waved her finger at him to say no. Boomer hung his head and settled back down for another nap.

Bess *was* hungry. The last few months, she had grown so quickly, she was always hungry. But it sur- prised her that Mammi was willing to shell out money to pay for premade food. Her father said that his mother's cooking skills surpassed most every- one in the county. And she was thrifty! Mammi never bought anything new or threw anything away; even her letters were written on the backs of old bills.

Bess followed and waited in line behind Mammi at the bakery counter. An older woman standing at the counter gave a double take when she saw Mammi. The woman had a massive pile of braided hair, like a coiled snake, on top of her head. Bess wondered how she managed to sleep at night.

The woman recovered from her surprise. She put a hand to her chest. "Bertha Riehl, as I live and breathe."

"Dottie Stroot," Mammi said. "And I hope you are still living and breathing."

"Have you finally decided to let me sell your rose petal jam in my bakery?"

"I have not," Mammi said firmly.

Mrs. Stroot sighed. "Folks are asking me for it all the time, Bertha. They can't always find you to buy it up at the farm."

"I'm busy."

"I'd give you a generous cut."

"For my own jam?" Mammi stared her down, and Bess saw Mrs. Stroot start to crumble.

In a longsuffering voice, Mrs. Stroot

asked, "Is there something you came in for today?"

"I want to talk to that one." Mammi pointed in the kitchen area, to the back of a girl in an apron and uniform who was putting a pie in a pink box, then carefully tying it with string.

Mrs. Stroot looked puzzled but called out, "Lainey. This lady wants you to wait on her." An oven buzzer went off and Mrs. Stroot quickly forgot Mammi to hurry to the kitchen.

Without looking up, the girl named Lainey called out, "Be with you in a minute." Bess saw her write something on top of the pink box and slip the cap back on her pen. The girl whirled around to face Mammi and froze. Then she stiffened up straight and swallowed hard. Bess was getting the feeling that people often had to swallow hard when they encountered her grandmother. She felt the same way.

"Bertha Riehl," Lainey said, faint and far off.

Bess had it wrong. Lainey wasn't a girl at all. She was a small woman, probably in her mid-twenties. She was very pretty. Her hair—nearly coal black—was cut short and curly. Her thickly lashed eyes were the color of blueberries that grew in her father's garden. Her complexion was perfection, as delicate as bone china.

"Lainey O'Toole," Mammi said flatly in return. "Last time I laid eyes on you, you were ten years old and so thin I could almost see the sun shining through you. You've gone and grown up."

Lainey swallowed again. "It's good to see you, Bertha."

"This here is Bess." Mammi indicated Bess with a thumb, without saying she was her granddaughter. Mammi never told more than the minimum.

Lainey gave Bess a brief nod, then turned back to Mammi. "I've been meaning to pay you a call since I came back to Stoney Ridge."

"Good. I'll expect you for Sunday noon dinner." Mammi looked through the glass counter. She pointed to a cherry tart. "You make those?"

Lainey nodded. "Just this morning."

"I'll have one. Make it two. And a

cup of coffee." She glanced at Bess. "What about you?"

"A Danish please," Bess answered. "And a coffee too."

"Make it milk," Mammi said. "And best stick to those cherry tarts. If those are as good as I remember, you'd be a fool to miss 'em." She paid Lainey for the baked goods and took her coffee to a small table by the window.

Bess asked her grandmother how she knew her.

"Who?" Mammi asked, the picture of surprise.

"The bakery lady. Lainey."

"She grew up around here. Then she left."

Mammi didn't offer up another word. She ate with the fork in one hand, the knife in the other, polished off her two cherry tarts and then eyed Bess's. Bess quickly stuffed it into her mouth. It was the finest cherry tart she had ever tasted, with a crumbly crust and cherries that were sugared just right and still tart. Soon, Mammi was ready to go, and she looked at Bess pointedly.

Bess guessed that when Mammi was ready, she'd better be.

That was another odd thing about Mammi—as big as she was, she could move like greased lightning. In a twinkling, she was at the door, pointing at Lainey. "Sunday noon, then." It was a statement, not a question.

The bakery lady looked a little pale but gave a nod.

Lainey O'Toole watched Bertha Riehl walk out the door and climb into the buggy. Bertha had always been a big, husky woman, now even bigger than Lainey remembered. Older, too, but she still moved along like a ship under full sail. And beside her was the young girl with platinum blond hair under an organza prayer cap that was shaped differently from the Lancaster heart-shaped cap. She had white lashes that framed her wide blue eyes. They made an odd pair. The girl turned back to wave at Lainey, as if she knew she was being watched. That young girl seemed as jumpy as a cricket. But those blue eyes—they were the color of a sapphire.

As surprised as Lainey was to see Bertha Riehl walk into the bakery, she was relieved too. She had wanted to see Bertha again and wasn't sure how to go about it. She'd already been in Stoney Ridge for two weeks and hadn't mustered up the courage to head to Rose Hill Farm. Bertha wasn't the kind of woman you could just walk up to and start asking personal questions. She could just imagine the way Bertha would stare her down, until Lainey's mind would go blank and she would forget why she was there. Like it did only fifteen minutes ago, when she turned and found herself face-to-face with her in the bakery.

Still, there were things only Bertha could tell her. It was the reason she was in Stoney Ridge in the first place.

Lainey had a plan. She was on her way to attend the Culinary Institute of America in upstate New York—she had scrimped and saved every penny for tuition since she was eighteen. She finally had enough money, was accepted, and was eager for her new life to begin. The school term didn't start until September, but she wanted to find a place to live and get settled. She thought she could pick up a wait-ress job to tide her over. Lainey liked planning her future. It was a trick she had learned years ago. Making plans gave her great comfort; she always felt better with a plan in place—like she had some control over her life.

Two weeks ago, Lainey packed up everything she owned and said a teary goodbye to her two best friends, Robin and Ally. She was going to make a quick pass through Stoney Ridge on her way to New York. At least, it was going to be a quick stop until her eleven-year-old VW Beetle sputtered to its death in front of The Sweet Tooth and she went inside to borrow the phone. Ap-parently, the bakery owner had just put up a sign for help wanted and as-sumed Lainey had come in to apply.

"Can you bake?" the owner, Mrs. Stroot, asked.

"Once I won first prize at the county fair for my cherry tart," Lainey said

truthfully. She was just about to explain that she only came in to make a
phone call, when Mrs. Stroot cut her
off and gave a decided nod.

"You're hired," Mrs. Stroot said. "I'm
desperate. My best girl quit this morning and my other best girl is out with
bunion surgery. I'm busier than a one-
armed wallpaper hanger. Here's an
apron and there's the kitchen."

Lainey tried, several times, to inject
that she wasn't going to be in town
very long, but Mrs. Stroot was more
of a talker than a listener. She pointed
to a building across the street as she
dialed the phone. "See that brick building across the street? The landlord happens to be my very own sister—" she
held a finger in the air when someone
answered the phone—"Ellie? I found
you a boarder for that room you got
available. What's that? Turn your telly
down." She rolled her eyes at Lainey
and whispered, "She doesn't appreciate being interrupted during *General
Hospital*." Ellie must have said something because Mrs. Stroot's attention
riveted back to the phone. "A lady

boarder. Uh-huh, uh-huh." She covered the mouthpiece. "Do you smoke?"

Lainey shook her head.

"No, Ellie. She doesn't smoke." Mrs. Stroot covered the mouthpiece again. "Any pets?"

Lainey shook her head again.

"Weekly or monthly?"

"Weekly," Lainey said. "Definitely weekly. I don't plan to be here long, you see . . ." She gave up. Mrs. Stroot wasn't listening. She was asking her sister for today's update on *General Hospital*.

Lainey had to admit that God had a funny way of answering her prayers. As she set out on her road trip to New York, she had prayed that God would direct her path while she drove through Stoney Ridge. She wanted to visit only one person—Bertha Riehl. Here she was, just a few hours later, and she was employed—even though she wasn't looking for a job. And it happened to be doing the one thing in the world that Lainey loved to do: bake.

Less than ten minutes after arriving in Stoney Ridge, Lainey had a place to live and a job to bring in some cash so she wouldn't have to dig into her culinary school tuition money. Her car, the mechanic said, was a lost cause. She thought that was God's idea of a joke. He directed her path all right. To a dead stop.

The house was painfully quiet. Jonah glanced at the clock in the kitchen and counted forward an hour. Bess would be in Stoney Ridge by now, probably at Rose Hill Farm. There were hundreds of reminders of his daughter throughout the house, more than he had ever been conscious of. Dozens of images of Bess at different ages rolled through his mind: taking her first wobbly steps as a toddler, dashing to the mailbox each afternoon to meet the mailman, running barefoot from house to barn and back to house.

Taking a sip of coffee from his mug, he lifted the pages on the calendar hanging by the window and counted off. Just twelve weeks to go and she'd be back.

He wondered how Bess and his mother would be getting along. He hoped Bess would let him know just how sick his mother was. He felt worried about her, and that was a new feeling for him. In the letter, his mother said she was pining for her granddaughter and off her feed. It troubled him, that letter. It wasn't like his mother to pine. Or to be off her feed. She had a mighty appetite. He never remembered her ailing, not once, not even with a head cold.

He sighed. Something wasn't adding up. Either his mother's health was truly a concern or . . . she was up to something.

Just then, Jonah saw his neighbor and particular friend, Sallie Stutzman, coming up the drive with a casserole dish in her arms. He set down the coffee cup and went to see what Sallie had in that dish. It had been only a few hours since Bess had left, and he was already tired of his own cooking. And he was lonely.

❈

Bess was a quick learner. After one buggy ride with her grandmother, she had already figured that she should hold tight to the edge of the seat so she wouldn't slide off and land on the buggy floor when Mammi took the curves. Her grandmother drove through those country roads like a teenage boy, the buggy leaning precariously to the side. She made a tight right turn and, suddenly, there it was: Rose Hill Farm.

The farm sat in a gentle valley surrounded by rolling hills, with fields fed by a secluded, spring-fed pond. The farmhouse—a rambling house with white clapboard siding and a brick foundation—was even prettier than Bess remembered. Three years ago, when she was here for her grandfather's funeral, she remembered being impressed by the neatness of the fields, the trimmed hedges, and the cherry trees that bordered the drive. It was the same today. Her grandmother may be ancient, but she had kept up the farm in good condition, that was plain to see.

A perfume wafted past Bess, and

her eyes traveled to the fields that surrounded the house: acres and acres
of blooming roses in what used to be
pastures. The roses were at their peak.
Pinks and reds and yellows and or-
anges blurred together to create a col-
lage of color. Bess remembered that
her grandmother had written awhile
back that she had started a small business selling rose petal jams and jellies.
But *this*—this was more than a small
business.

Mammi stopped the horse under a
shade tree next to a hitching rail. "We'd
best get to work."

Oh no. Bess clutched her forehead.
"On my first day here?"

Mammi lifted a sparse eyebrow. "Es
hot sich noch niemand dodschafft."
Nobody ever worked to death.

Boomer let out an ear-busting woof
and leaped out of the buggy to run to
the fields. Mammi hopped out of the
buggy and reached a large hand to pull
Bess forward by the arm. She stopped
dead and aimed a stern look at Bess.
"A little work might put a little muscle
on them bones."

There were moments, like this one, when Bess thought it would be simpler to be English. On the bus this morning, a little girl wanted her mother to give her a snack, and when her mother refused she broke down and bawled. That's just what Bess would like to do right now, break down and bawl. Of course, she couldn't.

But oh! she was hot and tired from the bus trip and frustrated at what she had just figured out. She came to Stoney Ridge on a mission of mercy for her ailing grandmother, and the truth was that she was nothing more than another pair of hands—to pick roses. For an entire summer! Her father was right. Her grandmother was sneaky. Bess wished she had just stayed home and worked with her father on their farm. She missed him terribly. Far more than she had expected she would.

Bess heard Boomer bark again and she looked to see why the dog was causing such a ruckus. Boomer was standing on his hind legs, licking the face of a boy—or was it a young man?—and ended up knocking off his straw hat.

"That's Billy Lapp," Mammi said. "He's my hired help."

The boy pushed Boomer off of him and reached down to pat the dog's big head. Then he bent down and picked up his straw hat, knocking it on his knee a few times to shake off the dirt. Billy Lapp looked to be about seventeen or eighteen years old. Man-sized. When he stood and his eyes met hers, Bess felt her heart give a simple thump. Clearly Amish by his clothes and haircut, he was tall, broad-shouldered, with curly brown hair and roguish eyes rimmed with dark eyebrows. Hands down, he was the best-looking boy Bess had ever laid eyes on. Her heart was beating so strangely now, she thought she might fall down and faint.

Things were looking up.

2

By the time Bess woke the next morning, she could hear Mammi banging pots and pans down in the kitchen. She dressed fast, already worried by yesterday's hints that her grandmother thought she had a lazy streak. She flew down the stairs expecting to encounter a hands-on-the-hips disapproving frown, but Mammi stood in front of the range at her usual place, on gray-speckled linoleum that was worn to the floorboards. With her thumb, she pointed to the table, already set with two places. Bess slipped into her chair and Mammi slid a belly-busting breakfast in front of her.

"How do you like your eggs poached?"

"Is there more than one kind of poached egg?" Bess asked.

"Runny, soft, or hard?"

Bess looked startled. "My yolks always end up hard."

Her grandmother flipped an egg timer. "Three minutes for runny, four for soft, five for hard."

"Dad and I poach eggs for fifteen minutes."

Mammi snorted. "A yolk like that could double for a rubber ball."

Bess grinned. Blackie had done just that with a yolk, patting it around on the ground with his paws. Her father had suggested Blackie be included in a game of kickball after church one Sunday.

Where was Blackie, anyway? He had disappeared the moment he was let out of that hamper and caught full sight of Boomer, head to tail. Mammi told her not to worry, that Blackie would find a place to live in the barn. Bess was horrified. She tried to explain that Blackie was a house cat and

Mammi only scoffed. "Animals belong outside." Boomer apparently didn't qualify as an animal, because he had followed Mammi right into the house and stayed by her side like a shadow.

They bowed their heads and then dug into the meal. They ate in silence for a long while until Mammi asked, "What's your father got growing in his fields right now?"

Bess cracked the poached egg with her spoon and pulled off the shell in pieces. "He's leased out the fields to a neighbor."

Mammi broke up her egg over a piece of toast so that the yellow yolk oozed over it. "He's not farming?"

Bess looked up, surprised. "Well, his bad back made it too hard for him. So last year he started a furniture-making business and it's done well. He has orders piled up for months." Bess poured molasses into her oatmeal. She would have thought Mammi would have known such a thing. She seemed to know everything, often before it happened. But her grandmother was stunned to silence, a silence so thick that Bess could hear a wasp buzzing on the windowsill.

Mammi remained deep in thought. "It wonders me. To think of my Jonah without a farm to tend." She took off her spectacles and polished them. Then she reached into her apron pocket and pulled out a handkerchief to blow her nose. A loud honk that rattled the windows. "Allergies," she muttered, but Bess couldn't be fooled that easily. It shocked her, finding a tender spot in her grandmother. Mammi quickly recovered. She handed Bess a jar of pale pink jam. "Put that on your toast."

Bess spread some on it and took a bite. Her eyes went wide. "Oh Mammi. Oh my. Oh my goodness. Is this your rose petal jam?"

"It is," Mammi said. "It's the food of angels, if they have a choice."

Bess took more jam from the jar and spread it all over her toast, right to the edges. She took a large bite and chewed thoughtfully. It was the most delicate, delicious flavor she had ever tasted.

Mammi tried to hide a smile at Bess's

rapturous expression with a swallow of coffee. "So what else is your dad doing?"

"Not much," she said, reaching for a spoonful of jam. "Well, except . . . he's given some thought lately to getting married again."

Mammi raised an eyebrow. "About time."

She shrugged. "You know Dad. He acts like a sheep that spooks and runs off at the slightest mention of marriage. He says it's because his heart belonged only to my mother."

Mammi nodded.

Bess took a bite of toast. She took another bite, chewed, and swallowed, then frowned. "But there's a neighbor lady who's wearing down his matrimonial resistance." She hoped the glum note didn't sound in her voice.

"En grossi Fraa un en grossi Scheier sin kem Mann ken Schaade." *A big wife and a big barn will do a man no harm.*

Bess shrugged. "It's not that. I want Dad to find a wife . . ."

She felt Mammi staring at her, hard. "What's wrong with her?"

"Oh, nothing. She's . . . real cheerful. And talkative. Cheerful and talkative." *Professionally cheerful.*

Mammi raised an eyebrow. "Our Jonah is a catch."

Bess knew that. Her dad was a fine-looking man. Even her friends said so. And he was young, only thirty-five. He was well thought of in their community, by men and women alike, and nearly every single female in their district—plus two neighboring districts—had set their cap for him. Cookies and pies, invitations to dinners and picnics, one father even boldly hinted to Jonah that his dairy farm would be passed down to his only daughter if Jonah married her. But Jonah never took the bait.

Until now.

That was half the reason Bess decided to come to Stoney Ridge this summer. Her father was spending time with Sallie Stutzman, a man-hungry widow with twin six-year-old boys—and the whole notion turned Bess's stomach inside out. Sallie had a heart of gold, everyone said so, but her very presence set Bess's teeth on edge. It wasn't that there was anything wrong with Sallie, other than the fact that she never stopped talking. *Not ever.* She even talked to herself if no one was around to listen.

Bess had a hope that her father would fall in love again, and she just didn't think he was in love with Sallie. That didn't seem to be a worry for Sallie, though. Bess saw how she was weaving her way into her dad's life. She asked him for rides to church and frolics, so often that other people assumed they were a couple since they always arrived together. Sallie stopped by every day with a casserole or cake or pie. The everydayness of it all was what made the difference between Sallie and other persistent female suitors. Even Bess found herself counting on Sallie's fine cooking. Sallie usually dropped broad hints about how it would be so much easier to cook for Jonah and Bess in their own kitchen. About how their new cookstove was so much more reliable than her old temperamental one.

Her father always paled a little when

Sallie dropped those hints. Sallie kept at it, though. Bess overheard her point out to her father that every girl needed a mother, and poor Bess—poor Bess, she always called her, as if it was one word—had gone without one far too long. She needed a mother's love before it was too late.

And what could her father say to that? Sallie's dogged determination was causing her father to weaken. Just last week, he asked Bess what she would think about having a little brother or two around the house.

The truth of the matter was that Bess thought it would be a terrible idea. Sallie's twins weren't like most Plain boys. Sallie's twins were as tricky as a box of monkeys. Their idea of fun was spreading Vaseline on Bess's toilet seat. But to her father, she only said, "Well, now, that's certainly something that needs serious thought." *Long and hard.*

Her father grew pensive at her response. And that was the moment when Bess decided to come to Stoney Ridge for the summer. She may not be able to stop a marriage with Sallie from happening, but she didn't want to watch it happen.

Bess suddenly realized that Mammi's gaze was fixed on her, and she was sure her grandmother could read the dark thoughts that were darting through her mind. Her cheeks grew warm and she looked out the window. Billy was coming up the drive and gave a wave to them before he disappeared into the barn.

Mammi smacked her palms down on the table. "We got us some roses to tend." She was on her feet now, making short work of the dishes.

Not ten minutes later, they joined Billy out in the rose fields. Mammi repeated the rose petal–picking instructions she had given out yesterday. Bess didn't interrupt her to say she understood; after all, her grandmother was older than the hills.

"The best time is in the late morning, after the dew has dried and before the strong afternoon sun." Gently, Mammi held a large pink rose with the tips of her fingers and pulled it off the base. "Trim the white sections with scissors—this will save you time." She quickly snipped the white part off of each petal and then let them shower into the basket by her feet. "Next, cut the stem to the next five leaves. That's where the next bud will form."

It amazed Bess to see Mammi's chapped, man-sized hands handling the roses like they were made of spun sugar. Her own hands looked like a child's next to her grandmother's. And she was embarrassed by how soft her hands were. As careful as she tried to be, thorns kept pricking her. Within fifteen minutes, her hands were covered in cuts and scratches. And how her back ached, bent doubled over!

When they had harvested a large basketful, Mammi gave a nod to Bess to come along, and they went to the barn. Boomer trotted behind, never more than a few feet away from Mammi. Inside, Bess stopped abruptly when she noticed that the cow stanchions and horse stalls were empty. There were no animals other than Frieda, the buggy horse. She had been so distracted by the sight of Billy Lapp yesterday that she hadn't even gone into the barn.

"What happened to the animals?" The last time she was here, this barn had been filled with horses, mules, cows, and even two ugly sows.

"Couldn't take care of them without my Samuel, so I sold them at auction," Mammi said matter-of-factly. "I buy milk from a neighbor. Still have my ladies, though." She meant her hens. She loved those chickens and called each one by name. She slid the door shut behind Bess. In the center of the barn were rows of sawhorses with screen doors laid on top. "This is how we dry the petals. Lay 'em out so they can air dry. No overlaps or else they'll mold. They need to get as crisp as cornflakes."

"Why don't you just put them out in the sun to dry?" Bess asked. "That's what we do with apricots and peaches. Apples, even."

"No. I keep them in the barn and out of direct sunlight."

"Have you ever thought about drying them in a warm oven?" Bess asked.

"Once when it rained all summer, Dad put sliced up fruit in the oven to finish drying." She felt pleased with her suggestion. Maybe that was one way she could be helpful to her grandmother this summer: by pointing out ways to improve the farm. Being fifteen, Bess had some pretty good ideas about modernizing, and her grandmother had lived here since Noah's ark reached Mt. Ararat. She could use Bess's help with such things. *Like indoor plumbing.*

Mammi cast her a look as if she might be addle-brained. "Might work for fruit but not for my roses. You'll lose oil. Lose oil and you'll lose fragrance." She straightened and pressed a hand against the small of her back. "Go bring me another basketful." She handed the empty basket back to Bess. "Be quick about it. We can't pick flowers in the afternoon. It's gonna be hotter than hinges today."

Bess took the basket and went out to join Billy in the fields. Yesterday, he had left soon after she arrived so she hadn't had time to get acquainted with him. Mammi said he usually only worked a few hours a day, then needed to get home to tend to his father's farm. Bess was looking forward to getting to know Billy. She followed behind him as he worked. He culled roses from the right row of bushes, she from the left. She could see he was concentrating on the work. He kept peering at the roses as if he was learning something from them. She racked her brains for an interesting thing to say, but nothing bubbled up to the surface. Finally, Billy stopped for a moment to gaze at a golden eagle flying overhead and seemed surprised to discover she was there.

"So, Bess, where are you from?" he asked.

"Berlin, Ohio."

Billy went back to examining roses, so Bess hastened to add, "Some folks think it's Ber-Lin, like the place in Germany. But it's really pronounced Burrr-lin. Folks changed the way they pronounced it during World War I, so it would seem less German." She could tell Billy wasn't really listening. Silence fell again. She tried to come up with a topic that would create conversation. Something that would make him notice her and realize she was bright, intelligent, deep. Nothing came to mind.

He stopped at a bush and examined a few blossoms, then started picking them. "You sure don't look anything like your grandmother."

That was a good thing, in her mind. Mammi must be nearly six feet tall and half as wide.

He eyed her bright blue dress. "Is it different in Ohio? Being Amish?"

"What do you mean?" She shrugged one shoulder. "Amish is Amish."

He snorted. "That's like saying roses are roses." He put a hand on his lower back and stretched, looking out at the wide variety of blooms. "What color is your buggy?"

"Black." So maybe there were differences. Lancaster buggies had gray tops.

"Some folks think Ohio churches are more worldly than ours." He shook the basket so the petals spread out. "Can you ride bicycles?"

"Yes."

"Telephones?"

"Only in the barn."

"You drive a car?"

"Gosh, no." Billy looked so disappointed that she added, "Once I drove a neighbor's tractor, though. And I take a bus to the public school."

He whipped his head up. "You go to public school?"

"High school." Bess had just sailed through ninth grade and was in shooting distance of high school in Berlin. All that stood in the way was that dreaded algebra class. That was the other half of the reason she changed her mind about spending the summer at Mammi's. On the day she took her final exam for algebra, she decided Stoney Ridge didn't sound so bad, after all. And if she hurried about it, she could leave Berlin before report cards would be mailed home, which suited her just fine. That way, she wasn't being deceitful. She didn't know for sure that she had failed the class. She had a pretty good idea that she did, but until that report card arrived, there was a slight hope she had squeaked by.

And had she failed, well, if she were in Pennsylvania, then she couldn't possibly attend summer school in Ohio.

She searched for something—anything—to pique Billy's interest. "My dad got arrested for letting me skip school," she blurted out. Then she clapped her hand against her mouth. Why in the world did she say *that*?

Billy spun around to look straight at her.

Oh my! but he was fine looking. Those dark brown eyes nearly undid her. She felt her cheeks grow warm. "Last September, Dad said I didn't have to go to school anymore. Kids in the county right next to ours had stopped going the spring before and no one bothered them, so a few families in our district decided to quit too. But it didn't work. The truant officer came knocking on the door and took Dad to the county jail."

"What happened then?"

"He was fined and let go. And now I have to go until I'm sixteen. Ohio law." Her dad wasn't going to mess with the law anymore, he'd said more than once when she tried to convince him to let her stay home. "I can't imagine stopping school at the eighth grade." She couldn't imagine it, but she sure would enjoy it. She had often thought she had about all the education she could absorb. Especially math.

A look came over Billy's face, as if he thought she might be a very dense child. "What makes you think an education has to stop?"

That was a new thought for Bess. She gave his backside a sharp look. A book stuck out of his back pocket. She never thought it any fun to be bothering about books when you didn't have to. "My teachers say you need a formal education to get ahead in the world." Now, why did she say that? Why did her mouth not seem to be connected to her brain today?

Billy took his time answering. He pulled a few more rose blooms, snipped the petals, and tossed them in the basket. Then he lifted his chin and looked at her. "I guess it all depends on which world."

They picked blossoms in silence for

a long while. When the basket was full of rose petals, he picked it up and leaned it against his hip. "Have you followed the Wisconsin trial?"

"No."

He shook his head as if she had just arrived from the moon. "*Wisconsin vs. Yoder*. It's a big court case going on in Wisconsin right now. Might bring about changes for us."

She hated to seem ignorant, but curiosity won out over pride. "What sort of changes?"

"It's possible that we won't have to attend public schools. That we could have our own schools right in our districts. Schools that would stop at eighth grade."

Such a thought made Bess's heart sing with gladness. She . . . would . . . be . . . done . . . with . . . algebra!

He handed her the basket to take into the barn. She broke into a skip on the way there, so thrilled by the news of *Wisconsin vs. Yoder*.

Billy and Bess picked rose petals for a few more hours. The sun had already begun to punish them when Billy said it was time to quit.

"I'll be on my way," Billy told Mammi as he handed her the last basket. He put his straw hat back on. "But I'll be over tomorrow morning, first thing."

He nodded goodbye and tipped his hat slightly in Bess's direction, which made her knees feel weak. The boys in Berlin would never dream of tipping their hats to a girl.

Mammi watched him go and said to no one in particular, "He's a good one, that boy."

Bess wanted to ask Mammi more about Billy Lapp, but then she thought better of it. Mammi saved herself a lot of bother by not being the kind of person who answered nosy questions.

Mammi closed the sliding door of the barn to keep it cooler inside. "After lunch," she said, "we got us an errand to do."

❧❀❧

A few hours later, Bess hurried to keep up behind Mammi as she breezed through the Veterans Hospital in Lebanon. On the bus ride there, Mammi told her they were going to pay a visit to her brother, Simon, who was seriously ailing. Bess had heard terrifying stories about Simon, bits and pieces of his life woven together from tales her cousins whispered to her at her grandfather's funeral. She knew he was Mammi's only brother, was the youngest in the family, had always been a black sheep, and—worst of all—that he had been shunned.

But Simon was nothing like Bess expected.

She had prepared herself for a hulking brute of a man, with eyes narrowed into slits and teeth sharpened into points and horns sprouted on his head. A monster.

Instead, before her was a tired, pale-skinned old man who looked as if he was weary of living and ready to die.

Bess and Mammi stood by Simon's bedside in the ward, trying to determine if he was awake or asleep. Bess had a fleeting thought that he might have passed.

She looked at her grandmother and whispered, "Should I get a nurse?"

Mammi ignored her and leaned over him. "Wake up, Simon!" she boomed, and the room echoed.

Simon's eyes flew open. "Oh Lordy. It's the town do-gooder." He glanced at the basket Mammi held in her hands. "Did you bring your jam?"

"I did," Mammi said.

"Homemade bread?"

"It's in there." She put the basket on his bedside table. "You always did take better care of your belly than your soul."

Simon squinted at Bess. "Who's that?"

"That's Bess," Mammi answered. She eased her big self into a hard-backed plastic chair.

"Jonah—your nephew—he's my father," Bess filled in. She shifted her weight awkwardly from foot to foot while standing at the end of the bed. There wasn't any other chair to sit in. "So I guess that makes you my great uncle."

Simon's eyes opened wide, full of

mockery, as he looked Bess over. "Another holy howler." He looked at her long and hard with cold blue eyes.

She'd never seen eyes so cold. There was a touch of meanness in his thin smile. Bess felt a bead of sweat run down the valley between her shoulder blades.

Mammi was watching her. "Bess, en rauher Glotz nemmt'n rauher Keidel." *A rough log requires a rough wedge.* "Never forget that."

How could Bess remember it when she couldn't even understand it? Bess looked at her, confused, but Mammi had turned her attention back to her brother.

"Simon, you never did know beans from honey," Mammi said. "If you could put two and two together, you'd figure out by now that Bess is a relation."

"So?" Simon asked.

"So mebbe she'd be willing to get a blood test and see if she can help you out. Mebbe her bone marrow could be a match for you."

Bess's eyes went wide as quarters.

"If she's willing, that is," Mammi repeated, avoiding Bess's eyes.

※

The ride home on the bus was a silent one.

Mammi had been told by the nurse that since Bess was underage, the hospital required a parent's consent before her blood could be tested. Mammi hadn't expected that, Bess could tell. But Bess was thoroughly relieved. It wasn't easy to say no to Mammi, and yet she wasn't at all sure she wanted to have her blood tested. The blood test was pretty simple, she knew that, but what if she were a match? Giving blood was one thing. Bone marrow was entirely different. She wasn't even sure what that meant and didn't want to ask. Her only experience with bone marrow was to cook up a pot of soup and simmer the bones for a good long while. Besides, even if Simon was her great uncle, he was not a nice man. He was downright mean-hearted. Maybe it all worked out just fine, Bess decided happily. Since she was only fifteen and

her father was in Ohio—with no intention to come to Pennsylvania—there
was no possible way she could have
a blood test. Bess looked out the window and smiled. Things had a way of
working out.

"Bess," Mammi asked, one sparse
eyebrow raised, "have you ever driven
a car?"

Bess shook her head. "Just a tractor."

Mammi gave up a rare smile. "Same
thing. When we get back to Stoney
Ridge, we got us another errand to do."

Lainey O'Toole reread the letter she
had written to her friends one more
time before licking the envelope and
sealing it shut. She had written and re-
written this letter during her break today until it sounded just right.

Dear Robin and Ally,

*A moment of silence, please,
for the passing of my Beetle. It
sputtered to a stop in a little town
called Stoney Ridge, but it didn't*

*die in vain. It took its final breath
in front of a bakery called The
Sweet Tooth just as the owner
put out a help wanted sign. I kid
you not! One thing led to another
and . . . well, instead of hunting
for a temporary job in upstate
New York, circumstances dictate
that I am going to spend the
summer here. But do not worry! It
is just a short-term turn of events.*

*Love you tons and miss you
more,*
Lainey
*P.S. Did I ever mention that my
mother and I had lived in Stoney
Ridge until I turned ten?*

Satisfied, Lainey dropped the envelope into the mailbox before she
crossed the street to head to her little
rented room.

When the bus dropped Bess and
Mammi off in Stoney Ridge, Mammi
told her to keep up as she made her
way through the streets. Finally, her

grandmother found what she was looking for. She made a beeline straight to
the sheriff's car, parked by the hard-
ware store.

Mammi peered in the open window
of the sheriff's car and saw the keys
dangling in the ignition. She turned to
Bess. "Come on, big talker. Show me
what you know."

Bess's jaw dropped open. "Mammi,
you don't mean . . ."

"I do." Mammi got into the passenger seat. "Sheriff won't mind a bit.
We're good friends. I've known that
boy since he was in diapers."

"Still . . ." Her father was forever
warning her to avoid stepping into
moral mud puddles, and here she was
jumping headfirst into one of his mother's own making!

Mammi reached over and pushed
open the driver's side door. Cautiously,
Bess slipped in.

She glanced at her grandmother with
a worried look. "Seems like there are
rules . . ."

Mammi turned to give Bess one of
her surprised looks. "Es is en schlechdi

Ruhl as net zqwee Wege schafft." *It's a bad rule that doesn't work both ways.* "Never forget that." She looked straight ahead. "Let's go."

Bess sighed and prayed God would understand. She turned the ignition and the car roared to life. She opened her mouth to try once more to talk her grandmother out of this notion, but Mammi only pointed down the road. "That way."

As if Bess was driving a car made of eggshells, she shifted the gear, took her foot off the brake, and the car lurched forward. This wasn't at all like driving a tractor in an open field. She was terrified she would hit something or somebody. She drove so slowly that a few shopkeepers came outside and stared at the sight of two Plain women inching a police car down the street.

"That'll do," Mammi said after one block. "Park it over there." She pointed to the curb.

Bess pulled over and shifted the gear to park. The car lurched to a halt and the engine died. She exhaled with relief. She knew she could start the car, but she wasn't quite sure about stopping it. Her grandmother's eyes were on the rearview mirror. On her face was another of those rare smiles. Running up the road was the portly sheriff, waving his fists in the air. Mammi opened the door and climbed out of the car, prepared to meet the sheriff head-on. Bess slowly stepped out, wondering how many years a car thief would spend in prison.

The sheriff slowed to a jog and reached them, panting heavily. "Miz Riehl! What the Sam Hill were you thinking?"

"Hello there, Johnny," Mammi said, friendly as anything. "Have you met my granddaughter?"

Still panting, the sheriff looked Bess up and down without a smile.

Bess stood there, nearly dying of shame.

The sheriff hooked his hands on his hips. "*Why* would you take my police car?"

Mammi looked unusually innocent. "Bess here is visiting from Ohio. She's driven a tractor before. We just got to wondering—"

We? Bess wondered.

"—if it seemed like the same thing . . . driving a car or driving a tractor. I don't know too many folks with cars. So I figured you wouldn't mind if we borrowed yours."

"Borrowed the car? Miz Riehl, what you did was to steal a police officer's car! That's larceny! I could have you arrested."

Mammi nodded agreeably. "So be it." She stretched out her hands so that he could handcuff her.

The sheriff looked down at her fists thrust in front of him, then looked up at her, bewildered. "Miz Riehl, I'm *not* going to throw a widder lady into the pokey."

"The law is the law," Mammi said. "But I get one phone call."

"Miz Riehl, I just don't want you moving my patrol car."

"Stealing," Mammi said. "You called it stealing."

The sheriff sighed, exasperated. "Seeing as how it was recovered and no harm was done, I'll just give you a warning this time." He got in the car, closed the door, and stuck his head out the window, jutting his round chin in Bess's direction. "I've got my eye on you, young lady. You should know I got E.S.P. Extrasensory perception. I see things before they happen." He glared at her. "I don't know what kinds of trouble Amish teens get into in Ohio, but you can't get away with those shenanigans in Stoney Ridge." He looked disgusted and shook his head. "Hoodwinking a sweet little old lady into taking a joyride. You oughta be ashamed."

Bess's eyes went wide with disbelief. *Mammi? A sweet little old lady?*

Mammi frowned. Then she marched through town and down the road that led to Rose Hill Farm. Bess hurried to keep up with her, wondering what in the world her grandmother was up to and how she could ever explain this to her father.

3

Dear Dad,

Mammi and I are getting along fine, just fine. She seems to be fully recovered from her female surgery. I didn't realize that pulling a tooth or two would be considered female surgery, but she said it definitely falls under that category. And one thing I'm learning about her, it's best to just agree.

Did you know Mammi's rose business is taking over Daadi's pasture land? Those roses of hers—they're something else. In full bloom! Lots and lots of rose

*blossoms. To handpick and hand
trim. Each and every day. My
hands have been pricked by so
many thorns they look like a pin
cushion.*
  Love,
  Bess

❧

Jonah was rubbing a final coat of
stain on a picnic table ordered by Mrs.
Petersheim. She was one of his best
customers, and he had promised to de-
liver the table for a family reunion she
had planned this weekend. The humid-
ity was working against him and the
stain wasn't absorbing like it should.
He put down the rag and opened the
workshop door to let the breeze in. It
had been a hot June. Even after thirteen years, he still wasn't quite used
to the extremes of Ohio weather. Hotter in the summer than Pennsylvania
and colder in the winter. He stood by
the door, looking out over the fields of
oats planted by his neighbor. It still ate
at him, to not be able to work his fields

anymore. He missed farming. Like his father, he had always marked his year by his growing crops. He planted alfalfa on the day after the new moon. Then oats and clover went in. Corn in April, when the sap was rising in the maple trees. The seasons turned like a wheel.

It used to give him great satisfaction to see crops growing in the fields, as if he was part of something bigger. But he didn't have the physical capability to farm anymore. He had tried to keep up for years now, but it was too much for him. He wasn't the same man he was before the accident. The doctor warned him he would end up in a wheelchair if he kept asking too much from his back. "Jonah," the doctor said, "if I were you, I would consider that limp a small price to pay for still being alive."

A small price to pay? What about losing the only woman you've ever loved? What about trying to raise a child alone? What about the fact that his daughter never knew her mother?

He had worked so hard to honor

Rebecca's memory and raise Bess the way she would have wanted her raised. He created a new life for himself and Bess, and the Lord had blessed his efforts. When he finally decided to lease the fields and try his hand at furniture making, the business took off. So much so that he had taken on a partner, Mose Weaver. Mose was a lifelong bachelor, an older, quiet man who spoke with a lisp when he talked, which was seldom. Most knew Mose was silent as a tomb, a man of deep thoughts, none of them revealed. Some thought that was because he had no thoughts at all, but Jonah knew better. Mose lived with his parents, worked hard, and wanted for little. He was a fine business partner for Jonah. There was more than enough work for both of them.

Jonah had no complaints about his life. But with Bess gone this summer, and with the painful awareness that she was growing up, he knew that things were going to be changing soon. He never did like change.

And what would life look like after Bess was raised? Sallie was forever pointing that out, as if he didn't wonder about it himself.

Jonah wiped the sweat off the back of his neck. Sallie had been making loud suggestions lately about getting married. He was fond of Sallie, but the thought of getting married made his throat tighten up. There had been a time, four or five years ago, when Jonah had tried to find a new mother for Bess, but his heart wasn't in it. He wanted to love again the way he had loved Rebecca.

Sallie had different ideas about marriage. She had been a widow for less than a year and was already moving on with her life, eager to marry again. That was one thing he admired about her. She didn't hold on to the past. Just last night, she had told him that she never expected a second marriage to be like the first. "There's no feeling like that first love, when you're young and carefree and life seems filled with possibilities," she said. "But that doesn't mean that a real good friendship isn't a fine start for a marriage."

Sallie thought his ideas of marriage

were unrealistic. And she should know—she'd been married twice before.

Her boys needed a father, she had told him frankly, and his Bess needed a mother. It made perfect sense, she said.

He picked up the rag and dipped it in the can of stain, ready to finish up that table for Mrs. Petersheim. Maybe Sallie was right.

❦

The Sunday after Bess arrived in Stoney Ridge was an off-Sunday, so no church would be held. Earlier this morning, a chicken—whose pet name was Delilah—lost its head when Mammi had picked it out specially and wrung its neck off. It happened so fast that Bess felt woozy. Mammi was feeding her ladies by tossing cracked corn on the ground, making little clucking sounds at them. Suddenly, she reached down and picked up a chicken by the neck and spun it over her head, snapping its neck. Within seconds she had it on a tree stump. After plucking off the feathers and saving them in her pillow bag,

Mammi dipped those chicken parts in buttermilk and bread crumbs, fried it, whipped up biscuits to mop up the gravy, added snap beans and sliced tomatoes from the garden. Bess was sure she'd never seen a chicken go from the yard to the table so quickly. It was record time.

Mammi asked her to set the table and get it all ready for Sunday dinner, so Bess took out three servings of utensils.

Without looking up from the fry pan, Mammi said, "Make it for four."

"Why four?" Bess asked.

"You never know," Mammi answered with an air of mystery. She tucked in a wisp of gray hair that escaped her cap. In English she added, "Mebbe I got extra-century perception like the sheriff."

So Bess set the table for four. What was the point of asking?

Jonah loved this time of year. On the way to pick up Sallie and her boys for church on Sunday morning, he passed by a neighbor's house and saw the straight rows of crops in the fields, tended lovingly. He loved summer best of all. The first fruits of summer gardens would be making an appearance for lunch after meeting: deep red beefsteak tomatoes, sliced thick; cucumber salad; a pyramid of pickled peaches; bowls of luscious, plump strawberries. Yes, this was a good time of year.

He was especially looking forward to meeting today. It had been nearly a week since Bess had left, and he was starting to talk to himself just like Sallie did, he was *that* hungry for company. He felt a familiar warm feeling spread over him as he pulled into Noah Miller's yard: dozens of buggies were lined up, shoulder to shoulder, like pigs at a feeding trough.

After meeting, the men and boys ate first at the set-up tables, then cleared out of the way so the women could eat. A softball game had been started by the big boys and Jonah watched for a while. He noticed Sallie's twins were sent off to the outfield to catch fly balls. They had been pestering the big boys until they were finally given a job to do and could be out of harm's way.

Jonah walked over to join Mose, standing with a few other men under the shade of a large oak tree. Jonah half listened to the men's grave analysis about the weather they'd been having. Too little rain, they worried, a drought in the making. But then, farmers always worried about the weather. He could hear the murmur of women's voices—including Sallie's laugh, for she was always laughing—through the open kitchen window, along with the clinking of plates and forks, the thumping of bowls and platters onto the tabletops to be taken home.

Young Levi Miller sidled up to him, kicking at the ground. Levi was an awkward boy, but he adored Bess, and for that, Jonah admired him. "Any word?" Levi asked in a low voice. He began to blush, a bright red trickling its way up from his collar to the middle of his ears. They were sizable ears. They stood straight out at the side of his head.

Jonah smiled. "Nothing yet. But I'm sure she's having a good summer."

Levi was crestfallen. "All summer? Bess is going to be there all summer?"

Jonah felt the same way.

Mose placed his large and gentle hand on Levi's shoulder and steered him to the softball game. He helped Levi find a spot in line to have a turn at the bat, then he jogged to the outfield to help Sallie's boys field balls.

Without a car, Lainey O'Toole had no option but to walk the entire way to Bertha Riehl's farmhouse. In her arms was a pink box—a lattice-topped gooseberry pie she had made last night at the bakery. She knew the way to Rose Hill Farm as if she'd been there yesterday. As she turned onto Stone-leaf Road, she slowed her pace and turned down the dirt lane that led to the cottage where she had lived with her mother and her stepfather. The cottage was set back from the road. When she saw it, her heart slowed and pounded. It had been fifteen years since she laid eyes on it. She squared her shoulders and approached the cottage. Her throat felt tight and a weight settled on her chest. She looked up at the worn clapboards, without a speck of paint, the rusted gutters, broken windows covered with nailed boards. It was even shabbier close up than it looked from the road. Like nobody cared.

She stopped for a moment and took her time looking. When she was little, she had tried to imagine it was pretty, but now she saw that it had always been just a poor man's house, with crooked shutters and a sagging front porch. The porch roof had a vicious slant to it, as if a strong burst of wind might carry it away. An old grape arbor, overgrown like everything else, sat at the end of a broken flagstone path. A crow shrieked in the distance and a few more answered back by telling it off. A mother deer and her baby were grazing under a tree and lifted their heads at the same time, startled to see someone in the yard. They froze, their stiff forelegs splayed out to the sides like stilts. They inspected Lainey with their black-tipped ears, worried she might be a threat. Then finally, deeming her harmless, they looked away and resumed grazing. Otherwise, the place looked lifeless.

She walked up on the front porch and tested the door handle. It wasn't locked, but she didn't go in. It was hard to even imagine walking through the door, so she stepped back and peered in the windows. There was nothing to see there, just an old, forgotten cottage, yet she had the strangest feeling about it. Like she was home.

She stepped off the porch onto the walkway and nearly tripped on a fallen-over For Sale sign. She tried to set it upright, then made her way through the weeds, back to the road that led to the Riehls' farmhouse.

Lainey smiled when she saw the old hand-painted sign hanging on Rose Hill Farm's mailbox: "ROSES FOR SALE. NO SUNDAY SALES." She'd forgotten all about that sign. It had always seemed odd to folks that a woman like Bertha Riehl—as tough as old boots—grew delicate roses to sell. Samuel Riehl was the tenderhearted one, most folks presumed. But Lainey knew better. Bertha Riehl might be tough on the outside, but she was as soft as a marshmallow on the inside.

She walked slowly past the leafed-out cherry trees that lined the long drive, mesmerized by the sight of endless rosebushes in full bloom. Those roses were the most glorious sight she had ever seen in her life. She felt sure that the path to the Pearly Gates of Heaven couldn't be any more inviting than the one leading up to Rose Hill Farm.

Lainey saw Bertha first. She was shaking out a wet dishrag to dry on the kitchen porch railing. Lainey stopped at the bottom of the porch steps and looked up at the big woman, wearing a shapeless plum-colored dress with a black apron stretched around her vast girth. "I've never seen such beauty, this side of heaven. It's like . . . God is showing off a little." She looked out toward the barn. "You've added so many roses. Doesn't your husband object to your converting his pastures to roses?"

"Samuel passed three years ago come October the tenth," Bertha said in a matter-of-fact voice. "I couldn't keep up the farm, but I could do one thing."

Lainey smiled. "Grow roses."

"That's right. And now I'm selling jam made from my mother's rugosas over there." She pointed to shrubs of pink, multiflowered roses.

"I remember those rugosas," Lainey said. "I remember your jam."

Bertha nodded. "I keep adding more and more stock. Filling the pastures with roses. I got a hired boy who has a knack for grafting roses, so he started grafting those rugosas onto heartier root stock." She nodded in the direction of a small greenhouse next to the barn. "Folks come from all over to buy my rosebushes and now they're after my jam and tea."

Lainey nodded. "Mrs. Stroot is hoping I'll talk you into selling some at The Sweet Tooth. She wants me to find out what you'd say to a barter arrangement."

"Such as?" Bertha lifted an eyebrow. She was interested, Lainey could see.

"Maybe you could have your pick of things from the bakery—like a credit— in exchange for letting her sell the jam and tea."

Bertha sized that up for a long moment. "Tell Dottie Stroot I'll think it over."

Lainey felt pleased. She had expected a flat-out no.

Bertha eyed the pink bakery box in Lainey's hands. "What's in there?"

"Gooseberry pie. Your favorite, if I remember right."

"You do." Bertha turned to go back to the house and Lainey took that as an invitation to follow.

Lainey was surprised to see the same young girl standing in the kitchen who had come with Bertha into the bakery the other day. Today she was steeping teabags in a blue speckled pitcher. "You're Bess, aren't you?" she asked. "Have you been working for Bertha for a long time?"

"Just this week, but it seems like forever and a day," Bess said. She held up a hand covered with Band-Aids. "She's wearing me to a frazzle."

Bertha looked unimpressed. "The poor child hardly knows a tea rose from a China rose."

Bess hooted. "But you're giving me a crash course on all things roses." She took out some glasses, filled them with ice, and set them on the counter, next to the pitcher. "Help yourself to the sugar. I like sweet tea, myself." She pointed to the sugar bowl.

"Too much sugar will make your teeth fall out like a picket fence," Bertha said. "I never have it, myself."

"Except for every day," Bess muttered.

"Mebbe just a little on Sundays," Bertha said, spooning heaps of sugar into her glass.

Lainey noticed Bess rolling her eyes and had to bite her lip to keep from smiling. When she first met Bess at the bakery, she thought she had seemed frightened of Bertha. Today, though, she was clearly at ease, gently teasing and joking with her. Lainey could tell Bertha enjoyed Bess's company too, though she would probably never say so. Bess was like a filly, all legs and arms. Watching Bess reminded Lainey of herself at that age, when she had grown several inches in one year and became awkward and clumsy, as if she couldn't get used to the new dimensions of her body.

Bess was pouring Bertha a second glass of iced tea when the kitchen door opened and in walked a very good-looking young man, straw hat in hand. He looked curiously at Lainey, then his gaze turned to Bertha. "Am I late?"

"Right on time," Bertha answered. "The very pineapple of punctuation." And with that, the glass slipped out of Bess's hand, shattered on the floor, and spilled tea everywhere.

Billy knelt down and began to carefully pick up broken glass. Lainey and Bess grabbed dishtowels to mop up the tea.

"Being barefooted, I ought not to help," Bertha said, sprawled in her chair, the picture of ease. "But I don't mind having a floor mopped clean, now that Bess's cat has moved in."

Lainey hadn't seen any sign of a cat, just a big dog sleeping in the corner and a rooster standing guard just outside the kitchen door.

As soon as the broken glass was picked up and the tea wiped clean, they sat down to dinner. The chicken was delicious, but Lainey had little appetite for it. Too nervous. She needed to have a talk with Bertha. How could she bring up anything private with Bess and Billy here? Bess, Lainey noticed, never gave up another word once Billy arrived. Lainey caught her studying Billy, aware of his every word and movement. Lainey fought back a smile. She was glad she wasn't fifteen anymore. Billy and Bertha seemed to be completely unaware of Lainey's anxiety or Bess's discomfort. They ate everything but the pattern on the plate.

Billy concentrated on his food until the subject of grafting roses was brought up, then he didn't stop talking. "Some rose varieties put on a lot of top growth and few roots, which makes them liable to be weak-wooded and short-lived," he said to Lainey with professorial patience, as if she had asked. "But we can graft that rose onto a better taproot so that it puts down a good deal of roots. Doing that makes a rose plant liable to be long-lived, grow better and bigger blooms, and be more resistant to stresses and strains, like a hard freeze."

"Where'd you learn how to graft roses, Billy?" Lainey asked when he finally stopped talking long enough to fill his mouth with roast chicken.

He shrugged and looked over at Bertha. "She told me if I could figure out how to graft, I could have a job. So I went to the library and read up on it and gave it a whirl." He spooned the rest of the pickled peaches onto his plate and looked around the table to see if there was anything left to polish off.

"Gave it a whirl?" Lainey asked in disbelief. "Why, I've heard people go to college to learn how to graft plants!"

"His mother was a Zook," Bertha said, as if that explained everything.

Billy looked embarrassed but pleased. "Roses aren't difficult to graft because they're compatible with nearly all other roses."

When Bertha served the gooseberry pie, silence fell over the table. Lainey started to worry that something was wrong until Billy looked up and said, "This is the best pie I've ever had. Better even than yours, Bertha, if you'll pardon me for saying so."

"Pardon accepted," Bertha said, helping herself to a second slice. "You're right. This pie is unparalyzed."

Bess's spoon froze, midair. She looked at Bertha, confused. Lainey swallowed a smile. Only Billy took it in stride, as if accustomed to Bertha's way of twisting English words around.

"I taught Lainey how to make a flaky pastry shell when she could barely reach over the counter," Bertha said.

Now it was Billy's turn to be surprised. He looked at Lainey, curious.

"It's true," Lainey said. "I used to live nearby. Bertha would let me come visit and help her in the kitchen. She taught me how to bake. Once she could get that black iron range fired up, she could do some serious cooking."

"Still can," Bertha said between bites.

They wolfed down the pie so quickly that Lainey knew it was good. Just as Billy had his eye on another helping, a horse nickered from the barn. Lainey looked out the window. A horse and buggy had turned into the drive, and Bertha's horse knew company was coming. Lainey had forgotten how horses always seemed to know things that people didn't.

Billy jumped up from the table. "That'll be my cousin, Maggie. She was coming by to get me for a youth gathering at the Smuckers' this afternoon."

"Good," Bertha said. "It will give Bess a chance to meet some other young folk."

Billy froze. A look of mild panic lit his eyes. He spoke hesitantly. "She seems awful young for a gathering—"

"I'm nearly sixteen!" Bess said indignantly.

Billy looked unconvinced.

Bertha waved that concern away. "Die Yunge kenne aa alt waerre." *The young may grow old too.*

That only confused Billy.

"Besides, your Maggie Zook is only twelve or thirteen and she's welcome," Bertha said.

"But . . . it's Maggie! You know Maggie. She's thirteen going on thirty. Besides, she's the bishop's daughter. Who's going to tell her she can't go?"

As Bess saw Billy's hesitation, her face clouded over. Bravely, she lifted her chin. "Actually, I had plans of my own this afternoon."

"Like what?" Bertha asked.

Bess looked around the kitchen until her eyes rested on a jar of homemade jam. "You were going to show me how to make rose petal jam."

"Can't," Bertha said. "It's Sunday."

Billy still looked uncomfortable. He scratched the top of his head. "She really shouldn't . . ."

"Sure she should," Bertha said, clamping her granite jaw. "Besides, Lainey and I got us some visiting to do." She shot him a deeply dangerous look.

Defeated, Billy slumped to the wall, plucked his hat from the peg, and held the door open for Bess. She grabbed her bonnet and brushed past him, head held high.

Lainey went to the window to watch them drive off in Maggie's buggy. When they were out of sight, she turned to Bertha, who was still seated at the table, halfway through a third slab of pie.

Lainey sat back down at the table. "There's something I'd like to tell you."

Bertha picked up the blue speckled pitcher and refilled their glasses. Then she added three teaspoons of sugar into her glass and stirred. "What's that?"

"I've never thanked you for helping me like you did, years ago. You always made me feel welcome in your home, and you took an interest in me and helped me and my mother out. It's thanks to you that I'm a Christian today."

Bertha picked a loose thread from her apron front.

Lainey could have been talking about the weather. She tried again. "Bess is a lovely companion for you."

"She's a nervous little thing. Jumpy

as a dog with fleas. But time will fix that."

Then quiet fell again. How could Lainey shift this conversation in the right direction without making Bertha suspicious? A stray thought fluttered through her mind, something she hadn't noticed before. She cocked her head. "When Bess left just now, she called you Mammi."

"So she did." Bertha took a sip from her glass.

"Isn't that the Deitsch word for grandmother? I . . . thought she was your hired girl."

Bertha snorted. "Not hired. Doubt I'd hire her—she oozes away like a barn cat when there are chores to be done." She looked straight at Lainey. "But she is my girl. My only grandchild."

Lainey was confused. "I thought Jonah and Rebecca and their daughter were in Ohio."

Bertha smoothed her skirt and pulled in her lips. "Rebecca died in that buggy accident, long ago."

"Oh no," Lainey said. That news was a shock to her. "I'm so sorry. I didn't . . . I thought she had survived it." She stood and went to the window, then turned to Bertha, confused. "So Jonah remarried?"

Bertha shook her head. "Not yet. Far as I know."

"Are you . . . ?" Lainey's voice cracked and she had to start over. "You can't mean that Bess is Jonah's daughter? That girl with the blond hair?"

Bertha nodded. "Bald as an egg until she was two years old."

Understanding flooded through Lainey and she felt her face grow warm as blood rushed to her head. She sat down in the chair to steady herself. "I never knew her name," she said in a faraway voice. "I knew Rebecca had her baby, but I never knew the baby's name. It was the same week my mother died . . ." The words got stuck in her throat and she couldn't continue.

Bertha leaned back in her chair and crossed her arms over her chest. "Jonah and Rebecca's baby was named Bess, so that's what he called this little girl." She took a deep breath. "That's what he called the little baby girl you switched on us, Lainey. Fifteen years ago."

Lainey felt as if her heart was pounding so loudly that Bertha must be able to hear it. She looked down at her lap and saw that her hands were trembling. It was such a hot day, but she was suddenly cold. For a brief second, the room started to spin and she thought she might faint. "How long . . . ?" Her voice drizzled off.

"How long have I known?" Bertha leaned forward, cool as custard, to take a sip of iced tea. "From the moment I arrived at the hospital, after the accident." She smoothed out the oilcloth on the table. "Think I wouldn't know my own grandbaby? And Mrs. Hertz told me—told the whole town— about your baby sister's passing and you getting shipped off to a foster home. Wasn't beyond my apprehension to put two and two together."

Lainey chanced a look at Bertha. "Samuel knew too?"

For the first time, Bertha seemed mildly distressed. She slipped off her spectacles and polished them. Then she blew her nose, loud. "That rain we had last night was hard on my sciences."

Lainey frowned. "Your what?"

"My sciences." She gave her nose a honk.

"I think you mean your sinuses."

Bertha huffed a small laugh. "That's what I said." She stuffed her handkerchief in her apron pocket.

Lainey tried again. "Did Samuel know?"

Bertha took her time answering. "No. The very week Rebecca had her baby, Samuel's brother in Somerset was laid up in the hospital for a bleeding ulcer. Samuel went to go help finish up spring planting on his brother's farm. He hadn't laid eyes on his own granddaughter yet. But he came back as soon as I sent word about the accident."

Lainey felt the words lock in her throat. "Why . . . why didn't you ever tell?"

"When Jonah found out that Rebecca had died, it was like the light had gone out of him. His back was broke to smithereens."

Lainey's eyes went round as quarters. "He's paralyzed?"

"No. His spiney cord wasn't hurt, but his lower back was broke. He had to learn to walk all over again. Knowing Bess needed him was all that kept him going."

Lainey stared at Bertha for a long time. She rubbed her forehead. "Are you saying that Jonah doesn't know?"

Bertha shook her head and looked away. "You know how fast babies change and grow. By the time Jonah was able to see her and hold her, she was already holding her head up and rolling over." She sighed. "But Jonah never knew. I planned to tell him. I meant to. But there never seemed to be a good time. And then weeks and months turned into years."

Lainey closed her eyes and squeezed her fists tight. She should have realized! She should have known! The color of Bess's hair—white blond—and those turquoise eyes. Simon's hair color.

Simon's eyes. She looked at Bertha. "So . . . Bess . . . is my half sister?"

As Bertha nodded, a single tear fell on Lainey's cheek, followed by another and another, until she couldn't hold them back anymore. She covered her face with her hands and wept.

⁂

When Bertha Riehl invited Billy for Sunday lunch, even then, he felt a pang of unease. He should have known that she would have something up her sleeve. She had a reputation for doing the unexpected. He had been working for her for over two years now, and she had never once invited him for Sunday dinner . . . until today. Normally, he got a kick out of Bertha's unpredictable methods of getting what she wanted. But he had never been the object of her finagling. He liked working for her. She paid him well, and he knew she needed his help around Rose Hill Farm. But now he was stuck babysitting her granddaughter for the rest of the afternoon—a girl who acted as nervous as a cottontail and had a hard time stringing more than two words together that made any sense. He found younger girls to be tiresome: they giggled a lot and refused to take anything seriously.

A horrible thought darted through his mind. He hoped Bertha wasn't trying her hand at matchmaking. He was real fond of Bertha, even if she was crafty, and he didn't want to lose this job. It was more than a job to him. It was his future. This was what he wanted to do with his life. He could never work up much enthusiasm pushing a plow behind a team of mules, but this—experimenting to create a better plant—this felt like something he was born to do. He studied books about roses, he wrote away to experts and asked their opinions, and he kept precise records—something Bertha had no interest in. It was a sin to be prideful and he was careful not to indulge in it, but it did please him when folks said they drove long distances to buy rose stock from Rose Hill Farm. Last week, an English lady came all the way from Pittsburgh because someone at Penn

State told her this was the only place to buy a rose that smelled like one grown a hundred years ago. "The hybrids might be the rage," the lady told Billy, "but they have no fragrance. But these roses"—she scanned the fields—"you can tell they're grown with passion."

How his father and older brothers would laugh at that comment. They thought his ideas were nonsense, so he stopped doing experiments and bringing his horticulture books home from the library. But his mother had understood. She and Bertha had been good friends and neighbors. His mother must have told Bertha the kinds of things Billy liked to learn about, because at his mother's funeral, she asked him to come work at Rose Hill Farm.

But as much as he liked and admired Bertha Riehl, as much passion as he felt for the roses, he knew he would never be passionate about this skinny girl sitting on the buggy seat next to his cousin Maggie. He guessed Bess could hardly weigh ninety-nine pounds soaking wet. She had an unnaturally scrubbed look, like she'd been dipped in a bottle of bleach and came out with ultra blond hair and white eyelashes. And that anxious-to-please expression on her face made him nervous.

He was glad his cousin was with them. Maggie could talk to a brick wall and never notice it wasn't answering back. At least he was off the hook from trying to come up with any more painful attempts at conversation, like he had to do—just out of politeness—when Bess was out helping him pick roses.

Still, the least he could do was to be nice, for Bertha's sake, so he took the long way to the Smuckers to show Bess his favorite spot on earth, Blue Lake Pond. A little jewel of a pond with pine trees that lined the shores. It was deserted, just as he expected. That was another thing he loved about this lake. He stopped the horse, hopped down, and tied its reins to a tree branch. He took a few steps and then stopped to wave to the girls. "Well, come on."

"Not me. I'm going to stay here," Maggie said, pushing her glasses up on the bridge of her nose. "I don't want to get my shoes dirty."

"Suit yourself," he said. "What about you, Bess? Every visitor to Stoney Ridge needs to get acquainted with Blue Lake Pond."

Thrown that small morsel of encouragement, Bess leaped off the buggy and trotted behind Billy.

Down by the shoreline, he put his hands on his hips and inhaled deeply. "This is the best lake in the county. In all of Pennsylvania. I spend every free hour on these shores—swimming in the summer, skating in the winter. Fishing in between." He picked up a rock and skimmed it across the pond. He gave Bess a sideways glance. "Me and my friend Andy go skinny-dipping here every summer." He paused for her reaction.

Bess's eyes went wide and her cheeks flamed scarlet.

Billy grinned.

Clearly mortified, Bess turned away from him and walked along the shore. Billy kept skimming rocks. After a while, she stopped to look up in the treetops. "It's the quietest place in the world."

"Sure is. Quiet and peaceful."

"I didn't mean it that way. I meant it in a strange way."

He tilted his head. "What's so strange about a quiet lake?"

"There are no birds singing."

He searched the skies and the trees. "Huh. You're right." He shrugged. "Maybe it's the time of day."

She walked further along the shoreline. "You'd think there'd be some sign of wildlife. A loon or a duck or a goose. Even a crow or scrub jay." She looked all around. "Nothing."

Maggie hollered to them she wanted to get to the Smuckers' before the gathering was over, if they wouldn't mind, so they turned around to walk back to the buggy. Before Billy left the shoreline, though, he shielded his eyes from the sun and scanned the lake. He saw plenty of dragonflies skating over the surface of the pond, but he was looking for some sign or sound of a bird in the trees or skies. Not one.

❧❧

Billy disappeared to join his friends the minute they hitched the horse at the Smuckers', but Maggie stuck to Bess like glue. She reminded Bess of a pixie, small and dark, with eyes darting here and there, forever watchful. She could talk a person to death. Bess didn't mind at all; she'd grown accustomed to half listening after being around Sallie Stutzman so much. As they walked around the yard and watched some boys pegging out a game of horseshoes, Maggie pointed out names and gave Bess the full rundown on each person. Bess nodded, vaguely interested, but she kept one eye on Billy the entire time.

Someone tapped Bess on the shoulder. "*Who* are you staring at?"

Bess whirled around to face a tall, shapely girl with sandy-blond hair and dark brown eyes. If it weren't for the fact that she was glowering at Bess, she could even be called attractive.

Maggie intervened. She hooked her

arm through Bess's and pulled her along. "I should have warned you about Esther Swartzentruber. She set her sights on Billy awhile back and hasn't let go. Well, most every girl has her sights on Billy, but Esther is the only one bold enough to tell every- one. She watches him like a hawk." She looked back at Esther who was scowling at both of them. "With you here, Bess, I think it's going to be a real fun summer. Esther thinks she's got all the boys pining for her, but look at how they're sizing you up like a hog at auction."

Bess was absolutely sure no boy was looking at her, but such a loyal remark earned Maggie a spot in her heart.

Right at that moment, a buggy wheeled into the driveway and pulled to a stop. Out poured four girls. It was the fourth girl who caught Bess's eye. Actually, it was Billy's reaction to Girl #4 that she noticed. He stopped playing horseshoes and walked over to greet Girl #4, lingering over her. But- who wouldn't? She was *that* pretty.

Maggie leaned over and whispered,

"That's Betsy Mast. Every boy in Lancaster County is wild over her."

A wave of pure jealousy came over Bess, shaming her. She said nothing. She was afraid it might show in her voice.

"How could they not be?" Maggie continued. "Look at her big eyes and gigantic pouty lips. Her chest looks like the prow of a ship! I call her Busty Mast. Have you ever seen such enormous—" She clasped her hand over her mouth. "Oh, I *shouldn't* have said that! Jorie—she's my stepmom—she's always telling me to think before I speak. But my mouth does run away from me."

Bess looked down at her own flat chest and up again at Betsy Mast. She sighed.

"Fellows sure do seem to love the prows of ships. They're always talking about them." Maggie spoke in a wise, mature woman-of-the-world voice and patted Bess's shoulder. "I know these things." She gave a sly grin. "I have a gift for eavesdropping."

For the rest of the afternoon, Billy

hovered around Betsy like a bee around a flower.

❦

For hours, listening to crickets in the thick, muggy silence, Lainey lay in bed and stared at the ceiling. Bess was her sister. *Bess was her sister!* She still couldn't believe it. She never dreamed she would see her again. Her thoughts bounced back to that terrible night, when she made a snap decision that altered lives. She had made a bold promise to her mother, who lay dying just two weeks before, that she would take care of her baby sister, Colleen. But within a few days, Lainey was overwhelmed and exhausted. And sad. Terribly sad. She missed her mother. She had found a small amount of cash tucked in the back of her mother's dresser drawer, but that was disappearing quickly after buying two weeks of baby formula. By now, she had been sure Simon would have returned. She was starting to panic.

When she heard the screech of tires

and the horse whinnying and then that horrible crashing sound, she grabbed her baby sister out of the cradle and ran outside to see what had happened. The buggy had flipped to its side. She bolted over to it and her heart lurched with recognition—Rebecca and Jonah Riehl. She called their names, but they didn't respond. They both looked pale and still. Rebecca was bleeding from her ear.

The truck driver who had hit the buggy climbed out of his cab. He walked up to Lainey in shock. "I didn't see them! It was so dark and I was trying to pass . . ." He looked as if he expected her to tell him what to do next.

Lainey took a deep breath. "Go down the street until you come to the intersection. Find the gas station and call for an ambulance."

The man just stood there, looking at the horse trying frantically to get up, panting heavily. Its leg was twisted grotesquely. Then the man looked at the buggy, at the bodies in it, as if he couldn't believe his eyes.

"Go!" Lainey shouted, pointing her small finger down the road.

The man backed up, staggering, then started to run down the road.

Lainey heard a sound and turned to Rebecca, whose eyes opened halfway. "Mein Boppli," Rebecca whispered. "Meine Dochder." *My baby. My daughter.*

Lainey looked around and found a small bundle, thrown from the buggy. She hurried to the bundle and felt her stomach reel. The baby looked nearly identical to her own baby sister—same size, bald like Colleen, the same wide blue eyes. The face was unmarked, but the baby's chest appeared to have caved in. Her eyes were wide open, showing no signs of life. There was no breath. She didn't blink at all, even when Lainey touched her cheek. She put her hand on the baby's tiny chest but couldn't find any heartbeat. She had seen enough of farm life to know that this baby was dead. She heard the horse whimper in pain and shock— she would never forget that sorrowful sound as long as she lived—and she looked back at the buggy, at Jonah and Rebecca, and then down at the dead baby. Nausea rose in her throat and she coughed, retching. There weren't many times she wished Simon were home, but she wanted him here now, to help her. She was frightened, so frightened, and didn't know what to do next.

Lainey heard Rebecca call out. How could she tell Rebecca that her baby was dead? Slowly, she walked back to the buggy and saw Rebecca's eyes flicker open again. Impulsively, hoping to give Rebecca comfort, she tucked Colleen into her arms. "She's here, Rebecca," Lainey lied. "She's just fine."

Rebecca's eyes tried to open, but Lainey could see she was fading. "Denki," she murmured. *Thank you.*

Lainey hoped that truck driver could figure out where the gas station was. She stayed by the buggy, telling Rebecca and Jonah to hold on, that help was coming. When she heard an ambulance siren in the distance, she exhaled with relief. As she reached down to pick up Colleen, she had a heart-thudding moment. Her infant sister looked up at her with wide blue eyes, oddly serene and peaceful despite this gruesome scene.

A plan took shape in Lainey's ten-year-old mind.

She saw the red flash of the ambulance's siren as it turned onto the street. Then she kissed her sister goodbye and picked up Rebecca's baby before running into the house. She spent the next hour by the window, shaking like a leaf, watching the ambulance workers and the police. She tucked Rebecca's dead baby in her sister's cradle and curled up in the corner of the old brown couch that smelled like mold. When she heard a single gunshot ring out—knowing the policeman had to put down the horse—she threw up again.

She didn't sleep at all that night. As soon as dawn broke, she walked down the road to tell her nearest neighbor, Mrs. Hertz, that her baby sister had died in the night, peaceful as can be, in her sleep. Surely God would punish her for all of these lies she was telling. Surely somebody was going to figure out what she had done. But all Mrs. Hertz said was, "God was merciful, Lainey. He knew no child should have to endure Simon Troyer as a father." She grabbed Lainey into her generous-sized bosom for a hug. "I never did understand why your sweet mama ever married that poor excuse for a man, anyhows."

They both knew the answer. A single mother, poor as a church mouse, didn't have a whole lot of choices in 1957.

Mrs. Hertz made one call to the county coroner and the next one to a county social worker. A bead of sweat trickled down Lainey's neck when the coroner arrived. She was petrified he might ask questions about the baby's death, but he just came and took the baby away, like he did two weeks before when her mother passed. She figured the coroner didn't concern himself with poor folks like them. In fact, he acted as disinterested as Simon had the night Lainey's mother lay dying. The day after his wife was buried, Simon told Lainey to take care of the baby and he went off deer hunting, though that couldn't be right because it wasn't hunting season. But maybe he *was* deer hunting. Rules were always optional for Simon.

As the coroner left, the social worker arrived. She took one look at Lainey's living conditions, at the absence of any adult in the home, and whisked her off to a foster home. When Simon didn't appear at the court date to claim Lainey, she became a ward of the state of Pennsylvania. She lived in three different foster homes until she was eighteen. After graduating from high school, she was on her own. She worked for a department store in Harrisburg and saved her money. She had a plan. Her two friends, Robin and Ally, gave her a hard time for being so serious and saving every penny, but Lainey knew what could happen to girls without goals and dreams. Her mother had warned her. She wanted a different life for herself.

All the while, Lainey had never forgotten her baby sister. Giving Colleen up was the hardest, best thing Lainey had ever done. Not a day went by when she didn't wonder a dozen questions about her sister—what did she look like? was she happy?—but she didn't feel plagued with guilt about whether it was the right thing to do. She couldn't think of a better life for a child than to grow up Amish. And now God in his mercy was giving her a chance to see that her sister had a childhood just as she had hoped for her: happy and loved.

Lainey gave up trying to sleep and went to the window to open it wider. The room she had rented from Mrs. Stroot's sister faced west and was hot and stuffy by evening. She sat on the sill for a while, looking up at a sliver of the new moon. Her feelings felt jumbled. She had come to Stoney Ridge to try to find out information from Bertha about how her sister was doing, but she never planned to reveal her secret. She never wanted to upset her sister's life.

Today, that noble intention turned upside down.

Bertha said she was going to tell Bess and Jonah the truth this summer. It was high time. Bertha said when she saw Lainey in town a few weeks ago, she decided she would do all she could to get Bess out here as soon as she could. Now the time was right, she said. Maybe not today, but soon.

At least Bess would be here all summer. And so would Lainey.

Lainey's thoughts bounced to Jonah. Bertha didn't offer up much information about him—typical of her—but she did say that Bess was his only family. Lainey was sorry to hear that Rebecca hadn't survived the accident. Rebecca had always been kind to Lainey. It gave Lainey comfort to think she might have given her peace in those last moments, laying Colleen in her arms. She remembered Rebecca had been a beauty—small and delicate. It was plain to see how much she and Jonah loved each other. She had thought they were the luckiest two people on earth . . . until the accident.

As she thought about all Bertha

had told her today, she found it hard to believe. But life could be like that, she had learned. A single decision, a moment in time, and the ground could shift beneath your feet.

4

When Bess came into the kitchen the next morning, Mammi was pouring batter on the waffle iron while the coffee perked. Mammi had finally relented to Bess's pleading and allowed her to drink coffee, as long as it was half milk. Peering out the window, Bess noticed Billy was already out in the fields among the roses. Unlike other mornings, she wasn't in any hurry to join him. She picked up her fork as Mammi brought her a waffle, then put it down as Mammi sat down and bowed her head. Mammi's prayers were never short.

When Mammi lifted her head, she

said matter-of-factly, "You got in awful late."

Bess poured syrup over her waffle. "By nine. You were asleep in the rocker. I didn't know if I should wake you to outen the lights." She had decided against it when she realized that her grandmother had taken out her false teeth. The sight made Bess shudder. Mammi's mouth had looked like a shrunken apple.

"I never sleep."

Bess rolled her eyes.

"Did you have a good time?"

Bess nodded, distracted, and chewed slowly.

"Then why are you sitting there with a face as long as a wet week?"

Bess rested her chin on her propped-up hand. "I'm all at sea."

"What's making you so mixed up?"

"Do you know a girl named Betsy Mast?"

Mammi raised an eyebrow at Bess, then her gaze shifted through the window to Billy in the fields, bent over a blooming rose. "Es schlackt net allemol ei as es dunnert." *Lightning doesn't strike every time it thunders.*

"I'm not so sure, Mammi. You know boys." Bess sighed dramatically and took a sip of her coffee-laced milk.

Mammi nodded. "Boys are trouble. But girls is worse." She started filling up the sink with soapy water.

Bess gave up a smile, in spite of her grim mood.

One sure way of surviving heartache was to stay busy, Mammi told her, and shooed her out to join Billy by the roses. Bess picked up a basket on the porch and slowly went out to the field.

Last night, with her chin propped on the windowsill watching the moon rise, she had given her runaway feelings about Billy some serious thought. She'd barely known him a week. Now was the time to reel her heart back in, before she found herself falling off the edge of no return—the way Billy's face looked when he caught sight of Betsy Mast.

So that's the way things were going to be. She thought she had found the man of her dreams . . . but it was only an illusion. A tragic illusion. She sat in the moonlight and shed a tear or two. It didn't take much to set her off, now that she was fifteen. Her feelings were as tender and easily bruised as a ripe summer peach. Even Blackie, her cat, had declared his independence and had taken up barn living. She shed a tear for Blackie too. She missed her father, missed her home and her own bed. She even might miss Sallie and her boys a little. *No, scratch that.* But she did regret ever coming to Stoney Ridge. Even summer school looked more appealing than being stuck here, picking roses near a beautiful boy who hardly noticed her. She sighed, deeply grieved, and climbed back into bed, sure she would never sleep. She turned over once, and it was morning.

As Bess walked out to the roses, she decided that she would avoid Billy as much as possible, picking roses in rows far from him. She bent down to examine a blossom.

"Hey, what are you doing way over there?" Billy called out to her.

She bounced back up.

He picked up his basket and joined her in the row she was working on, making her heart turn in somersaults. "You were right about birds missing from the lake. I went back later last night, to see if I could hear any owls hooting. Nothing. What do you make of that?"

What did she make of that? Looking into his dark eyes, she couldn't make sense of anything. She couldn't think of a single thing to say—she was that tongue-tied around him. He looked particularly fine today too, with his cheeks turning pink from the sun and his shirtsleeves rolled up on his forearms. The wind lifted his hair. He looked so handsome she wanted to reach out and stroke his cheek. Her spirits soared.

Billy Lapp wasn't making it easy for her to fall out of love with him.

⁂

Jonah walked out to the shop in his barn, reviewing the facts for the hundredth time. He had tossed and turned last night trying to figure it out.

What exactly had happened last night to lead Sallie to the conclusion that they now had an Understanding? He had dropped her and her boys off after church, and she had invited him to stay for dinner. There was nothing different about that scenario. He and Bess had often taken Sunday suppers at Sallie's. He remembered saying that the house was awful quiet without Bess. Then, as he said good night, Sallie told him that she was just thrilled they had an Understanding. He was mystified. What had he said?

The morning was so warm that he opened up both doors in his workshop to have air circulate through. As he slid open the barn door, a thought seized him. Sallie was so . . . overly blessed . . . with the gift of conversation that he often found himself not really listening to her. Maybe he was asking himself the wrong question. Maybe the question wasn't what he had said. Maybe it was: what had he not said in reply?

When Lainey heard the bakery door jingle, she looked up, surprised to see Bess. Her blond hair was covered by a bandanna knotted at the nape of her neck, just below her hair bun. She wore a lavender dress under her white apron and she was barefooted.

"My grandmother has a craving for your cherry tarts and sent me down to get some," Bess said, peering into the bakery counter. She looked up, disappointed. "But they're all gone!"

The store was empty and Mrs. Stroot had gone home, so Lainey grabbed the chance to encourage Bess to stay. "I was just going to whip some up. What would you think about staying to help?"

Bess looked delighted. "I'd love to! Mammi is canning zucchini, and the kitchen is so hot that it's steaming the calendar right off the wall. One thing I've learned, if I don't make myself scarce, Mammi will find me some chores." She followed Lainey to the back of the bakery.

Lainey pointed Bess to the sink to wash her hands while she got out the flour and sugar and lard. She felt her heart pounding hard and tried to calm herself. It still seemed like a miracle to her, to think that her sister was right there beside her.

❧❦

Mammi was waiting out on the porch, arms akimbo, when Bess drove up the drive to Rose Hill Farm. Bess felt a little nervous because she'd been much longer than she said she would.

"Where have you been?" Mammi asked when Bess pulled the buggy horse to a stop by the barn.

"Lainey taught me how to make cherry tarts!" Bess handed Mammi a big pink box before she got out of the buggy, which, she thought, was a smart move. "The bakery was empty and she was just about to make a fresh batch. So she asked if I could help and I thought you wouldn't mind, seeing as how you love them so much."

Mammi opened the box and looked over the tarts. "Well, as long as you were helping her and doing something useful." She took a bite out of a tart and closed her eyes, as if she were tasting heaven.

"Lainey didn't even let me pay for them. She said I earned my keep and she hoped I'd come back again. She said late in the day the bakery is usually empty and she could use my help." Bess hopped down from the buggy and started to unbuckle the tracings on the horse. "Would you mind if I go see Lainey at the bakery now and then? Dad would sure love it if I could bake something new. I told her you wouldn't mind. You don't, do you, Mammi?" She backed the buggy up from behind the horse and leaned it upright against the barn.

There was no answer, so Bess chanced a look at her grandmother. Mammi's mouth was too filled with another cherry tart to talk.

Three o'clock in the afternoon had become Lainey's favorite time of the day. For the past two weeks, like clockwork, Bess came through the door for another baking lesson. Normally, Mrs.

Stroot closed the bakery at three, but when Bess started coming by at that time, Lainey asked if she would mind if the store stayed open a little longer. "I'm here anyway, getting ready for the next day," she told Mrs. Stroot, "and each afternoon we end up selling a few more baked goods. Better first-good than day-old prices."

Mrs. Stroot couldn't argue with logic that turned a profit, but she did say she needed to go home and start dinner for Mr. Stroot. Lainey promised her that she would lock up. So each afternoon, Bess drove Bertha's buggy to the bakery, parked the horse under the shade tree, and spent two hours with Lainey, baking and talking. More talking than baking.

Oh, the things she was discovering about Bess! She learned about Jonah and how he was going to marry his neighbor, Sallie Stutzman, who had twin boys no one could tell apart. And she learned about the boy at school who liked Bess overly much. "Levi Miller is nothing but a bother and a nuisance, Lainey. So . . . childish," Bess said, sounding so very adult. "But we're the only two Amish ninth graders at our public school, so he thinks we're destined for each other." And with that, Bess made a sour face.

There were also things about Bess that Lainey picked up without being told. Earlier in the week, Bess was in the middle of mixing cookie dough when she froze, eyes wide, as she stared out the window. Eventually, she turned back to the cookie dough, but sadness covered her like a blanket. Carefully, Lainey craned her neck to see what had caught Bess's eye out the window. It was that young fellow who worked for Bertha, Billy Lapp, carrying packages for a very attractive Amish girl.

"You're every bit as pretty as she is, Bess," Lainey said. She wasn't just saying that. Bess was going to be a beauty. She was unusual looking, with lovely cheekbones and skin like peaches and cream. And those eyes! They were extraordinary. When she wore a dress of a particular shade of blue, those eyes looked like the waters of a tropical island.

"No. I'm not," Bess said, sounding miserable. "It's hard on an ordinary moth when a beautiful butterfly comes around."

Lainey couldn't help but laugh. "Give yourself a little time. You just turned fifteen!"

Sadly, Bess said, "I don't have time. The summer is flying by."

Lainey's stomach gripped tight. She didn't want to think about that.

Bess looked up at her, a question on her face. "How did you know how old I am?"

And Lainey had no answer for her.

❧❧

Over two weeks had passed since the Understanding, as Jonah came to think of it, had been formalized with Sallie. By Sallie. He still felt a little stunned, yet the idea of marrying again wasn't altogether unpleasant. It was starting to grow on him, the way Sallie sort of grew on a fellow. She was cheerful, that Sallie. And her boys certainly did need a father's influence. Sallie thought their antics were adorable, but most people ran the other way when they caught sight of those twins. Just the other day, they stripped Jonah's tree of apples and tossed them at passing cars. Mose caught them in the act and quietly took them home to Sallie. If Jonah had caught them, he would have wanted to tan their hides. Yes, those boys needed a father. And living alone this summer gave him a pretty good idea of what the future would hold for him once Bess was grown and gone. He hated it.

❧❧

Over a month had passed since Lainey had arrived in Stoney Ridge. This July afternoon Bess came into The Sweet Tooth looking pale and worried, with arms crossed tightly in front of her as if she were shivering despite summer's muggy warmth. Lainey tried to teach her how to roll a pie crust, but she could see Bess couldn't concentrate. Bess kept rolling and rolling until the crust was so thin, it was nearly see-through.

Lainey quickly rolled it into a ball and put it in the refrigerator to chill. "You can't let pastry get warm. The shortening needs to be in layers when it bakes, not mixed in."

Bess looked as if the thought of ruining the pastry made her want to cry.

"Is something troubling you, Bess?" At first, Lainey was sure it had something to do with Billy Lapp. But then she had a horrible premonition that maybe Bertha had finally told her the truth.

"No. Yes." Bess's eyes met Lainey's, wide and sea blue. "I'm dying."

"What do you mean?"

"I'm bleeding to death."

Lainey looked her up and down. She didn't see any signs of hemorrhaging. "Where?"

Bess pointed to her stomach. "Here."

"Your stomach?"

Bess shook her head. She pointed lower.

"Oh," Lainey said. Then her eyes went wide as it dawned on her. "Oh!"

She put her hands on Bess's shoulders. "Oh Bess, you're not dying. Hasn't anyone ever told you about getting the monthly visit from Flo?"

Bess looked at her, confused. "From who?"

Of course she hadn't been told! She had no mother. Her father certainly wouldn't discuss such a personal thing. Lainey went to the door and locked it, turning the closed sign over. She sat down and patted the chair next to her. "Let's have a talk."

⁂

Later that afternoon, as soon as Bess returned to Rose Hill Farm, Mammi showed her a black bonnet she had made for her.

"It's bigger than a coal scuttle!" Bess said miserably. "Mammi, are you trying to turn me into Lancaster Amish?" Her Ohio bonnet was much smaller.

"Nothing of the sort," Mammi said, tying the ribbons under Bess's chin.

Bess could hardly see from side to side. "I feel like a horse wearing blinders."

Mammi didn't pay any attention. "We got us another errand in town."

"Oh Mammi," Bess said, too worried to stir. She didn't think this day could get any worse, but it just had.

Sure enough, Mammi was on a mission to search out that poor sheriff's car. Mammi spotted the empty car out in front of the five-and-dime store and pulled the buggy over.

"Why? Why are you doing this?" Bess asked.

"I got my reasons."

"Then why don't you do the driving?"

"Can't," Mammi said. "I'd be put under the ban." She gave a sideways glance to Bess. "You're safe."

Bess sighed and got into the driver's side. Refusing Mammi anything never worked. She started up the car and drove down the road, a little faster this time—after all, she might as well enjoy this—until Mammi pointed to an empty parking spot and Bess pulled over.

Just like last time, the sheriff came running up the street, huffing and puffing. "Dadblast it, Miz Riehl! You did it again!"

"Did what?" Mammi asked, the very picture of surprise. She pushed open the passenger door and eased out of the car. Bess hopped out and stood beside her.

The sheriff's face turned purple-red. "Now, Miz Riehl, don't be like that."

Out of nowhere, Billy Lapp stepped in front of Mammi and Bess and made a patting gesture with both hands. "You'll have to excuse Bertha Riehl, Sheriff Kauffman. She's feeling her age these days." He made a clocklike motion around his ears with his hands. "I'll make sure these ladies get right on home so they don't cause any more trouble for you."

The sheriff turned to Billy with one hand on his gun holster. "You do that. And make sure that yellow-haired gal stops tempting her granny to a life of crime."

Mammi glared at Billy as he steered them by their elbows to the buggy. Billy tried to help her into the buggy, but she batted away his hand. "Feeling my age, am I?"

He rolled his eyes. "I was only trying

to keep you out of jail. What were you thinking?" Mammi wouldn't answer, so he turned to Bess. "And just what do you think you're doing? Why would you ever drive off in a sheriff's car?" He reached out a hand to help her climb up in the buggy.

Still mindful of seeing Billy drive Betsy Mast in his courting buggy the other day, Bess shook his hand off her arm. "We have our reasons," she said huffily as she climbed into the buggy. As soon as they had left the main street, she turned to her grandmother. "Just what *are* our reasons?"

"Why, no reason at all," was all Mammi said, jutting out her big chin.

Later that week, Bess was in the barn, spreading rose petals. She took off her bandanna and wiped her forehead and neck. It was already hot and only nine in the morning. She opened the barn doors to get a crosswind and leaned against the doorjamb for a moment. She scanned the farm as she tied her bandanna in a knot at the nape of her neck. She saw Billy in the fields, Mammi in the kitchen. Hot breezes sighed in the cornfield across the road. A row of crows on the fence line told each other off. A woodpecker was hard at work somewhere high in a treetop. The morning was going on around them.

Suddenly she heard Billy holler like he'd seen a ghost. "Aphids! Bertha! We got aphids!"

The kitchen door blew open and Bertha stood there, arms akimbo. "Aphids?!" She marched out to the rose fields like a general to the front lines. She bent over the rose that Billy was working on, then looked around her. "Why, they're everywhere!"

From the look on her face, Mammi had just declared war on the aphids. She pointed at Billy. "Scoot uptown and bring me back Coca-Cola. Bring back as much as you can carry." She turned on Bess, who was walking over to see the aphid invasion up close. "Run in the kitchen and get five dollars from my special hiding place. You go with Billy to help him carry the soda pop."

By the time Bess figured out that Mammi's special hiding place for her money was an empty Folger's coffee tin—the same place her father kept his money—Billy had the horse harnessed to its traces and was waiting for her. She hurried to join him, delighted at the turn of events that gave her time alone with him. Usually, Mammi was within shouting distance and added her two cents to their conversation. Bess tried to think of something interesting to say, something witty and wise. Just last night, she had been working out a few imaginary conversations with Billy, just in case an opportunity like this—driving together in a buggy—presented itself. But now her mind was empty. She couldn't think of a single thing to say. They were getting close to the store when she blurted out, "Why Coca-Cola?"

"Kills aphids," Billy said without even glancing at her. And then he fell silent.

"What do you suppose it's doing to your belly?" Bess said quietly.

Billy turned to her, a surprised look on his face, before bursting out with a laugh. "Good point." He flashed a dazzling smile at her. His smile seemed as if he had never smiled for anyone else in the world.

Bess felt pleased. She had made Billy Lapp laugh.

❊❊

Satisfied that the aphids were done in, Mammi spent the rest of the afternoon on another project. Instead of drying the rose petals from today's pickings, she said she was using them to make rose water. She filled a pot with clean rose petals. Then she poured boiling water over them and covered the pot with a lid. She turned off the heat and let the petals stand until they cooled.

Before bedtime, Bess helped Mammi strain the petals from the water. They ended up with the most beautifully colored liquid a person would ever see. The liquid would be kept in the cooler and used whenever they would bake something that called for rose water,

and Mammi would sell it in small ma-
son jars. "And we'll charge double at
Dottie Stroot's," she told Bess.

Some nights, like tonight, it was
so hot that Bess couldn't sleep. She
threw off her sheets and went downstairs, finding her way by touch because it was so dark. She opened the
back door and stepped into the yard.
Boomer followed her out and disappeared into the shadows.

She stood still for a moment. Ohio
summers were even hotter, lacking the
fresh breeze that seemed to always
come through Stoney Ridge. There
was just a sliver of a moon and the
night was not totally black. She could
make out vague shapes: the henhouse,
the barn, the greenhouse, the cherry
trees.

Blackie slid out of nowhere and wove
himself between her legs. Bess picked
him up. "You're getting fat! You must
be feasting on barn mice."

Blackie jumped down and oozed
away, insulted.

She looked up at the velvety night
sky, filled with star diamonds. It was a

peaceful time. She still went back and forth about being there, but tonight she was glad to be here in Stoney Ridge with her grandmother.

She thought of the things she had already learned to do this summer: how to pick roses and get rid of aphids, how to dry rose petals to make tea and jam, how to make rose water. And how to make a fair profit. How to bake a cherry pie. Mammi told her that was just the beginning of things she needed to learn.

How much more learning can I take? she wondered as she rubbed her head.

✿✿

Later that week, Mammi made one more valiant effort to steal the sheriff's car. Bess tried to talk her out of it all the way into Stoney Ridge, but Mammi went right on merrily ahead with her plan.

"But why, Mammi? You're going to give that sheriff a heart attack! Why would you want to kill the poor man?"

Mammi set her jaw in that stubborn way and wouldn't answer.

This time, as Bess coaxed the sheriff's car slowly onto the road, Mammi flipped a switch and the siren went on. In the rearview mirror, Bess saw the sheriff run out of the bank and into the road. She pulled the car over and hung her head. Her grandmother was certifiably crazy and she was the accomplice.

The sheriff opened the passenger door for Mammi and helped her out. "Miz Riehl, you are turning into a one-woman crime wave."

Mammi's eyes were circles of astonishment. Stoically, she stiffened her arms and offered her wrists to the sheriff for handcuffing. "Do what you must, Johnny."

Now a crowd started to gather. The sheriff paled. "Aw, Miz Riehl, don't make me do this."

"You are sworn to uphold the law." Mammi clucked her tongue. "Think of all them voters, watching their tax dollars at work. You can't be playing favorites."

"Dadblast it, Miz Riehl! If I didn't know better, I would say you are try-

ing to get yourself thrown in the clink."
His face was shading purple.

"Nothing of the sort! But I do get one
phone call."

The sheriff narrowed his eyes and
thought hard for a moment. "Get in the
patrol car, Miz Riehl. You too, missy."
He meant Bess.

Mammi slid into the back of the patrol car and patted on the seat beside
her for Bess. Bess wanted to die, right
there on the spot. But Mammi looked
as content as a cat sitting in cream.

The sheriff drove them to his office
and took them inside. He pointed to
two chairs by his desk. "Can I get you
two anything to drink?"

"Nothing for me," Mammi said politely, lowering herself into a chair, "but
my Bess here would like a soda pop."

Bess didn't want a soda pop, the
way her stomach was turning itself inside out. The sheriff went to the back
of his office and brought back a warm
Tab. He eased himself down into his
chair and leaned back, lacing his fingers behind his head. "Now, Miz Riehl.

Let's cut the cackle and come straight to the point. Who do you want to call?"

"Oh, I don't want to call anyone," Mammi said. She pointed at him. "But you can call someone."

The sheriff picked up the receiver. "What's the number?"

Mammi turned to Bess. "What's the phone number to Jonah's barn?"

Bess's jaw dropped open. "Oh no, Mammi, no! You can't tell Dad about us getting arrested! He'll be on the next bus to Stoney Ridge!"

Mammi pushed a few loose gray wisps of hair back into her prayer cap. "Do tell."

5

As Jonah hung up the phone on the wall of the workshop in his barn, he had to sit down. He couldn't believe what he had just heard from the sheriff. His mother and his daughter were in jail for stealing a police car. In jail! If he hadn't recognized the sheriff's voice, he would have even thought it might be a prank call. Bess had been in Stoney Ridge for only a few weeks. What in blazes had been going on back there?

He had to get there. He had to go, get Bess, and bring her home. As soon as possible. The thought of his precious daughter locked up in a city jail, surrounded by drug addicts and cat burglars and pickpockets and murderers, sickened him. He shuddered. Then he had a comforting thought. No one would bother her as long as his mother was nearby.

He went in search of Mose to tell him that he would be in charge of the furniture business for the next few days.

❧❧

When Mammi and Bess returned to Rose Hill Farm that afternoon, freed from the sheriff after promising that they would stop taking his car, they found a bucket of water sitting on the porch, two big catfish, mad as hornets, swimming inside. "They are sure ugly fish," Mammi said, "but they make good eatings." She picked up the bucket and took it in the house, but turned toward Bess at the door. "My ladies need feeding. And take the big pail for eggs. Lift *every* hen."

Bess always gathered every one she found, but maybe some days she didn't look as hard as she might. She picked up the pail by the kitchen door and turned to Mammi. "Aren't you wondering where those fish came from?"

"Billy left 'em," Mammi said. "He's done it before."

Bess took off her big black bonnet and hung it on the porch railing. She walked across the yard to the henhouse, cataloging her woes. Her father, understandably, had been astounded to hear that she was at the police station and said he was on his way to Stoney Ridge. He would probably be here by morning, if not late tonight, to take her home. Just when she was starting to feel encouraged about her developing friendship with Billy Lapp.

On the buggy ride back to Rose Hill Farm, Bess had fought back tears. She asked her grandmother, why didn't she just say she wanted to send her home? Why go to all that trouble to aggravate the poor sheriff?

Mammi gave her a look of pure astonishment. "I *don't* want you going home." She turned her gaze to the back of the horse. "I want my boy to *come* home."

"But why?"

"It's high time." Then her jaw clamped shut in Mammi's own stubborn way and she didn't give up another word all the way home.

What troubled Bess the most was that she understood Mammi's logic. In fact, even more worrisome, she thought it was pretty smart. Her father wouldn't have come back to Stoney Ridge under any other circumstance than an emergency. And finding out his daughter was thrown in jail for stealing a sheriff's car would definitely constitute an emergency.

She got a scoop of cracked corn from the feed bin and tossed it around the ground as the chickens tried to peck at her bare toes. Life just wasn't fair, wasn't fair at all. Under the late afternoon sky, all life seemed wrung out.

From the kitchen window came the smell of catfish sizzling in the frying pan. Suddenly, Billy came flying out of the barn, pounding for the house, face first, bellowing like a calf, "No! No! Don't eat it!"

With eyes as big as quarters, Bess

watched him jump the steps into the kitchen. She threw the corn on the ground and ran up to the house. Inside, Billy grabbed the frying pan from a startled Mammi and tossed it into the sink. Then he yelped in pain, "Eyeow!" and hopped on one leg. He had burnt his hands from picking up the pan without a rag.

With unusual presence of mind, Bess thrust his hands in the bucket of water the catfish had been in. "*What* is the matter with you?"

He yanked his hands up and she pushed them back in the water. "Those fish. Something's wrong with them. I shouldn't have left 'em on the porch, but that black cat of Bess's was eyeing them in the barn."

"What makes you think something is wrong with them?" Bess asked. She was putting ice from the icebox into a rag and tying it up to make an ice pack.

"Didn't you see them?" he asked.

"They were just as ugly as any other catfish," Mammi offered.

"They didn't have whiskers," he said,

taking the ice pack that Bess offered to him. He leaned against the counter, holding the ice pack between his hands. "And one was missing its eyes. A few weeks ago Bess noticed that birds weren't singing at the lake. So I've been back a few times. She's right. There's no birds up there anymore. And this time, I found these fish up on the shore, practically dead. Something's wrong with that lake."

"Blue Lake Pond?" Mammi put a hand against her chest. "That place is teeming with wildlife. My Samuel used to say he only needed to hold out a pail on the shore and fish would jump in."

"Not anymore," Billy said mournfully.

"What were you planning to do with the catfish?" Bess asked.

"I don't know," he said. "I hadn't gotten that far."

"Something like that happened in Berlin. A company dumped chemicals in a lake. Birds ate the fish and they ended up with strange-looking babies."

Billy's dark eyebrows shot up. "Someone is *polluting* the lake."

"Maybe so," Bess said. "But you need proof." She held up some B&W salve to put on his hands.

He held out his palms. "I don't know what shocks me more." He looked at Bess as she put a dab of salve on his hands. "Someone ruining my lake—" he gave her a sly grin—"or hearing you speak a full entire paragraph that makes sense."

Mammi snorted. "Come around here for breakfast sometime. She babbles like a brook. A person can hardly drink a cup of coffee in peace."

Bess wrapped a rag around Billy's hand and tied it so tight he yelped like a snake bit him and yanked it away from her.

"So how am I going to get some evidence that someone is polluting my lake?" he asked.

Bess put the salve back in the kitchen drawer. "You have to go out there and look for tracks. Maybe even stay out there awhile and watch, at different times of the day. Even at night."

"Trapping!" Mammi said happily, clapping her big red hands together.

"Haven't gone trapping in years. Used to be my favorite thing in the world. We'll go tonight."

❧❧

Later that evening, Jonah Riehl was on the bus heading to Pennsylvania. He gave Mose a note to give to Sallie, telling her he had a sudden errand to attend to. He didn't explain the circumstances. He felt too ashamed of what had happened. He leaned against the window on the bus and tried to sleep, but his thoughts kept him awake. He had been back in Stoney Ridge only once in the last fifteen years—for his father's funeral—since he left it that year after Rebecca died.

It was the trial that made him decide to leave Stoney Ridge for good.

The truck driver who crashed into the buggy, killing Rebecca, had been driving under the influence of alcohol that night. Jonah had to testify against him. It tore Jonah up—he was grieving so deeply for his Rebecca, yet he couldn't ignore the anguish in the truck driver's eyes. He saw the driver's wife at the trial every single day, looking as if she was barely holding herself together in one piece. Who was he to ever judge another man? If he couldn't forgive that man for what he had done, how could he ever expect God to forgive him? In a letter presented by Jonah's bishop, he had asked the judge for mercy. "He has suffered, and suffered heavily. It was a tragedy, not a crime. Sending the defendant to prison would serve no good purpose, and I plead leniency for him."

The state was less generous. The truck driver was sentenced to six years in prison for reckless driving and involuntary manslaughter.

Jonah also asked the judge to dismiss a petition for a wrongful death settlement because he was receiving all the financial help he needed from the church. The judge looked at him as if he thought Jonah might have endured more than broken bones in the accident—maybe he had been brain damaged.

The insurance company representing the truck that had struck their buggy and killed Rebecca had offered Jonah a settlement of $150,000. Jonah returned the check to the insurance company with a statement: "I'm not seeking revenge. Our Bible says revenge is not for us."

Someone in the insurance company, astounded by Jonah's letter and returned check, leaked it to the press. Newspaper writers and photographers swarmed to Rose Hill Farm like bees to a flower. Jonah couldn't even go out of his house without someone trying to take his picture and ask for comments. He thought it would blow over, but the story was picked up and reported across the nation. He received hundreds of letters expressing sympathy. And then ordinary folks started arriving at Rose Hill Farm, knocking on their door and wanting to see Bess. That was when he couldn't take it any longer. Every day brought reminders of what he had lost. It was just too painful to stay in Stoney Ridge. Even more so because he knew better. His people were known for yielding and accepting God's will. Yet, deep inside, he was angry with God for what had happened. It made it worse still for him to be among his people and feel like an outsider.

His father understood why he had to move, but his mother didn't. She felt that family belonged together, through thick or thin. Maybe that was why he agreed to let Bess go this summer. It was time to smooth things out with his mother.

His eyes jerked open. How could he possibly smooth things out when his mother got his daughter tossed into jail?

❧❧

When a round and creamy moon rose above the barn later that evening, Billy came back to Rose Hill Farm to pick up Mammi and Bess in his open courting buggy. It was so small that it tilted to one side when Mammi climbed up on it. Bess was squished between Mammi and Billy and tried not to notice how good Billy smelled—like pine soap. He led the horse up to the turn-off to the lake and drove the buggy to the edge of the trees. Then he hopped out. "I thought we would walk the perimeter and see if we find anything out of the ordinary."

Bess climbed out behind him.

"I'd better stay alert for us all and keep a lookout on things at this end of the lake," Mammi said, stretching out in the buggy seat. She yawned. "I've got eyes like an eagle and ears like an Indian scout." She dropped right off.

Billy and Bess had hardly gone a few hundred yards when they heard the rhythm of Mammi's snores echoing off the still lake water.

"She's as loud as an air compressor," Billy said.

"This is just the prelude snore," Bess said. "Wait till you hear what it sounds like when she's sleeping deep. She rattles the windows. And if you think that's loud, you should stand clear of her sneezes. If I sneezed like Mammi did, I would fly apart."

A laugh burst out of Billy and he stopped to turn around and look at Bess, amazed. "It's nice to hear you finally talking, Bess. Kinda made me nervous at first when I thought we were going to be stuck picking rose petals together all summer."

Bess's knees suddenly felt as quivery as Mammi's green Jell-O salad. Her heart was pounding so loudly she was sure it drowned out her grandmother's snores. She hurried to keep up with Billy's long strides. There weren't many perfect moments in life, she thought happily, but this was surely one of them. Here she was with Billy Lapp, on a moonlit summer night, at a beautiful lake.

"Whatever happened with that lake in Berlin?" Billy said, turning his head slightly to call back to her.

Oh. Apparently she wasn't exactly on the top of his mind like he was on hers. "Well, someone found out it was the chemical company that was dumping their waste in the lake. So then the state of Ohio got involved and the chemical company was fined a bunch of money and had to clean up the lake. Took a few years to come back, but now it's just like it was before."

"How did the state of Ohio get involved?" Billy asked.

"I guess someone notified the police."

Billy stopped abruptly. "Oh," he said flatly. He looked crestfallen.

"What's the matter?"

"Even if we found something tonight, I'm not sure what I would do with the information. You know I can't go running to the police."

Bess snorted. "Tell that to Mammi."

Billy took a few steps and whirled around. "This is no joking matter, Bess. What's the point of trying to find out who's polluting the lake if we can't turn them in?"

"Well, how are you going to protect the lake if you don't find out what's causing a problem?" She walked a few steps to catch up with him. "Maybe you're getting ahead of yourself, assuming it's a person doing wrong. Could be something else entirely."

"Like what?"

"Well, like algae growing. In science class, I learned about some kinds of algae that grow so thick they wipe out any oxygen in a pond, so all the plants and fish die. That might explain what happened to the birds. No fish, no birds." Bess liked science much better than math.

Billy took off his hat and ran a hand through his hair. Then he put his hat back on. "I guess what you're saying is not to get ahead of myself." He started walking again, scanning the shore for some sign of human activity. Too soon, they had walked the rim of the lake and were back at the buggy. Mammi's head was rolled back and she was sawing logs. Billy helped Bess up into the buggy, which startled Mammi out of her deep slumber.

"Sorry to wake you," Bess said.

"I was just resting my eyes," Mammi said. "Find anything suspicious-looking?"

"Nothing," Billy said, untying the horse's reins from the tree. "Not a thing."

"What about that?" Mammi pointed behind Billy. There, on the ground, was a pile of sawdust in between two wheel ruts, as if it had spilled from the back of a vehicle.

Billy bent down and rubbed the sawdust between his fingers. "It's fresh. I can smell the sap." He picked up some more and looked up at the trees. "It's not from these pines. It's from a different wood. Someone brought it here."

"Could sawdust ruin a lake?" Bess asked.

"If there's enough of it," he said.

"I'm feeling a little peckish." Mammi rubbed her big red hands together. "And when I get hungry, I get cranky."

And heaven knows, Bess thought, they couldn't have *that.*

Jonah got off of the bus in Stoney Ridge at five in the morning. He walked down Main Street straight to the sheriff's office, but the doors were locked and it was pitch black inside. The town was silent. It drove him crazy knowing that Bess was just yards away from him, locked up in a dirty jail cell. Frustrated, he turned and bumped right into a young English woman as she came around the corner.

"I'm sorry," Jonah apologized and picked up the purse she had dropped. "What are you doing out at this hour of the morning?" he asked. The birds weren't even singing yet.

She looked at him cautiously, then seemed to relax as he handed her the purse. "I work at the bakery. This is when the workday starts. What about you?"

He pointed up the street toward the bus stop. "I just got off the bus. Waiting for the sheriff to arrive."

"You might have a long wait. His hours can be very . . . casual."

Her gaze took in his straw hat and his jawline beard. Her face was lit softly by the streetlight and she smiled. To his surprise, so did he.

"You look pretty harmless. Why don't you wait for the sheriff in the bakery?" She crossed the street and unlocked the door to The Sweet Tooth, then turned on the lights.

He followed her inside but stood by the door. She put on her apron and turned on the lights in the kitchen. He hadn't really noticed what she looked like out in the dark street. He didn't usually pay much attention to English women, but there was something appealing about this one. That face . . . it seemed vaguely familiar. Where had he seen her? He studied the woman more closely as she bustled around in the kitchen. There was a cautious quality in her eyes that made him suspect she'd seen more of life than she wanted to. He felt as if he'd met her before, but of course that was impossible. She was quite a lovely woman, he realized, with fragile, finely carved features and a long, slender neck. And she had been kind to him, even after he nearly knocked her down in the street.

She poked her head out from the kitchen. "If you don't mind waiting a minute, I'll start the coffee."

"I don't mind," he said. He was famished. He hadn't eaten dinner last night; he was too busy trying to pack and get to the bus station in time. He sat down in a chair at a small table and stretched out his legs.

She set down a mug of coffee and a cinnamon roll on Jonah's table. "Cream and sugar?" she asked, glancing at him. Then she got a startled look on her face and froze.

He felt a spike of concern, wondering what had caused her to suddenly look so alarmed. Had he done something wrong? She dropped her eyes to the floor and spun around, returning to the kitchen to get started on the day's baking.

Jonah decided he should leave, that he must have made her uncomfortable, but she started to ply him with questions. Where had he come from? What was it like living there? She was mixing dough and rolling it out and the oven was starting to send out some delicious smells. Before he knew it, she was asking about his family and he found himself answering. He began to talk: slowly at first, like a rusted pump, then things started spilling out of him in a rush.

"Rebecca and I met when we were both only sixteen. She lived in a neighboring district. I courted her for four years, driving my buggy two hours each way to see her on Saturday nights. Sometimes, I would barely arrive home in time to help my father milk the cows on Sunday morning." He gazed into his coffee mug as the bakery lady refilled it. She poured herself a cup and slipped into a chair across from him, listening carefully.

As Jonah lifted the coffee mug to his lips, his mind floated to a different time. "As soon as her father gave us his blessing, we married. Rebecca came to live at Rose Hill Farm and a year after that, our Bess arrived." He glanced up at the bakery lady, wondering if she was listening to him only out of politeness, but the look on her face suggested otherwise, as if she was anxious for him to continue. "Most men wanted a son, but I was glad the Lord gave us a daughter. I knew Bess would be good company for Rebecca." He stopped then and looked out the window at the empty street. "You see, I thought there would be plenty of time for sons. But there wasn't."

"Life can be that way. Things have

a way of not turning out the way we expect." She said it so softly, he wondered if it was more his thought than her voice he'd heard.

Jonah caught her gaze and gently smiled. "No, you're right about that."

Then, in a voice that hurt him with its gentleness, she asked, "How did she die?"

His smile faded and he took his time answering. He'd never spoken aloud of Rebecca's accident, not with his parents or Bess, nor Mose. Not even with Sallie. Yet on this morning, the morning he returned to Stoney Ridge, he found himself wanting to talk about Rebecca. "It was a warm April night, just a week or so after Bess had been born. Rebecca wanted to go visit her folks—they were moving to Indiana— and truth be told, my mother was making Rebecca go a little stir crazy. She was always afraid of my mother, was Rebecca." He gave up a slight smile. "My mother can be a little . . . overbearing."

The bakery lady nodded sympathetically, as if she understood perfectly.

"The baby was in Rebecca's arms, sound asleep, and Rebecca had nodded off. The baby's blanket had slipped to the floor. I reached down to pick it up. I took my eyes off the road for just a moment . . ." His voice drizzled off and he closed his eyes tight. "It was the last thing I remember." He covered his face with his hand, but just for a moment. He came to himself with a start and glanced cautiously at the bakery lady. She didn't say a word, but the look in her eyes, it nearly took his breath away. It wasn't pity, nor was it sorrow. It was . . . empathy. As if she understood what a horrific moment that was for him, and how that moment had changed his life.

He hadn't meant to reveal so much to an English stranger. It shocked him, the things that spilled out of him in the predawn of that day. Maybe he was just overly tired and overly worried about Bess and his mother, but talking to that bakery lady felt like a tonic. His heart felt lighter than it had in years.

But this lady had work to do and he had stayed long enough. He stood to leave. "I don't even know your name," he said at the door. "I'm Jonah Riehl."

"I know," she said, giving him a level look. "I know who you are." She put out her hand to shake his.

He took her hand in his. It surprised him, how soft and small it was.

She took a deep breath. "My name is Lainey O'Toole."

Jonah's dark eyebrows lifted in surprise. "Lainey? Lainey O'Toole. I remember you. You were just a slip of a girl. Simon's stepdaughter."

She nodded.

"You disappeared. After your mother died."

She nodded again.

"What happened to you?"

"I became a long-term houseguest of the state of Pennsylvania."

He must have looked confused because she hastened to add, "Foster care system. Until I was eighteen."

He leaned against the doorjamb. "What then?" Jonah asked. He was sincerely interested.

"I worked at a department store in customer service. That's a fancy way

of saying I listened to people complain. I didn't want to do that forever
and a day, so I saved my money to go
to culinary school."

"I remember you and my mother baking together in the kitchen at Rose Hill
Farm." Those eyes of hers, they were
mesmerizing. Full of wonder and wisdom for a woman barely twenty-five,
if he counted back correctly. "Are you
back home now, for good?"

She didn't answer right away. "I'm
trying to do good while I'm here." She
gave him an enigmatic smile then. She
had flour on her cheek, and without
thinking, he almost brushed it away. It
shocked him that he would even consider touching a woman like that. There
were ten years between them, and a
world of differences in every way that
mattered.

Still, something about Lainey O'Toole
stirred him. He remembered her as a
small, worried-looking girl. Simon was
a bad-tempered man, lazy and cyni-
cal. Even though he lived down the
street and passed the house almost
daily, Jonah kept a wide path from

Simon, and his parents shunned him completely. Jonah saw Lainey's mother only a few times, tossing food out for chickens that lived under the front porch. He remembered her as a faded-looking woman who had probably been pretty in her youth. Lainey used to slip up to the fence that lined the house, quiet as a cat, and just watch him and his father work in the fields or around the barn. It wasn't long before his mother coaxed Lainey into the kitchen, teaching her how to bake. Just taking an interest in her, because no one else seemed to.

And here Lainey O'Toole was, a grown woman, standing in front of him.

"Jonah . . . ," Lainey started. Just as she opened her mouth to say something, the sheriff drove by in his patrol car. She snapped her mouth shut.

And now his thoughts shifted to Bess. "I'd better go. Thank you, Lainey O'Toole." He held her eyes as he put his straw hat back on his head, then tipped his head to her and hurried down to the sheriff's office.

✻

Jonah Riehl had a crooked gait. The good leg did most of the work while the weaker one shuffled to keep up, twisting stiffly from the hip. Lainey knew, from Bertha, that was a lasting result of the accident. Her heart swelled with compassion for the man as she watched him walk down the street, leaning on his cane.

She had nearly told Jonah about Bess. That first Sunday afternoon, when Bertha told her she knew Bess wasn't Jonah's daughter, she had made Lainey promise not to tell him or to tell Bess, either. "I'm the one who needs to do the telling," Bertha insisted. "And I will. When the time is right."

Lainey had agreed, reluctantly. Now she regretted that promise. She hadn't expected to be spending so much time with Bess, nor did she ever dream she would meet Jonah face-to-face.

It took her awhile to recognize him this morning, yet once she did, she saw him as he was fifteen years ago, with laughing eyes and a quick wit. When she was just a girl, he used to tease her like a big brother. Never mean-spirited, though. She remembered how kind he was . . . so very kind. He was still kind. And he still had that wavy dark hair, snapping brown eyes, and good-looking face, slightly disfigured by a broken nose. She remembered the day it was broken. He was pitching in a softball game and got hit in the face by a ball. She'd watched from afar and thought she'd never seen a nose bleed so much.

As she saw Jonah head into the sheriff's office, she leaned against the doorjamb and crossed her arms. This summer was turning into something she had never expected. Everything—all of her carefully designed plans—was turning upside down. Would things right themselves again? The oven buzzer went off and she went to check on the bread. Or maybe, she thought as she pulled the loaves from the oven, maybe things had been upside down and were turning right side up.

She set the loaves on cooling racks and pulled off her oven mitts. Either way, she had trusted God with all of this years ago, when she was only ten. And she wasn't going to stop trusting him now. She would see it through.

❦

While Bess was making her bed, she heard a car turn onto the driveway of Rose Hill Farm. She looked out the window and felt her stomach twist into a knot. It was the sheriff. With her father.

She ran downstairs to tell Mammi but found her already on the front porch, ready to greet her son. Like she had been expecting him all along. Bess went outside and stood behind Mammi as the sheriff's car came to a stop and her father opened the door. He climbed out, pulled his suitcase from the backseat, and turned to the sheriff to shake his hand.

"My work here is done," the sheriff said, leaning out the car window. "Stay out of trouble, Miz Riehl." He pointed to Bess. "You too." He made a motion with his hand, two fingers splayed, pointing from his eyes, as if to say "I'm watching you."

After he drove off, Jonah took a few strides to the kitchen porch.

"Jonah," Mammi said calmly.

"So, Mom," Jonah said, just as calmly. "Care to tell me what's been going on?"

Then an awkward silence fell, until Billy appeared out of nowhere. "If they're not going to tell you, I will. Bess had a notion to take the sheriff's car out for a few spins," he said. "Three times, from what I hear."

Bess popped out from behind Mammi and glared at Billy. What had she *ever* seen in him?

"Billy," Mammi said firmly. "Time to move the bees out to the fields. Take Bess with you." She turned to Bess. "Get your bonnet. You'll need it."

Bess went into the kitchen and grabbed her big black bonnet from the wall peg. As she passed by her father, he held his arm out wide to her. "Don't I even get a hello?"

She leaned into him and felt a wave of relief that he was here. She hadn't realized how much she missed him. He wasn't nearly as upset about the police car borrowing as she had expected him to be. But then, her father wasn't quick tempered. She had never seen him angry, not once. Still, she would know if he was upset with her. This morning he looked relaxed, even a little pleased to be here in Stoney Ridge. She hadn't expected *that.*

"Maybe when you're done with moving your grandmother's bees," Jonah said with one dark brow raised, "we can talk about your algebra grade."

She dropped her head. She hadn't expected *that* either.

❧❧

In the barn, before getting anywhere close to the beehives, Billy rolled down his sleeves, then tucked his pants into his boots. He took out a roll of mosquito netting and covered his hat and face with it. "Better cover up good, Bess," he said, but she didn't appreciate his advice. Billy lifted the mosquito netting to help her wrap it, but she turned away from him. "Bess, don't

be childish. You have to protect yourself." He turned her by the shoulders
to face him. As he wrapped the netting around her bonnet, she kept her
eyes on the ground. "What are you so
peeved about, anyway? I was only telling the truth."

She locked eyes with him. "Well,
you were wrong. It was Mammi who
wanted me to borrow that sheriff's car.
I tried talking her out of it . . . but you
know my grandmother."

Billy tucked the netting into the back
of her apron. "No kidding? That's too
bad." He sounded genuinely disappointed. "A couple of fellows were
asking me all about you. They think
you must act all quiet and shy, but
underneath . . . they say . . . sie is voll
Schpank." *She is daring.*

Oh no. That meant that everyone
in town knew about Mammi's car
thievery. "Tell them I'm neither." She
pushed his hand away from her waist
and rolled her eyes. They both looked
ridiculous, covered up with so much
mosquito netting, and she couldn't

help but laugh at the sight, which got Billy grinning.

"Well, I'll pass that information along." He put the netting on the shelf and picked up a matchbox and the smoker, then placed it on the wheelbarrow. "So what's this about algebra?"

"I see no reason to study math," she said firmly. "No reason in the world."

"I love math," Billy said.

Bess looked at him. "What is there to love?"

"Math is . . . entirely predictable," he said. "There's always a right answer."

"Only for those who make sense of it in the first place."

"You're not looking at it in the right way. Math is based on all the patterns around us. They are constant and repetitious and dependable, like . . ." He looked out the barn window. "Like rows in the fields, ripples in a stream, veins on a leaf, snowflakes. Man-made or natural, those patterns are there. Math is always the same."

She had never thought of math like that. She didn't like to think about math at all.

Billy picked up the wheelbarrow handles and pushed it out the barn door. He waited until Bess joined him, then slid it shut behind her. They walked down the path to the rose fields. "Isn't there anything about learning you love?" he asked.

"Words, I guess. How you can tell by the root the way words get started in the first place. And then how they change over time."

"See? Not so different. You're looking for patterns too."

She pondered that for a while and decided he was probably right, but she still felt suspicious about math.

"Since you're over being mad, I need some advice."

Her heart skipped a beat. Billy came to her for advice? Her madness melted away. "What kind of advice?"

"I'll tell you more when we're done. I need to concentrate." Billy pushed the wheelbarrow down to the beehives in the back of one rose field. As they approached the hives, the buzz grew louder. He lit the smoker and waved it all around the stack of hives. She noticed that he sang softly to the bees as he worked. It touched her, that gentle singing. It was one of the hymns from church, sung in a slow, mournful way. He told her his singing calmed the bees; that they were smart creatures and appreciated a good tenor voice when they heard it. She rolled her eyes at that but couldn't hold back a smile.

Carefully, Billy lifted a hive onto the wheelbarrow as Bess held it steady. A few stray bees buzzed around them, curious. They rotated the hives among the fields where the roses were in bloom. It made for more honey, Bertha had taught him. The bees didn't have to work so hard on the gathering and could concentrate their energies on the honey making. He took one more hive and gently placed it on the wheelbarrow. When he was finished, he emptied out the smoker and they headed to the barn. About halfway there, Billy stopped to make sure the bees weren't swarming, indignant that their homes had been moved. Satisfied, he told Bess she could take off the netting now.

He helped her unwind it from around her bonnet, carefully rolling it up again to reuse. "Yesterday afternoon, I went to the lake and saw the truck dumping the sawdust. Backed right up to the shoreline and lifted the truck bed up and dumped. Deep enough so that it all sank."

She pulled the big gloves from her hands. "Did you say anything to the driver?"

He shook his head. "No. I stayed out of sight."

"What are you going to do with that information?"

"That's what I don't know. That's the part I need your advice about."

Her heart skipped another beat. Maybe Billy was finally starting to notice her. She admired how much he cared about the lake. He was genuinely troubled about it.

"If I tell my father about it, he'll only say that we need to let English problems be English problems, and Amish problems be Amish problems."

"Is that what you think?" she asked.

"I can't just do nothing and let the

lake die. God gave us this earth to care for properly. But my father is right about one thing too. It's not my place to get the law involved. It's not our way to demand justice. We leave those matters in God's hands."

Bess shrugged. "It's just letting consequences have a place. There's nothing wrong with that."

"Still," he said, hesitating, and she knew. These kinds of situations were complicated. How could they care for God's earth and not want the lake to be protected? And yet by protecting the lake, they would need to get involved with the law. Billy lifted the wheelbarrow handles and started walking carefully to the rose fields. Bess followed behind, thinking hard.

She stopped as a new idea bubbled up. "Maybe there's something in between."

He turned his chin toward her. "I'm listening."

She took a few steps to catch up to him. "Every afternoon, I've been going to the bakery to visit with Lainey. There's a newspaperman—Eddie Beaker—

who comes in after three so he can buy Danish for half off. He's always asking Lainey if she's heard any big news stories. Even not-so-big stories. Any story at all, he said. Just yesterday I heard him complaining to her that he doesn't like summer. Said it's too hot and it always makes for slow news months."

Billy stopped and spun around to face her. "You think maybe he could break the story?"

She nodded. "Mammi says Eddie Beaker is 'a wolf in cheap clothing.'"

Billy smiled, then stroked his chin. "Bess Riehl, du bischt voll Schpank." He tapped his forehead. "Und du bischt en schmaerdes Maedel." *You are daring. And you're a smart girl.*

※ ※

Jonah leaned against the doorjamb at Rose Hill Farm and looked around the kitchen. It hadn't changed, which comforted him somehow. The wrinkled linoleum floor, the pale green walls and ceiling. Even the bird clock on the wall was the one he had grown up with. He used to think that clock was irritating. Now, it seemed endearing. "I see that the early rain has been good for the roses."

"Now we need sunshine to keep them dry and blooming," his mother completed his thought.

He hung his cane on the wall peg and put his straw hat on top, then sat in a chair. It was the same chair he had always sat in. He knew it would always be his chair. His place in the family. "Bess seems happy. She's as brown as a berry. Looks like she's gaining some weight from your good cooking."

Bertha nodded in agreement. "She came here looking as brittle as a bird. Now she's as fat as a spring robin."

Hardly that, Jonah thought, as Bertha poured two cups of coffee. But Bess's appearance had changed. In just a few weeks, she seemed older, more mature. "The sheriff gave me his side of the story. Mind filling me in on yours?"

Bertha eased into her chair. "I had to

do something that would get you back here."

"Why didn't you just ask?"

"I did," she said flatly. "Been asking for years."

So she had. Jonah leaned back. "What is so all-fired important that you need me to be back in Stoney Ridge? Right now?"

His mother took her time answering. She sipped her coffee, added sugar and milk, stirred, then sipped it again. "Simon's dying."

Jonah snorted. "Impossible. Dying would take too much work. He'll out-live us all."

"He's dying all right."

"Where is he? The cottage looked empty."

"He lost that years ago when the bank took it. It's been up for sale for a long time. He's at the Veterans Hospi-tal over in Lebanon."

Jonah sighed. "What's he dying of?"

"Some kind of cancer. Hopscotch disease."

"Hodgkin's?"

"That's what I said." Bertha stood

and went to the window, crossing her arms against her chest. "Them doctors are looking for family members. They want bone marrow for him." She turned back to Jonah. "They think it might cure him."

"Don't tell me you're getting tested to give your brother—a man who has done nothing for anybody his whole livelong life—don't tell me you're planning to give him your bone marrow?"

"I tried. I'd give it to him if I could. But I'm not a match." She sat down in the chair. "But you might be." She looked into her coffee cup and swirled it around. "And so might our Bess."

"Bess?" Jonah looked up in surprise. "She's a distant relation to him." He easily dismissed that notion. "What about your sisters? Why don't they get tested?"

"Two did. Three refused because he's still shunned. The two that did— Martha and Annie—they aren't a match." Before Jonah could even ask, she answered. "And their husbands won't let their children or grandchildren test for it."

"Because he's been shunned."

Bertha nodded. "You and Bess . . . you're his last chance."

Jonah exhaled. "What makes you think Simon would accept my bone marrow, even if I were a match? You always said he was as cranky as a handle on a churn."

"You leave Simon to me," she said in a final way.

❦❦

On the following Sunday, before church, Jonah was buckling the tracings on the buggy horse. Bess and his mother were upstairs getting ready to leave. His mind was a million miles away from churchgoing. He was thinking about what his mother had told him yesterday, about wanting him to take a blood test to try to cure Simon from his cancer. His mother rarely spoke of her brother—Simon had been excommunicated from the church years ago. He wasn't included in family gatherings, his name wasn't spoken, and he was ignored when he was seen, which was often.

Jonah could never figure out why Simon stayed in Stoney Ridge. He moved there right after he was discharged from the army due to an injury. Simon had been drafted in World War II and served as a conscientious objector, stationed as a maintenance worker in a base camp in Arkansas. He was accidentally shot in the foot. He claimed he was cleaning a gun, but the story was vague and changed each time he told it. Samuel, Jonah's father, said it probably went more like this: Simon was doing something he shouldn't have been, like hunting when he was supposed to be on duty, then blamed the Army for the accident. Using his disability pension, Simon bought a run-down home near his sister's farm and ran it down even further. It was as if he enjoyed being a thorn in everyone's side. But . . . that would be Simon. His father said Simon was born with a chip on his shoulder.

Jonah slipped the last buckle together on the bridle and looked up over the horse's mane to see Lainey O'Toole walking toward him.

"Bess invited me," she said, as she took in his confused look. "To church."

"Our church?" he asked, wondering why Bess would have put Lainey in such an unfair position. She might have meant well, but Lainey shouldn't feel obligated to come. "Our church . . . the service lasts for three hours." He knew enough about the English to know they zoomed in and out of church in scarcely an hour's time. Why, the first hymn was just wrapping up after an hour in an Amish church.

Lainey shrugged. "I'm used to that. The church I've been going to the last few years has long services, plus Sunday school."

"The preachers speak in Deitsch."

"I remember. I used to go with your mother." She smiled. "As I recall, those preachers can get a good deal across with just their tone of voice."

A laugh burst out of Jonah. She surprised him, this young woman.

"I can still understand a little bit of Deitsch. Growing up in Stoney Ridge . . . living with Simon those few years, I picked up a bit."

Jonah looked past her to the rose fields, then turned back to her. "Du bisch so schee." *You are so lovely.* Did he *really* just say that? Oh please no. He suddenly felt like Levi Miller, self-conscious and bashful and blurting out ridiculous, awkward compliments.

She gave him a blank look. "I guess I don't remember as much as I thought."

Oh, thank you, Lord! "I said, 'Well then, hop up.'" He offered her his hand and helped her into the buggy. He happened to notice that she smelled as sweet as a lemon blossom.

❧❧

This was how church was meant to be—pure and simple, Lainey thought as she followed behind Bertha and Bess. This must have been what church was like for the first disciples—no fancy church building with a steeple that grazed the sky. Just a home, shared, to worship in. And God was there.

Today, church was merely a well-swept barn. But God was here. She could feel his presence.

It was such a hot and humid July

morning that the host—the Zooks of
Beacon Hollow—decided to hold the
meeting in the barn, where it would be
cooler. The sliding doors were left wide
open to let the breeze waft through.

Lainey sat in the back row bench on
the women's side, in between Bess and
Bertha. Bess whispered to her that they
had to sit in the back row because no
one wanted to sit behind Bertha—she
was too big. She also warned Lainey
to watch her head. "Barn swallows
might swoop in and steal your hair for
their nest if they're in the mood. I've
seen it happen. Just two weeks ago,
to Eli Smucker's chin whiskers—"

Bertha leaned over and laid a calm-
ing hand on Bess, who snapped her
lips shut and tucked her chin to her
chest.

Lainey had to bite her lip to stop from
grinning. She could barely contain the
happiness she felt. It nearly spilled out
of her. There was no place in the world
she would rather be than where she
was right that minute. It was a miracle
of miracles. On one side of her was
Bertha, a woman who had always been

good to her, and on the other side was Bess, her very own sister. She could hardly hold back her feelings of praising God.

And to add to her happiness, she was still feeling a little dazed that Jonah had told her she was lovely. She was so startled by it that she pretended she didn't understand him. But she did. It was a phrase Simon said to her mother in those rare moments when he was at his best. Hearing it from Jonah made her stomach feel funny. She glanced at him across the large room. His dark head was bowed, preparing for worship, she knew. Unlike her mind, which seemed to be darting around the room like one of those barn swallows. Where had these new thoughts about Jonah come from? He had always been just Jonah to her, Bertha's son. She remembered that she had thought he was a good-looking young man. She had never been crazy about those scraggly Amish beards. Jonah's was a full, soft brown beard that he had worn since he was twenty. She thought back to being disappointed when he started to grow that beard after he married Rebecca and covered up that fine square chin. His face had so many other interesting features, though, such as high cheekbones and gentle brown eyes that looked at her with warm concern.

Then, as if Jonah had read her mind, he looked up and caught her eye, and she felt a nervous quiver in her belly. She reached down to smooth out her dress as a small, elderly man stood up. A perfect, pure note, as dazzling as a sunrise, floated from his open mouth. The men joined in, then the women, all singing the same slow tune, the same quavery note, almost a chanting. Two hundred voices rising to the barn rafters. They sang for the longest time. Then they stopped, as if God himself was the choir director and signaled to everyone the end of the hymn.

As Lainey inhaled the familiar barn smells of hay and animals, and heard that long, sad hymn, she felt a tidal wave of long-buried emotion. Songs and smells could bring a person back to a moment in time more than anything else. It was amazing how much could be conjured with just a few notes or a solitary whiff. Her thoughts drifted to the church service she had attended with Bertha just a few weeks before her mother had died. The wind that morning had the barest thread of warmth to it. It smelled of the thawing earth, of spring. Lainey suddenly realized that was the last true moment of childhood. The last moment she had been thoroughly happy. A sadness welled up inside her. She shut her eyes and pressed her fingers to her lips. She didn't want to cry, not here. Not now.

And then came the preaching. She was fine through the first sermon, given by an elderly minister. That sermon was told in a preacher's voice, hollow and joyless. It was the second sermon, given by Caleb Zook. She vaguely remembered him as a friend of Jonah's. Caleb was the bishop now, married to the small, copper-haired woman sitting in front of Lainey, who had a baby in her arms and a toddler by her side. Lainey was amazed at how quiet her children were, how quiet all of the children were. When it was Caleb Zook's turn to stand and preach, his eyes grazed the room and rested on his wife's face. Some kind of silent communication passed between them, because he shifted his eyes and noticed Lainey sitting in the back row. He delivered his sermon in English. For some reason, such kindness touched her deeply and made her eyes well with tears. An odd pang of longing pierced her heart. She felt overcome with a desire to belong to this—to these people—forever.

The woman with the child on her hip kept her back turned, slowly ladling the apple butter into small bowls. Bess wanted her to hurry, so she could take out the platter with bread and apple butter and serve the farthest table, where Billy happened to be sitting with his friends after the church service ended. Billy had smiled at her during the sermon. Twice. She thought that when he smiled, he really meant it.

She glanced nervously over at Billy.

Sometimes, for no reason, looking at him made her chest ache. It was the tall, strong, splendid sight of him, she supposed.

Bess cleared her throat, hoping the woman would notice she was there, waiting. But this woman could not be hurried. Bess chanced another look in Billy's direction and her heart sunk. Sure enough, Betsy Mast had gotten there first. She was leaning over Billy's shoulder, filling his glass with sweet tea. The dreamy look on Billy's face as he looked up at Betsy made Bess think about dumping the bowl of apple butter right on his head.

The woman spun around and handed Bess a platter of freshly sliced bread. Bess went to find where her father was sitting instead, to serve him. She looked all over and couldn't find him, so she set the bowl and platter at the nearest table. Then she spotted Jonah, still over by the barn, leaning one arm against the door, engrossed in a conversation with Lainey O'Toole. The way Jonah was looking at Lainey—standing a full foot taller than she did, his head bent down as if he didn't want to miss a word she was saying—something about the sight caught Bess in the heart. She stopped and stared. She'd never seen her father pay such rapt attention to a woman.

Her grandmother came up behind her and silently watched. Then she took in a deep breath and let it out with, "Hoo-boy. Didn't see that coming."

6

On Sunday evening, Jonah told Bertha he had decided to get the test to see if his bone marrow could be a match for Simon. "I'll have the test and wait for the results. But I'm not bringing any of this up to Bess," he told her. "There's no reason to. If I'm not a match, that will be the end of it. I won't let Bess get tested. She's barely related to Simon. The chance of being a match is remote."

Bertha gave a brief nod of her head. "One thing at a time."

He wasn't quite sure what she meant by that, but he needed to turn in for the night. He stood to leave but turned around to face her. "Mom, why are you going to such lengths for someone like Simon?"

"He's the only brother I got," was all she said.

That comment struck him as forever odd. It was similar to what Lainey said at church this morning when he told her that his mother lured him here to be a bone marrow transplant for Simon. She said that Bertha had told her all about Simon's illness, but she hadn't had the courage to see him yet. "I'd like to go with you to see him," Lainey told him. "It's my day off, if you don't mind going tomorrow."

"Are you sure?" he asked her. He knew Simon had treated her badly. Everybody knew. It amazed him that she would even bother with Simon.

"He's the only father I've known," was how she answered him.

So early Monday morning, Jonah met Lainey in front of the bakery and they walked to the bus station to catch the first bus from Stoney Ridge to Lebanon. He felt a little uncomfortable at first, spending an entire day traveling with an English woman, but she soon put him at ease. She started by asking him questions about Bess. It was as if she couldn't get enough of hearing stories about their life in Ohio. He found himself telling her all kinds of stories . . . Bess's first day of school when she came home and told him she quit, that one day was enough. Levi Miller, who overly liked her and left wilted flowers for her in the mailbox until the mailman complained. Her cat, Blackie, who seemed to have abandoned her at Rose Hill Farm and taken up the life of a barn cat. They both started laughing then and couldn't stop. He hadn't laughed that often in a long time, and it felt so good.

Just being with Lainey felt good. He hadn't enjoyed another woman's company so much since . . . well, since he first met Rebecca, he realized with a start. He had taken one look at Rebecca, in her pale green dress that set off her hazel eyes, and he knew she was the one for him. He never wavered, not once. He just knew.

And here he was, with feelings stirring for Lainey. Yet this made no sense.

No sense at all. It was downright wrong. Lainey was English. Besides, he felt with a sting of guilt, there was the Understanding he had with Sallie. Oh, this was wrong, wrong, wrong.

And yet . . . he couldn't take his eyes off of Lainey. He found himself memorizing every feature, every expression, of her lovely face. He marveled at her beauty, her glorious black hair that curled around her head like a wreath.

The hour-and-a-half bus ride to Lebanon flew by, and soon they were standing at a nurse's station in the hospital, filling out reams of paperwork. Then they had a long wait until a phlebotomist would be free to draw Jonah's blood for the donor test, so the nurse pointed them to the waiting room.

Lainey looked at Jonah. "Maybe I'll go see Simon while you're waiting to get your blood drawn."

"Not without me," Jonah said firmly. It worried him, having her meet up with Simon after all these years. He remembered Simon to be unpredictable. Granted, his love for the drink had much to do with those moods. But even at his best, Simon was not a pleasant person.

There was something in Lainey's expression right then—a sadness? A longing? He couldn't quite tell. Then she gave him one of her inscrutable smiles and sat down in the plastic chair. He sat down next to her.

"Jonah, why would you be willing to share your bone marrow with Simon?"

He set his cane on the empty chair next to him. "I guess I'm doing it for my mother. Since he was shunned all those years, there hasn't been much we could do for him. But this . . . well, maybe this would give Simon the push he needs to return to the church." He crossed his arms against his chest. "That's what she's hoping, anyway, to encourage him to make things right with God before it's too late."

"Did you ever know that Bertha used to bring us meals on a regular basis?" Lainey asked. "And she would slip my mother money to pay bills."

"What?" Jonah was stunned. "My parents . . . ?"

"No. Not your father. Only your mother." Lainey tilted her head. "Your mother . . . she's something else."

Jonah couldn't believe it. No Amish from their church went near Simon. To do so would risk their own good standing. They were quiet for a long time after that, until he finally asked, "So are you in Stoney Ridge this summer to see Simon?"

Her head was bowed as she quietly said, "He's part of the reason. I need to tell him something." She lifted her head and looked him in the eye, as if there was something she wanted to say. He'd had that feeling before when he was with her . . . as if there was something she was holding back. But then, how could he really know that? He was just getting to know her.

If Simon was part of the reason she was back in Stoney Ridge, what was the other part? He was just about to ask when a large graying woman in a nurse's uniform pointed at him from the door to the lab. "Jonah Riehl?"

He nodded.

"In here. Now." Her lips compressed

into a flat line. "Hope you got big-sized veins cuz I've had too many folks in here today with itty bitty veins. Had to poke 'em a hundred times."

His dark eyebrows shot up in alarm. "I'll be back soon," he told Lainey. "Real soon, I hope."

Fifteen minutes later, he came out, unrolling his sleeve. He looked around the waiting room for Lainey, but she was gone.

❦

As soon as Jonah left with the nurse, Lainey went to find Simon. She finally located him on a ward for terminally ill patients. He was at the far end of the ward, and she felt herself trembling as she approached him. When she was about ten feet away, she stopped and watched him for a while. He was sleeping and looked so peaceful. Simon had been handsome before alcohol had thickened his face. He had good features, high cheekbones, and deep-set eyes. Once, he had been a big man. Now, he seemed shriveled, like a grape left out in the sun. His face, once smooth and glossy, was like old shoe leather.

She used to be terrified of him. He could be sweet and charming, but then something minor could trigger an explosive rage.

She remembered one time when she served him a piece of cake she had made and waited by his side, hoping to see if he liked it. He had eaten it in its entirety. Then, instead of complimenting her, he yanked the blue ribbon she won at the county fair for her cherry tart off of the refrigerator and tore it into pieces. "You were getting too fond of that ribbon. Don't you think I've noticed?"

She didn't answer him, which had enraged him.

"Pride goeth before a fall. You should be ashamed!"

She glanced at her mother for help, but her mother looked away. "You're right," Lainey said meekly. "I was too fond of winning that ribbon."

Afterward, her mother had tried to explain to her that it was getting injured in the war that had made Simon

so quick to anger. Lainey wasn't so
sure. She thought he was born mad,
though he was the only Amish-born
person she'd ever known who had a
temper on him. They were gentle people, she knew that to be true. Gentle
like Jonah.

Simon opened his eyes and stared
at her. Then recognition dawned in his
eyes. Those eyes—icy blue—combined
with his mane of thick white hair had
always reminded Lainey of a Siberian
Husky. "Elaine?"

Elaine, her mother. Lainey supposed
she did resemble her mother, at least in
coloring. Certainly more than Bess did.
Bess took after Simon, that was plain
to see. "No, Simon. I'm not Elaine. She
died over fifteen years ago. I'm Lainey,
her daughter."

Simon peered at her, trying to com-
prehend what she was saying. He was
very ill, she could tell that. "I got married once," he said. "Long time ago,
she left me. That's when my life took
a turn."

"She didn't leave you, Simon. She
died having your baby."

He closed his eyes and was quiet for a moment. After a while, he opened one eye. "I don't suppose you have something to drink?" he asked her, licking his lips.

"There's some water by your bedside." She went to it and poured a glass, then held it out to him.

"I was hoping for something a little stronger," he said, brushing her hand away that held the water glass. "Course, I don't drink much as a habit. Don't have the taste for it."

She knew that was a lie. Simon drank like a fish.

He put his head back down on the pillow and gazed at her. "So, you're Lainey. All growed up."

She nodded.

"I don't have money, if that's what you're after."

"I don't want your money, Simon."

"You must want something. Showing up after all these years, without a word. You're after something. Everybody wants something."

"I don't want anything from you. I wanted to tell you that . . . I forgive you. That's all." She exhaled. "I just want you to know that I forgive you."

He snorted. "For what?"

She dropped her head and didn't see him grab her arm until he had it tight in his grip.

"For what?" he snarled, like an angry dog. "I put a roof over your head and food in your mouth. You weren't even my kid. You should be thanking me."

His grip was weaker than she would have expected. She peeled his fingers off of her arm as calmly as if she was peeling a banana, and stepped back. "You can't hurt me anymore." She took in a deep breath. "No matter what you think, Simon, you do need to be forgiven. And no matter what, I do forgive you."

He seemed not to care in the least. He pointed to the door. "Don't let the door hit you where the dog bit you," was all he said.

His sarcasm slapped her with surprise. She lifted her chin and marched toward the door. Her shoes made a clicking sound down the ward. As soon as she went through the door, she leaned against the wall, trying to compose herself. Hadn't she thought this all through before she even asked Jonah if she could join him today? Hadn't she reminded herself, over and over, not to expect anything back from Simon? And yet, here she was, deeply disappointed. She found herself shivering, as if she was very cold. She heard someone call her name, so softly she thought she might have imagined it. But there was Jonah, walking down the hall toward her. When he saw the look on her face, he held out his arms to her. She burst into tears and sank into him.

Dear Jonah,

Your note said you would be gone only a few days. It has now been nearly a week and I haven't heard a word from you. Should I be planting celery? Can't have an Amish wedding without celery!
Affectionately,
Sallie

"Today's the day, Bess," Billy said when she came into the greenhouse to bring him a glass of lemonade. "We're going to the bakery today to talk to Eddie Beaker."

Bess's eyes went wide. "We? What do you mean, we?"

He took a sip of his lemonade and wiped his mouth with the back of his hand. "You've met him. I don't have any idea who he is."

"I haven't *met* him. Lainey pointed him out, that's all. And you can figure out who he is. He wears a plaid blazer and his hair is slicked back with Crisco and he chews on a cold cigar." She shook her head. "You go. He gives me the creeps."

Billy blew air out through his lips like an exasperated horse.

"What would we say, anyway?"

"Bess, think," he said patiently, as if she were a schoolchild stumped on an easy problem. "We need to be talking about the lake just loud enough so that he overhears us. He needs to think it's his story to break."

She bit her lip. He made it sound simple, but she knew it wouldn't be. It was just like Mammi and the sheriff's car. Same thing.

"Come on, Bess," he said, as she hesitated. "We've got to try and save our lake! You're the one who found out it was polluted in the first place!"

The way he was looking at her, so passionate and fired up, made her fall in love with him all over again. And he had said "our lake," like it belonged to just the two of them. "Fine," she said. "I'll tell Mammi that we're going to buy some cherry tarts from Lainey. She'll be thrilled."

But there were no cherry tarts at The Sweet Tooth today. It was Lainey's day off, Bess and Billy discovered unhappily when they arrived at the bakery five minutes before three. Mrs. Stroot was trying to lock up for the day and seemed anxious for them to leave. Billy stood in front of the counter, stalling for time, pretending that he couldn't make up his mind about what to buy.

Bess kept looking down the street to see a man in a big plaid jacket head this way. Finally, just as Mrs. Stroot was about to shoo them out, in came Eddie Beaker. It was just like Bess had told Billy, he was chewing a cold cigar.

"You go first," Billy told Eddie as he walked up to the glass counter. "I'm still thinking it over."

Mrs. Stroot rolled her eyes.

Eddie pointed to the Danish. "How much?"

"Ten percent discount," Mrs. Stroot bargained.

"Make it half off and I'll take them all," he growled.

As Mrs. Stroot sighed deeply and started to pack the Danish in a box, Billy unrolled his spiel. "I was planning to go fishing, but there's just no fish at Blue Lake Pond." He motioned with Bess to pick up his lead.

"Still none?" Bess asked, too loudly.

"Just the dead ones on the shore," he said.

"Such a pity," Bess said. "And all of those birds gone too." She wished Lainey were here. She would have been able to engage Eddie Beaker into the conversation. He seemed far more interested in the Danish than in the missing wildlife.

Billy sidled closer to Eddie Beaker. "It's the strangest thing. Ever since that paper mill went in, there's been less and less wildlife up there. Now, there's virtually none. Can't figure it out." He looked at Eddie Beaker to see if he was taking the bait. What more of a morsel could he toss to a reporter hungry for news?

Eddie Beaker pulled out his wallet to pay Mrs. Stroot. He handed her a few dollars, took the change, put it in his pocket, and left the bakery.

Billy exchanged a defeated look with Bess. "Let's go home."

Mrs. Stroot groaned.

❧❧

Bess woke to the sound of bacon sputtering and popping in the pan. She lay in bed and smiled. Mammi said she would be making pancakes with maple syrup today.

Bess was delighted that her father

wasn't talking about returning to Ohio anytime soon. She had assumed they would be heading back as soon as possible, but no. Jonah had told her that he was waiting on blood test results to see if he could help out Mammi's brother with his cancer. And happily, there was no mention of Bess as a donor.

She was glad she didn't have to worry about returning to Ohio. She had enough worries on her plate without adding more.

Her main worry was Billy Lapp. He'd taken up the outrageous notion that Bess could give him advice about how to get Betsy to stop flirting with other boys and just concentrate on him. "I know she's sweet on me," he told her just that afternoon while they were bagging up dried rose petals from the drying frames.

Bess listened sympathetically with her face and about a third of her mind. The rest of her thoughts were on memorizing Billy's face. "How do you know that?" She bent down to scratch a mosquito bite on her ankle until it bled. "Well?" she asked defiantly.

"She tells me so."

Bess straightened up and rolled her eyes to the highest heaven at that comment. "If she's telling that to you, Billy, she's telling that to all the boys."

He scrunched up his handsome face. "Nah. You don't know Betsy like I do."

How could Billy be so smart in rose grafting and mathematics and so dumb when it came to understanding women? The way the male sex thought had her stumped.

Bess had tried to have a conversation with Betsy Mast after church the other day, just out of curiosity. She couldn't deny that Betsy was exceptionally pretty—even more so, up close—but she had a breathy, baby voice and answered questions with questions. Bess asked her if her parents were farmers, and she responded by saying, "Aren't all Amish farmers?" Well, no, Bess told her. Some build furniture, like her father. One fellow manufactures windows. Others even work in factories. Betsy looked at her as if she was describing life on another planet. Bess wasn't sure if Betsy's lantern in her attic wasn't lit or if she was just trying to pretend she was interested when she wasn't.

Billy nudged Bess to bring her back to his problem at hand. "What do you think I should do? Should I tell her I want her to stop seeing other fellows?"

They were working side by side. She enjoyed being this close to him. He smelled of earth and sweat and roses. "I don't know, Billy."

He lifted a frame and leaned it against the wall. "Sure you do. You're a girl, aren't you?"

Charming. At least he had noticed that.

"You can't *make* someone like you." She knew that to be true. "There was a boy in Ohio who drove me cuckoo, he liked me so much. Kept trying to walk with me to school and hold my hand and talked about getting married someday. He hung around me like a summer cold. He even had our children's names picked out. All ten of them!" She shuddered. "If he had just left me alone, maybe I would have taken notice of him." Probably not, though. Everything about Levi Miller was annoying to her.

Billy lifted the last empty frame and set it against the wall. He swiveled around on his heels, his head cocked. "Okay, I'll try it! I knew you'd have an idea of what to do. You're a peach." He smiled, exposing two rows of very white, straight teeth. Possibly one of his best features, Bess assessed. Either that or the cleft in his chin.

Bess turned away. *Don't tell me I'm a peach*, she thought. *Tell me I'm . . . what? Beautiful? Hardly. The love of your life? That would be Betsy Mast. A loyal friend? Oh, that sounds like a pet dog.* So what did she want? Why was she so determined to keep on loving him, knowing that he loved another?

She had no answer.

In the middle of her musings, Billy surprised her with a loud and brotherly buss on her forehead. He grabbed his hat and waved goodbye as he left the barn for the day. She went to the open barn door and watched him walk down the drive, hat slightly tilted back on his head, whistling a tune as if he didn't have a care in the world. Blackie— fatter than ever from hunting all those barn mice and birds and other things Bess didn't want to think about—came out of his hiding place and wound himself around her legs. She bent down to pick him up, the traitor.

She wasn't sure what she had said that gave Billy a better plan to woo Betsy, but she knew she wasn't going to wash that kiss off of her forehead for a very long time.

Billy hurried through his chores that afternoon to get home, shower, and change, so he could hightail it over to the volleyball game at the Yoders'. He was grateful to Bess for giving him such good advice. Bess was turning out to be a valuable resource. He hadn't really had a friend who was a girl before. Bess was easy for him to talk to, maybe because she was a good listener. When Bess told him the story about the fellow who overly liked her, it hit him like a two-by-four. That was just the way he'd been acting toward Betsy.

It made so much sense. Betsy was more than a year older than he was. The last time he had tried to talk to her about courting, she tilted her head and asked him how old he was.

"Eighteen," he said. "Nearly nineteen."

Betsy gave him a patronizing look. "You can't even call yourself a man yet."

"Years aren't everything," Billy said. "I'm taller and stronger than most grown men."

Betsy had smiled and let him kiss her on the cheek, but he knew she never took him seriously. Of course not. He'd been acting immature, fawning and obsequious. Girls didn't like that, Bess had told him. That came as a surprise, but most things about girls came as a surprise to him.

Starting tonight, he was going to ignore Betsy. Not talk to her. Not even look at her.

When Billy arrived at the Yoders', he found his friends huddled together in a sad circle. "Who died?" he asked his best friend, Andy Yoder, who claimed to also be head over heels in love with Betsy. But Billy wasn't at all concerned. Andy was always in love with somebody.

"Haven't you heard? Betsy Mast ran off. We think she's with an English fellow who works at the Hay & Grain. Guess they've been planning it for months now." Andy looked as if his world had just imploded. "She's just been using all of us as decoys, so her folks wouldn't catch on."

That night, Bess was sleeping deeply until a noise woke her. She opened her eyes and tried to listen carefully to the night sounds. She wasn't entirely used to Rose Hill Farm yet, the way the walls creaked or the sounds of the night birds, different from Ohio birds. At first she thought the sound must have been Mammi's snoring, but then she heard something else. Something thumped the roof by her window. She hoped it was a roof rat. Or maybe Blackie, finally coming out of that barn for a visit. Where was Boomer when she needed him? Probably snoring right along in rhythm with Mammi.

She tiptoed out of bed and looked out the window. Sometimes at night the leaves rustled branches at the window, but she didn't see leaves or branches. A shape was down there and it scared her half to death. She was just about to scream when she heard the shape calling up to her.

It was Billy, below her window, waving to her. He cupped his hands around his mouth and whispered loudly, "Get dressed and come down! I need to talk to you!"

Bess's heart sang. She never dressed faster in her life. She stuck herself twice as she pinned her dress together. She bunched up her hair into a sloppy bun and jammed her prayer cap over it, then quietly tiptoed down the stairs and slipped out the side door.

Billy was pacing the yard, arms crossed against his chest. When he

saw her, he stopped and motioned to
her to come. "Let's go to the pond."

He had left his horse and courting
buggy on the road so that he wouldn't
waken Mammi and Jonah, he said,
so they hurried down the drive and
climbed in. Bess looked back once,
but the large farmhouse looked silent.
Billy slapped the horse's reins and
kept his eyes straight ahead. He didn't
say a word, but Bess didn't care. Here
she was on a perfect, moonlit summer night, being secretly courted by
Billy Lapp. This was the most wonderful, splendid moment of her life. She
wanted to remember every detail of the
evening so she could relive it during
dreary moments—math class came to
mind—when she returned, inevitably,
to Ohio. The night was dark, so she
chanced a glance at Billy, admiring the
determined way his jaw was sticking
out, the stern set of his mouth, his two
dark eyebrows furrowing together.

All of a sudden, Bess's dreamy hopes
evaporated, like steam rising from a tea
cup. She felt something was wrong,
but then she was always feeling that

and it never was. "Billy, is something bothering you?"

He took in a deep breath. "She's gone, Bess. She ran off with an English fellow who worked at the Hay & Grain." He wiped his eyes with the back of his sleeve.

"Who?"

"For crying out loud, Bess! Who do you think? Betsy!" He jerked the horse's reins to sharply turn right onto the path that led to Blue Lake Pond. He pulled back on the reins and stopped the horse at the end of the level space, then hopped down and tied the reins to a tree. He sauntered down to the water's edge, looking bereft.

Bess stayed in the buggy, watching him, half furious, half delighted. A part of her was disappointed that Billy used her as a listening post for his troubles. The part that felt delighted Betsy was gone made her feel shamed. What kind of person took delight in another person's downfall? She knew that wasn't right and she breathed a quick apology to the Lord for her sinful thoughts. But from the start she knew what kind of girl Betsy was, that she never did care about Billy or see how special he was. Betsy Mast wasn't good enough for Billy Lapp. Then she caught herself. That, too, was a sinful thought, and she had to apologize again to the Lord.

Goodness. Love was a tricky business.

She could see that Billy was suffering, and she tried not to be too glad for it. She sighed and hopped down from the buggy to join him.

"This is the worst summer on record," he said mournfully. "My lake is ruined. My love life is ruined." The words gushed out of him, heartfelt. He pressed a fist to his breast. "I love her so, it's like a constant pain, right here in my chest." He glanced at Bess. "You probably don't understand that kind of love."

Oh, I understand it all right, Bess thought. Love that burns so hot and fast it makes you act crazier than popping corn on a skillet.

He was sitting at the water's edge with his elbows leaning on his knees. "It's your fault, you know."

Her jaw dropped open.

"It is. If you had only given me the idea of ignoring her before today, maybe she would have taken me more seriously." Billy looked up at the moon. "I should have told her how much I loved her. How I was planning on marrying her. I shouldn't have waited."

Bess rolled her eyes. One minute he's ignoring Betsy. The next minute he's professing undying love.

"It's just that . . . I've never felt like that about anyone before. And I'm sure she was in love with me. I'm just sure of it."

Bess plopped down on the shore next to him. "Lainey said she's seen Betsy zooming around town in that English fellow's sports car all summer."

Billy froze. "That's not true."

"Lainey wouldn't lie about that," she said softly. "And you must know she was spending time in other boys' courting buggies." She looked away. "Even I knew that, and I've only been here a little over a month."

"That is a lie!" Billy shouted.

"No, it is not. You know it's the truth.

I've seen Betsy in Andy's buggy and Jake's buggy and—"

Billy scrambled to a stand. "Aw, you don't know what you're talking about! She told me to my face that she was pining only for me!"

Bess rose to her feet and brushed off her dress. "Billy . . . you must have had some inkling—"

"Why am I even trying to talk to you about this? You're nothing but a child! What would you know about love?" He spun around and marched to the buggy.

Bess opened her mouth, snapped it shut. How *dare* he call her a child! She stomped up to the buggy. "Betsy Mast was never sweet on you! You got caught up like all the others with her . . . her curves and big lips and wavy hair. There was nothing in the attic." She tapped on her forehead. "Kissing don't last. Brains beats kissing every time."

Billy stared at her, as if he was trying to absorb what she had said. Finally, she threw up her hands in the air, turned, and marched up to the road to walk back to Rose Hill Farm.

She was halfway down the dark road and thought she heard a rustling noise in the berry bushes along the road. She stopped, slowly turned, looked back. The movement behind her also stopped. Each time she paused, it happened. Was Billy really going to let her walk all of the way home by herself? She was determined not to look behind her to see if he was coming, but now she was sure she heard a loud scruffling noise. Why, it was as loud as a bear, she started to think, though she had never actually come face-to-face with a bear. Bears liked berry bushes, she knew that for a fact. Yes, it definitely sounded like something was following her. A spooky owl hooted, wind cracked in the trees, and something else made a slithery noise that she hoped wasn't a snake, because she was afraid of snakes.

Just when she was about to run for her life, she heard the gentle clip-clop of Billy's horse pull up the road.

When he was beside her, he called

out in his soft, manly voice, "Bess, hop in."

She continued walking quickly up the road, stubborn but pleased he had come for her.

Billy slowed the horse to a stop and jumped out, putting his hand on her shoulder to turn her to face him. "Bess. Don't be like that. I'm sorry I called you a child. I'm just . . . upset."

He looked so heartbroken and sad that her madness dissolved. He guided her back to the buggy and helped her up. They rode home silently, and he let her off at the edge of the drive so she could sneak back in the house.

Morning came too early. Bess couldn't stop yawning throughout Jonah's prayer before breakfast. Mammi handed her a cup of coffee without any milk in it. When Bess looked into the cup, puzzled, Mammi said in her matter-of-fact way, "Awful hard to sleep with a full moon blasting through the window. Goings-on outside look as bright as daylight."

Bess froze. Her eyes darted between Jonah, who was spooning strawber-

ries onto his hot waffle, and her grandmother, quietly sipping her coffee with
a look on her face of pure innocence.
There was no end to what Mammi
knew.

7

The weather all week was sunny and mild with no sign of rain. Late one afternoon, Lainey found Caleb Zook out in his cornfield, walking among the rustling whispers of the stalks. He was a tall man, yet the green stalks nearly reached his chin. He waved when he saw her and came through the path to meet her by the fence.

"We met at church on Sunday," she said, putting out her hand to shake his. "I'm Lainey O'Toole."

"I remember." He smiled. "I remember you as a girl too. Bertha brought you to church now and then."

His warmth surprised her. She would have thought a bishop would act stern

and serious and cold with an Englisher.
But Caleb Zook wasn't cold. Not cold
at all. "I was hoping to have a talk with
you sometime."

"Now is as good as any," he said
kindly, though she knew she had interrupted him. "Shall we walk?" He
hopped over the fence and joined her
along the road. "What's on your mind?"

"There's something I've been thinking about. I've given it a lot of prayer,
and thought, and more prayer. And
more thought." She had too. It was
something she couldn't get out of her
mind. The more she tried, the more
she felt God pointing her in this direction. And it was a frightening direction.
She wouldn't be in charge of her life,
not anymore.

He cocked his head, listening intently.

"I want to become Amish."

Caleb took off his hat and spun it
around in his hands. "You want to become Amish?" he asked her. "Amish go
English, but English don't go Amish. At
least, not very often. I can only think of
a few converts." He looked up at the

sky. "Oh, lots of folks come and say they want a simpler life, but they don't last more than a few months. It's just too hard on them. The language, living without modern conveniences. They just didn't understand what they'd be giving up."

"Their independence," she said quietly.

"Yes. Exactly that." He looked at her, impressed. "Folks don't realize that being Amish is much more than simple living. It's giving up self for the good of the community. It's giving up individual rights because you're part of a whole. It's called Gelassenheit. There's not really a way to say what it means in English."

She nodded. "I know enough about the Amish to know what you're getting at. But that's the very reason I want to become Amish." Her gaze shifted past him to the corn in the fields, swaying in the wind. "For just that very reason— to be part of a whole. To belong." She crossed her arms against her chest. "I don't know if you can understand this, but I've never really belonged to anyone or anything. Until I was ten, I watched all of your families, always wishing I were part of one."

Caleb listened, spinning his hat. "Have you thought of joining an English church? Wouldn't that give you what you're looking for?"

She dropped her chin to her chest. "I've always belonged to God. He's been the one thing I've been able to count on. I've always gone to church, even on my own, even when I was living with different foster families." She lifted her head. "But there's still a part of me that wants something more. I thought finding a career would be the answer, so I saved up my money for culinary school. That's where I was heading when I ended up in Stoney Ridge this summer. But now that I'm here, I know it's something else that I want." She swept her arm out in an arc and gathered her fist to her chest. "I want this." She owed so much to the Amish. It was through them, years ago, when her sorry childhood was at its bleakest point, that she met the Lord. It was one of those mornings when Bertha let her tag along to church. Lainey couldn't understand much of the service, but there came a moment when she knew God loved her. It was during a hymn, a long, mournful Amish hymn, and it was as real as if God spoke to her, telling her that he knew her and loved her and not to worry. He would be watching out for her. She couldn't explain how or why, but she knew it was true, and that assurance had never left her.

Caleb looked at her with great sincerity. "Being Plain . . . it's not easy, Lainey, even for those of us born to it."

"I know more about being Amish than you might think," she said. "Do you remember Simon, Bertha's brother?"

He dropped his eyes. "Of course."

"Simon had it all wrong, about being Amish." Caleb was about to interrupt, but she put a hand up to stop him. She knew what he was going to say. "Oh, I know he was excommunicated. But he was raised Amish and thought he understood what it meant. He emphasized all the wrong things. He would rail against pride and then scold my mother for decorating a birthday cake for me with icing. He would say God was watching everything we did, like an angry parent, then he would go out drinking until the wee hours."

She could see Caleb wasn't sure what she was trying to say. She tried to make it more clear, but this was hard. She was telling him things she had never told anyone else. "Even back then, I knew he was missing the heart of it all. He didn't understand God the way I knew him, not at all."

Caleb raked a hand through his hair. "I have to ask. Does this have anything to do with Jonah Riehl?"

She looked at him, stunned.

"I noticed the two of you talking together after church on Sunday."

Her eyes went wide with disbelief. Why would talking together make the bishop think she wanted to join the church? "No! For heaven's sake, no! Nothing could be further from the truth. Jonah will be leaving for Ohio any day now. Bess said he's planning to marry someone there. I'm staying right here, in Stoney Ridge."

Caleb spun his straw hat around in his

hands, around and around. She could see he was thinking hard. "Spend one week without using electricity."

Lainey's eyes went wide. "What will I tell Mrs. Stroot at The Sweet Tooth?"

He smiled. "No. Not at the bakery. But at home. You might find yourself heavy-hearted in your soul for machine-washed clothes and flipping on a light switch and other things in life that you have taken for granted."

Lainey was sure she wouldn't be so heavy-hearted. She had grown up poor, accustomed to going without luxuries. "Before I came to Stoney Ridge, I worked at a department store, listening to people's complaints about the products they bought." She shook her head. "All day long, I listened to complaints. It struck me one day that people were hoping these products—these things—would bring them happiness and satisfaction. But they never did." She looked up at him. "Because they can't."

Caleb listened carefully to her. "One week without electricity. Then we'll talk again." He put his hat back on his head and laid his hand on the fence post. Before turning to go back to work, he added, "For now, Lainey, I'd like you to keep this to yourself. Just something between you and the Lord God to work out. I'll be praying too."

She did write weekly to her two friends, Robin and Ally, but she would never dare tell them about this new plan. They would think she was certifiably crazy. "Bess knows."

Caleb tilted his head and smiled approvingly. "Then we'll keep this between the three of us." He jumped back over the fence.

Lainey watched the top of his straw hat until he disappeared among the cornstalks before she started back down the road. The funny thing was, going Amish was Bess's idea in the first place, a week or so before Lainey went to church with her. Bess and Lainey were baking muffins one afternoon at the bakery and talking about what they imagined a perfect life to be. Lainey described growing up Amish, and Bess looked at her, surprised. "Well, why don't you become Amish, then?" Lainey laughed, but Bess persisted. "I mean it. Why not?"

Lainey hadn't taken her seriously, but she hadn't stopped thinking about it ever since. And then when she went to church last week, she felt an even stronger pull. So then she started to pray about it, long and hard, asking God to tell her all the reasons why she *shouldn't* become Amish. But all she sensed from God was the same question Bess had posed, "Why not?"

She ran through all the logical things: she didn't know their customs or language, she didn't dress Plain, she would have to give up modern conveniences. Many things that she took for granted would be forbidden, like listening to the radio or watching television for entertainment. Then there were the deeper aspects to being Amish: humility and obedience to authority and denying self. Those weren't exactly popular concepts in the world she lived in.

It didn't make any sense, yet she couldn't deny what was stirring in her heart: a deep-down longing to join the

Amish church and community. She wanted a place amongst them.

❧❧

For the rest of the week, Bess avoided Billy as best she could, but he was so sulky, he didn't even notice.

"That boy looks like he's been poked in a private place," Mammi noted, watching him walk to the barn one morning. She finished drying the last dish at the kitchen sink and hung the dish towel to dry. "Anything to do with Betsy Mast running off?"

How did Mammi know everything that went on in this town? "It's not fair! It's just not fair," Bess cried, dropping her head on her arms at the kitchen table. "How could he be so sweet on a girl who would leave her church and family?"

Mammi shot her a warning glance. They should be worried that Betsy's soul was in peril, not throw stones at her. Bess knew that, but it was hard not to feel despair over the situation.

"The only fair I know hands out ribbons for canned pickles and prize tomatoes," Mammi said calmly. She eased her big self down onto a kitchen chair. "Things happen for a reason. Best to leave it in the Lord's hands."

"Do you think Billy will pine after her *forever*?" Bess glanced out the window as he came out of the barn and went over to the greenhouse.

"Forever is a big word for a fifteen-year-old. No sense tearing through life like you plan on living out the whole thing before you hit twenty." She leaned back. Bess was sure she heard the chair groan. "But he's no fool, that Billy Lapp."

Bess had no desire to listen to Billy's woes about Betsy Mast, but the situation at Blue Lake Pond was another matter entirely. Last night, lying in bed, she gave the matter serious thought and had a brainstorm. In the morning, she took out a sheet of white paper and started to write. She described the vanishing wildlife, the sawdust on the shoreline, the truck seen coming in and out dropping a load of paper pulp. She even included the license plate of the truck. She signed the letter, A Friend of the Lake. She addressed the letter to the *Stoney Ridge Times*, attention: Letter to the Editor, put a stamp on it, and tucked it in the mailbox so the postman would pick it up. She hoped the good Lord would understand that she wasn't just doing this to help Billy Lapp. She really did care about that lake.

Then she waited. And waited. But there was no sign of any activity at Blue Lake Pond other than the truck dropping paper pulp into it on a regular basis.

After lunch one day, Bess and Mammi washed the dishes and swept the room, and now Mammi was mending a torn dress hem while Bess was cutting scrap material into quilt pieces. They sat close to the window for better light—it was raining again. Jonah was in the greenhouse fixing a broken window.

"Mammi, I've been thinking," Bess said.

"Mebbe you should have tried that in math class," Mammi said.

Bess paid no attention. She was getting used to her grandmother. "I just don't know what else we can do about Blue Lake Pond. Billy and I have tried to get the attention of the right people, and they just don't seem to care."

Mammi's brow was furrowed and she rubbed her forehead, thinking hard. Then a look came over her. You had to study hard to see any expression at all on Mammi's face, but it was a look Bess was coming to know. She could tell Mammi was having one of her sudden thoughts. Mammi slammed her palms down on the table, stood, grabbed her bonnet off of the hook, and opened the door. "You coming?"

Bess followed behind her to help get the buggy ready. It wasn't long before Mammi went flying into town and pulled the horse to a stop at the sheriff's office.

Bess's heart nearly stopped. "Oh no. Oh no no no. I am not telling that sheriff about this. I don't want to get the law involved and then have to testify and . . . oh no." Bess crossed her arms against her chest. "I am staying right here."

"Suit yourself," Mammi said agreeably. "Here he comes now."

From across the street came Sheriff Johnny Kauffman. "Well, well, well. It's Miz Riehl and her granddaughter. Out on another crime spree?"

Mammi ignored his question. "Johnny, it's time you came out to dinner at Rose Hill Farm. I was thinking catfish. Battered and fried."

The sheriff's eyebrows shot up. He was practically licking his chops. "Your cooking is legendary, Miz Riehl."

"Saturday lunch then. We'll be looking for you." She climbed back in the buggy. "You wouldn't mind bringing the catfish, would you? You being such a dedicated fisherman and all. From Blue Lake Pond? No better catfish than Blue Lake Pond."

The sheriff looked pleased. "I haven't been out that way all summer." He clapped his hands together. "What time you want me at your farm?"

Mammi whispered to Bess in Deitsch, "What time does that paper truck make the drop?"

"Two on Saturdays," Bess whispered back.

"Twelve noon," Mammi said decidedly. "I want those catfish still jumping."

"I'll be there, Miz Riehl." He looked pleased. "You can count on it."

As they drove off, Bess tried to object, but Mammi waved her off. "You leave him to me."

Bess spent the drive home trying to think up Mammi-proof, ironclad excuses to absent herself from Saturday's lunch. *Nothing.* Nothing came to mind.

୨⭑୧

On Saturday morning, Mammi picked out two plump chickens to roast. By eleven, they were plucked, dressed, and in the oven. At twelve thirty, the sheriff turned into the drive at Rose Hill Farm and parked, all riled up.

"There wasn't a fish to bite," he told

Mammi. "Something's *wrong* with that lake."

"Do tell," Mammi said, looking surprised. "Why, just last week, Billy Lapp said there's no birds out there anymore." She shook her head. "It's a misery, all right."

"She means mystery," Bess whispered to the sheriff.

"No, she's right," the sheriff said, looking quite bothered. "It *is* a misery. I sure was looking forward to Bertha Riehl's catfish, battered and fried."

"We'll have to make do with chicken," Mammi said. "Bess, go call your dad from the barn. Tell him dinner is ready."

The sheriff ate heartily, but as he left, Bess and Mammi noticed he turned left instead of going right into town. Mammi said she had a hunch he was heading back out to Blue Lake Pond.

❧

Early Wednesday morning, Billy came running up to Rose Hill Farm, hollering for Bess at the top of his lungs. Bess and Jonah and Bertha were having breakfast. He burst into the kitchen.

"Look at this, Bess!" He held a newspaper up in his hands. The headline read "SCHWARTZ PAPER COMPANY FINED FOR POISONING BLUE LAKE POND."

"Somehow, it worked!" Billy was overjoyed. "That Eddie Beaker took the bait!"

Jonah asked what bait he was talking about and Billy tried to explain. Bess opened her mouth to interrupt and point out that the story wasn't written by Eddie Beaker at all but by another reporter. But before she could cut a word in edgewise, Mammi shot her a silencing glance.

Jonah read the article aloud: "'The Schwartz Paper Company has been fined for discharging millions of gallons of untreated paper pulp into surface water at Blue Lake Pond. Sheriff John Kauffman of Stoney Ridge blew the whistle on one of the worst pollution offenders in Lancaster County. While fishing one day, he noticed that the lake seemed to be absent of fish.

The sheriff began an investigation and discovered that the Schwartz Paper Company had been dumping gallons of untreated pulp straight from their mill into Blue Lake Pond.'" His voice picked up the pace as he read through the more factual parts of the story: " 'Tremendous amounts of material discharged into the lake used up the oxygen in the water. Fish and aquatic life died from lack of oxygen. Mill wastewater also carries large amounts of suspended solids, such as wood fiber, that could smother underwater habitat for scores of fish and invertebrates such as insects and mussels . . .' " His voice trailed off. He scanned to the end of the article. "The company has admitted negligence and will pay the costs to return the lake to its original pristine condition." Jonah put the paper on the table and looked up. "The sheriff's been given a special commendation from the governor."

After Billy had left the kitchen, Jonah stroked his beard. "Curious, isn't it? Sheriff was here on Saturday. Story broke on Monday." He cast a sideways glance at his mother.

Mammi paid no attention. She stifled a rare smile and appeared pretty satisfied with the way things had turned out. "Well. That's that." She nodded, as if a great mystery had been solved.

Jonah had to leave a contact number for the hospital to call about the results of the blood test, and Lainey had offered the bakery's phone number since Bertha didn't have a phone. Plus, she said, someone was at The Sweet Tooth most every day. So Jonah had quickly slipped into the habit of dropping by the bakery very early in the morning—just to see if the hospital had called—when the town was still sleeping and Lainey was already at work. He would sit at the table by the window while she baked, and they would talk. Too soon, they would hear the noises of Stoney Ridge waking up, of the squeaky bicycle wheels that belonged to the paperboy as he rode down the street and the thump of the newspaper as it hit the shop doors. Of a car engine sputtering to life. Of a dog barking excitedly and another answering back. And then Jonah would get to his feet and prepare to go. He had to make himself leave. It seemed to him that the sweet smells that came out of that bakery—well, they could make a man forget everything in the world and follow its fragrance wherever it led.

As he shaved his cheeks, getting ready to head out the door this morning, his eyes fell on Sallie's letter, received just yesterday. It made his stomach hurt a little.

Dear Jonah,
It has been more than
two weeks since you left for
Pennsylvania. Mose Weaver is
working full-time taking care
of your furniture business. I'm
worried about the poor man,
he works so hard. You left an
abundance of undone work for
him. I need to bring him lunch
each day just to keep up his

strength so that your business doesn't suffer.
Fondly,
Sallie
P.S. I went ahead and planted celery. It is starting to come up. Plenty for the food, plenty for the table decorations.

He thought he would try to call the shop today and speak to Mose, just to make sure he wasn't overwhelmed by the workload. He was going to need to stay in Stoney Ridge awhile longer. For his mother's sake. For Bess's sake.

Oh, who was he kidding? It was for his sake. He couldn't get Lainey O'Toole out of his mind. It thrilled him to death. It worried him to death.

8

Early one morning, Mammi stood at the foot of the stairs to give Bess a wake-up call. She banged a spoon against a metal pan. "And bring down your sheets," she hollered up the stairs.

"I'm doing the laundry today," Bess hollered back down the stairs. Lainey had the morning off and was coming over. For once, Bess knew something that her grandmother didn't know. Lainey had told her she spoke to the bishop about going Amish, and Bess was so thrilled by the notion that she quickly offered to help. Today, she was going to give her a lesson on how to work a wringer machine. They had talked yesterday and picked out today for a laundry lesson because Jonah would be gone all day at an auction with Caleb Zook. And Mammi had plans to go to a neighbor's for a quilting frolic. Lainey wanted to keep quiet about her interest in going Amish. Bess wasn't sure why it was so important to keep it mum—she thought it was *wonderful* news—but she respected Lainey's wish.

"Good! I'll go back to bed and sleep till noon!" Mammi called out.

"Thought you didn't sleep at all!" Bess yelled back with a smile in her voice.

"Mebbe I'll just have to give it a try one of these days. See what Ohio folks find so appealing about it."

Bess laughed out loud. She looked out the window and saw her grandmother cross the yard to go to the henhouse, as she did every morning. A feeling of love for Mammi swept over her. How could she have ever been so frightened of her? She thought of those first few days when she arrived at Rose Hill Farm. She had been deathly worried her grandmother would be relentless about her getting a blood test for bone marrow to help Simon, but she never mentioned it after that first time. Not even when her father arrived in Stoney Ridge. She knew her grandmother continued to visit Simon at the hospital once a week, but she never discussed him with Bess. She didn't even ask Bess to go with her. In fact, Bess had nearly forgotten about Simon.

When her grandmother disappeared into the henhouse, Bess turned her attention back to her project. She had just finished writing out another list of Deitsch vocabulary words for Lainey to memorize. She looked the list up and down. Earth. *Erd.* Mountain. *Berig.* Ocean. *See.* It struck Bess that this might have been what Adam and Eve felt like, having to learn the names of everything. The first job God gave Adam: inventing language. *Not* math. She'd have to remember to point that out to Billy Lapp.

She folded up the list and stuffed it in her pocket. She glanced out the window again and saw Lainey coming up the street with a pink bakery box in her arms. Mammi saw her too. Good. Maybe Mammi would be too busy thinking about what was in that box to wonder why Lainey was here.

Not likely. Her grandmother didn't miss a thing.

Lainey had spent a week now going without any electricity in her little rental room. She had to admit, it was harder than she thought it would be. Bess was a big help, showing her that it didn't have to mean living *without* power—she just had to do things differently. Bess loaned her a gas lamp with a fierce-looking fabric wick and showed her how to fill it with kerosene. They bought a little propane camper stove to use for heating food.

"It's a small version of what we use," Bess told her. "If you can start getting comfortable with kerosene and propane, you'll find that most everything else comes easily."

Lainey had tried to make chicken corn rivel soup for dinner last night using the propane stove. The soup wasn't so bad, but the rivels were inedible. Instead of turning out like dumplings, they tasted like lumps of school paste.

One thing that took getting used to was sitting in a room so dimly lit. She kept the gas lamp close to her so she could read, and it cast its glow in a circle around her while the rest of the room remained dark. It seemed so different from the English way of lighting up the entire room and then some, especially on a rainy day.

Bess gave her fifty words to learn each day, then quizzed her on them and corrected her pronunciation. She said the easiest way to learn a language was to be just like a toddler again, matching words for objects, so your ear became attuned. Bess was a hard taskmaster, Lainey thought with a smile. Lainey had taken German in high school, so she had a head start, but Deitsch was a dialect of German. Similar but different. Everything was slightly skewed, like how you felt when you looked in a wavy mirror.

This morning, she followed Bess down to the basement. Two large galvanized tubs were waiting, side by side, filled with hot water that Bess had brought down from the kitchen. On one of the tubs was fastened a wringer.

Bess tossed in some shavings of Mammi's soap and swirled it around until it lathered. "Mammi's soap lathers up real good. Vile smelling, but it does lather up."

Bess took a sheet and placed it in the tub. Lainey's eyes went wide when she saw Bess pick up a plunger to swirl the water.

"I've only used that to unclog a toilet," Lainey said.

Bess snorted. "Not around here. Mammi still uses a privy." She rolled her eyes. "I've tried talking her into letting Dad put in indoor plumbing till I'm blue in the face. Now it's Dad's turn to persuade her." After a few minutes of plunging, Bess fed the sheet through the wringer, then put it in the second tub to rinse it. Again, she plunged and plunged, then fed the sheet into the wringer.

Lainey helped with the next sheets. By the end of wringing them, she was panting hard. "This takes some muscle, doesn't it?"

Bess laughed at that. "This is just bedding for three people. Imagine what it's like for most Amish families."

Now Lainey understood why she saw clotheslines up at Amish farmhouses every day of the week except Sunday. It must take an Amish housewife hours every day to keep a family in clean clothes.

Bess looked up at her over the wringer. "How do you do your laundry?"

"At the Laundromat. You have to sit there for a few hours so no one steals your clothes."

Bess's head snapped up. Lainey could see that the thought shocked her. Stories about the English fascinated Bess. To her, they seemed so complex, so filled with odd contradictions. Lainey knew what Bess was thinking: how could it be better to use electricity when it meant you had to worry about your clothes getting stolen?

By the time they got the big basket of sheets outside and hung on the line, the sheets were half dry and Bess and Lainey were wet through. Lainey's black hair hung in damp tendrils. Bess's blond hair was flying every which way out from under her prayer cap.

Lainey slipped a clothespin on the last sheet. The wind pushed against the damp sheet, making it fluff and lull in the air like a sail on a ship. The scent of roses lingered around them. For some odd reason, the morning's work was deeply satisfying. Far more satisfying than she ever felt at a desk, listening to people complain about their purchases. Their stuff. She wondered what Robin and Ally would say to that. They loved their stuff.

The Amish used time in a different way, Lainey thought, walking back to town after the laundry lesson with Bess. As she had watched Bess work, she noticed that her movements were unhurried. She never seemed to be rushing through a task so she could get on to something else, something better. To Bess, it was all good, all worth her time. Lainey thought of how she and her English friends would jam their schedules full so they could fit in more. And yet they were always running out of time! The Amish had the same amount of hours in a day, lived busy, productive lives, but somehow they seemed to have an abundance of time for all that really mattered. Lately, she felt as if she were on a fence, in between Amish and English worlds. Watching, evaluating. With every passing day, Lainey felt herself drawing closer to the Amish way.

Jonah had come up with an idea to build Mammi a roadside stand so folks wouldn't always be wandering up to the farmhouse. Bess knew Mammi didn't like to have English strangers wandering around Rose Hill Farm, mostly because they interrupted her work and they talked too long. Mammi was so pleased with Jonah's suggestion that she decided to expand her line of rose products to sell at the stand. Besides rosebushes, she sold rose petal jam, rose petal tea, potpourri, rose water, and now, she decided, she would add rose-scented soap.

Mammi had always made her own lye soap. It smelled like woodsmoke and could take the top layer of skin right off of a person. Bess thought it was a fine idea to try rose-scented soap.

Jonah told her that if she wanted to sell the soap, she should probably stop using animal fat and switch to vegetable shortening or coconut oil. Mammi looked shocked, and it wasn't often that she could be shocked.

"Where did you learn so much about soap making?" Mammi asked Jonah.

He told her he might have learned a thing or two in his life, and Bess thought he was starting to sound an awful lot like his mother.

When Mammi started to collect ingredients around the barn workshop for her rose soap project, Bess had a hunch she was going to have the raw end of this new business prospect.

To be sure, the very next morning Mammi set Bess to the chore of cleaning out the old soap kettle. That ancient kettle hadn't been thoroughly scraped out since it was new. Bess had to roll the cast iron kettle in the grass and climb halfway in with a wire brush to loosen the clinging, foul-smelling lye soap. Even Boomer wouldn't come near her. Blackie came to investigate, then scampered away before slowing to a stiff walk, his white-tipped tail arrogantly upstanding.

Near the barn, in the shade of a big tree, Billy was helping Jonah build the roadside stand. He walked past her once or twice and shook his head. It was hot and sticky work, and by the end Bess reeked of old lye soap.

When the kettle was finally scraped clean to her grandmother's satisfaction, Mammi brought out the ingredients for the rose soap. She cooked the soap outside, over an open fire, despite weather that had turned beastly hot and humid. The air felt so heavy it was hard to breathe, but Mammi soldiered on, which meant Bess had to also. Mammi experimented until she was satisfied with the right blends. Using rose water instead of plain water at the end of mixing the glycerin and oils together gave it a heavenly scent. Mammi wanted to get it perfect before they poured the soap into molds and let it cure in the barn for a few weeks. At last, she had the perfect combination.

"I need a victim," Mammi said, eyeing Bess's prayer cap. "Let's wash your hair."

Bess smelled of such sour smoke that she was happy to get her hair washed, but she hoped to high heaven Mammi's soap wouldn't leave her bald in the process. Mammi brought out a new wash pan and filled it with fresh water from the pump. Jonah and Billy had finished the stand and were building a foundation for it down by the end of the drive, so the two women had plenty of privacy. Bess pulled out her pins to let down her hair. Her hair fell

to her waist. She bent over a big wash-
tub and Mammi lathered her head.

"That burning your scalp at all?" she
asked Bess.

"So far, so good," Bess said. Actually, it felt good, so good, with gentle
suds and a sweet smell.

Mammi rinsed out her hair with clean
water, again and again, until it squeaked.
Then she took the tub and leaned it
upright against the house before she
went back inside. Bess wrung out her
hair and let the air dry it. She sat very
still, with her back to a tree, staring
into the sky as she combed her hair
out. The clouds were scudding overhead. There was quiet, and soft summer air, and time to think. She closed
her eyes, just for a moment, and drifted
to sleep.

Moments later, or maybe an hour, she
opened her eyes and there was Billy.
He was smiling at her with his thrill-
ing white smile. She hoped her white
blond hair looked like shining waves of
water, blowing gently in the breeze.

Her eyes closed again, and when
she opened them, he was gone.

Early the next morning, Lainey waited
for Jonah to come into the bakery. She
kept peering out the window, looking
for him. She smiled when she saw him
turn the corner. She looked forward to
their visits and was surprised at how
comfortable it felt to be with him. She
had a cup of coffee ready for him and
let him sit down before she gave him
the message from the hospital.

She sat down across from him.
"They said you're not a match. You
have three HLAs that match, but Simon
needs six HLAs." She scrunched up
her face. "I'm not really sure what that
means."

Jonah stirred his coffee solemnly. "It
means that even though we have the
same blood type, there are different
antigens in the blood."

She thought he would be relieved
by the news, but instead, he seemed
distressed. They amazed her, these
Amish. They genuinely cared about
people who were difficult to care for.
The timer for the oven went off and

she picked up her mitts to take the Morning Glory muffins out. She was ashamed to realize that she wasn't sure she would give Simon her bone marrow, at least not as readily as Bertha and Jonah had offered theirs. Had she really forgiven him, then? Or was it a conditional forgiveness? Only good as long as he didn't ask anything of her. Was that truly forgiveness?

Jonah was watching her face as she took the muffins out of the pan. He stood and came to her. "What's troubling you?"

She finished setting the hot muffins on a cooling rack. "I told Simon I forgave him for being such a pitiful father. But the truth is, I'd only given him a small piece of forgiveness. The part that benefited me. I released my anger toward him for how he treated me and my mother. But I don't want the best for him." She took off the mitts and placed them on the counter. "I'm not even sure if I care if he lives or dies." She looked away. "That must shock you."

He leaned his back against the

counter, his arms crossing his chest. "It doesn't shock me. I remember Simon's drinking and his get-rich-quick schemes. And his temper." He locked eyes with her then, and before she knew it, he brushed a curl of her hair away from her eyes.

His touch was so gentle, feathersoft, it nearly undid her. She was finding herself attracted to Jonah despite her best efforts to ignore—even stamp out—those feelings. Falling for Jonah didn't make any sense. But still, there was . . . just . . . something about him. She felt so safe with him, as if she could be entirely herself. She had never felt this way about a man before. But she couldn't forget about the Sallie woman back in Ohio. Jonah had never mentioned her to Lainey, and Bess didn't mention her either, other than that one time. But Lainey hadn't forgotten.

She tucked her hair behind her ear. "I'm amazed you don't feel relieved that you're not a match."

"I'm not relieved." He crossed his arms again. "I wish I had been a match. Since I'm not, my mother will be after

me to get Bess tested. She's brought
it up nearly every day. I keep telling
her there's no way it would work. Bess
is Simon's grandniece. But you know
my mother. She gets like a dog with a
bone over things."

Lainey felt a cold shock run through
her. She turned away from Jonah so
quickly that she dropped the empty
muffin pan and it clattered as it hit
the ground, echoing throughout the
bakery.

❄❄

Billy had offered to show Bess how
to graft roses, so when the weather
cooled off one day in late July, with
gray skies threatening rain, he told
her today was the day. Good grafting
weather. He showed her how to pick
out the strongest rootstock, healthy
and undamaged. Then they went out
to the rose fields to cut some slips.

"Your grandmother said she has an
order for ten plants of white sweetheart
roses," Billy said. He pointed out the
best plant. Then he pulled out his knife
and made slanted cuts from branches,

quickly wrapping them in a wet dish-rag. "Don't want the cut pieces to dry out."

Raindrops started to splatter their faces as they hurried back into the greenhouse. Inside, the air was warm and musty. Billy made an assembly line with rootstocks and slips. First, he dipped the slips into a powdery substance to help the root take, then carefully matched each slip to a root-stock branch before wrapping it with gauze. "Roots may not be glamorous, and they aren't even seen, but they're the source of a rose's strength," he told her, as if he were a teacher and she a student.

"Like people," Bess murmured.

"How's that?" he asked absently.

"It was in one of the sermons last week. 'If our roots go deep in the knowledge of God and our lives are hidden in Christ, we'll be strong. More likely to survive the storms of adversity.'" She surprised even herself by remembering what the minister had said. It was Lainey's influence. The more time she spent with Lainey, the more interested she became in spiritual things. Lainey quizzed Bess and Jonah after each church service. She understood more and more Deitsch now and was eager to piece together what she was learning. Her enthusiasm was contagious. "I'm thinking of joining the church," Bess said aloud to Billy. She had been considering it, but it gave her a shiver to say it aloud. It seemed more real.

Billy glanced at her. "I already did. Last year." He put away the powder. "If you know it's right for you, no point in putting it off, is the way I see it." He brushed one palm against the other. "But you are awful young. Not sure the bishop would allow it."

She rolled her eyes at that slight. She was, after all, nearly sixteen. She doubted Billy was much older when he became a member. He had joined at a younger age than most boys did, but that didn't surprise her. Billy wasn't like most boys. In many ways, he seemed already grown-up, solid and unwavering. Except when it came to girls. In that area, Bess thought, his judgment was quite poor. Abominable.

Billy liked to talk while he worked, and Bess loved listening to him. Today, he told her that he wanted to buy his own farm as soon as he turned twenty-one. "No mortgage, either. I've been saving every penny. I want to own my land free and clear. You see, land is a trust, Bess," he said, starting to sound like a preacher. "I think it's something you hold onto for a lifetime. Something a man passes on to his sons. And his sons pass on to their sons. Land should be cared for and improved in every generation—just the way your grandparents have done here at Rose Hill Farm—and that way, we're passing on a legacy."

Bess studied Billy as he worked. She felt keenly aware of every detail. She liked being this close to him. The rain was coming down hard now, soughing on the roof above them. She pretended for a moment that she and Billy were married, working side by side on their farm. Talking together, laughing together, making plans together. She wished this moment wouldn't come to an end, wished she could stretch the morning and make it last forever. Why was it that three hours in school felt like a week, but three hours with Billy Lapp felt like mere minutes?

The morning melted away too soon. The rain ceased and a bright sun flooded the space with light as Bess fell more in love with Billy than ever. Unfortunately, he showed no sign of feeling anything more for her than a kind of platonic friendship. But he hadn't mentioned Betsy Mast all morning. That thought made Bess happy.

And then it was noon and Mammi was calling to Bess to stop for lunch, which meant Billy would head home. She sighed. Time spent with Billy was always over too soon.

Dear Robin and Ally,

Work at the bakery is going well here in Stoney Ridge. So well that I've even given some thought to postponing culinary school.

*But don't worry; I haven't decided
anything for sure.*
   Love,
   Lainey

❧

At lunch one day, Bess mentioned
to Mammi and her father that Lainey
would be dropping by later in the afternoon. Afterward, as Bess was washing
dishes at the kitchen sink, she happened to glance out the window and
notice her father by the pump. His
head was under the pump. Then he
skinned off his shirt and was washing
his entire upper region. He was soap-
ing seriously and Bess grinned. Her
dad had never said so, but she had a
sneaking suspicion that he and Lainey
were growing sweet on each other.
They shared smiles with their eyes and
stole glances at each other when they
thought no one was looking. But Bess
saw and it suited her just fine. She
had a hope for her father and Lainey,
but she knew it was best to keep that
thought quiet. She knew when to leave
things be.

When Lainey arrived at Rose Hill Farm, Mammi was over at the Yoders', helping to clean the house for church that weekend. Another neighbor had come to ask for Jonah's help to catch a runaway horse. The house was empty but for Bess and Lainey. This afternoon was working out better than Bess had even hoped.

She told Lainey she was going to teach her how to sew using a treadle sewing machine.

Lainey looked dubious. "I can't even sew a button on my blouse."

"Good news," Bess said. "No buttons." She laid out a few yards of dusty plum–colored fabric and spread a thin tissue pattern over it. As soon as she had smoothed it all out over the fabric, she pinned one edge and pointed to Lainey to start on the other side.

"What are we making?"

Bess smiled mysteriously. "A dress."

After cutting out the pieces, Bess threaded the machine and started to push the pedal with her foot, causing the needle to go up and down at a steady speed. She sewed one seam and then turned it over to Lainey. "You do the other side. Just sew a straight line."

It took awhile for Lainey to get the rhythm, to pump her foot steadily so the machine would work. "You made it seem so easy, Bess. It's harder than it looks!" But then it came together. She held up the shapeless dress. "Done!"

"Not hardly," Bess said. She took two sleeves and pinned them to the main section. "Watch carefully. Curves are trickier." She whipped off one sleeve and let Lainey take her place.

After Lainey finished, Bess held it up and frowned. "Pull out the stitches and we'll do it again."

So Lainey did. Two more times until Bess was satisfied. They worked the rest of the afternoon and took the dress downstairs to press out the wrinkles.

Bess showed Lainey how to light the pilot light for the Coleman iron. They drank sweet tea while they worked in the kitchen. Lainey ironed the dress and held it up for Bess's approval. "There you go! A new dress for you."

Bess shook her head. "Not for me. It's for you."

Lainey looked stunned, so Bess added, "I don't know if or when you feel the time will be right to start wearing our garb, but I thought it would be good for you to have a dress. For when you're ready."

Lainey looked at the dress. "Should I try it on?"

Bess nodded, pleased. "There are pins on my bureau top."

⚜

Lainey felt strange, taking off her blouse and skirt and putting on this Amish dress for the first time. She wasn't even sure what kind of underwear they wore. She forgot to ask Bess. Did women even wear brassieres? Well, she would be wearing one today, that's for sure. One step at a time.

She slipped the dress on and tried to figure out how the pins should be placed so they wouldn't work themselves loose. She had heard a taxi driver who came into the bakery complain about all the loose pins he found in his cab's backseat after driving Amish women on errands. She folded the front pieces across each other and tried not to jab herself as she pinned them shut. Bess and Bertha never seemed to complain about the pins, but she knew they would take getting used to. Laid out on the bed were a prayer cap and a white apron. Lainey smiled. Bess had this all planned out ahead of time. She hesitated for a moment, but then decided to try them. She slipped the prayer cap on her head. It perched uneasily on her curls. She was growing out her hair, but she knew the covering probably looked silly. She tried to tuck her hair back under the cap. She had watched Bess do it one day and was shocked to see how long her hair was. Below her waist! She told Lainey it had never been cut.

Lainey put pins through the cap to hold it in place, the way she'd seen Bess do it. Then she pinned the apron into place and turned around slowly, trying to decide if she felt any different. She had pins holding her together from head to waist. There wasn't a mirror, so she wasn't as self-conscious. She had been wearing less and less makeup the last few weeks and hadn't even missed it. Well, the first day or two she had felt practically naked, but then she relaxed. She even started to like feeling less made-up, more natural. Maybe that's another secret the Amish have, she realized. If you aren't looking in mirrors all the time, you aren't thinking about how you look all the time. Your mind is freed up for other things.

She went downstairs to show Bess. Moving quietly as she always did, she found Bess washing dishes by the kitchen sink and said, "Well, what do you think?"

Bess whirled around, startled, dripping soapy suds on the floor. "Oh Lainey! Seller Frack bekummt dich!" *That dress becomes you!* Then her eyes darted nervously to the other side of the room.

Lainey looked to see what had distracted Bess. Jonah was standing by the door, staring at her. "Ya. Ich geb ihr allfat recht." *Yes, I agree with her.*

His smile got lost somewhere in that quiet moment.

Now, Lainey felt different.

❧

Dear Jonah,

It has been over four weeks since you left. Mose has been working as hard as a pack of mules for you, but he did take time out to stake the tomato plants in the garden for me. And take us for a picnic down by Miller's Pond. And he built a treehouse for the boys with leftover wood from the furniture-making business. He said you wouldn't object. Would you?

Yours truly,
Sallie

P.S. The celery patch is nearly six inches tall!

❧

It took Jonah a few days to get up his nerve to tell his mother about the blood test not being a match for

Simon. He had dreaded this conversation. He waited until Bess had gone to the barn, and then he quietly told her. He sat sprawled in his chair, one arm hooked over the back.

"I know," Bertha said. "They sent a letter with the results." Out of her apron pocket she pulled a letter from the hospital.

Jonah closed his eyes. "How long have you known?"

Bertha looked up at the ceiling. "Let's see. A week."

Jonah rubbed his forehead. "I know what you're thinking. And I'm not going to agree to it."

"Bess is old enough to make the decision for herself."

"She's still a child."

"Fifteen years old is no child. Why, when I was a girl—"

"I know, I know," Jonah interrupted. He'd grown up hearing plenty of hardship stories that started with that sentence. "There's a remote chance, anyway, that Bess would be a match. Why take the risk?"

Bertha slapped her palms on the table and glared at him. "Why not?"

Right then, Jonah realized that the simplest, easiest thing to do would be to have Bess take a blood test. That way, the results would show his mother what he already knew—that Bess could not possibly be a match. "Okay." He surrendered his hands in the air. "If she agrees to it, Bess can have the test."

He thought his mother would be ecstatic or, at the very least, satisfied. He was giving her what she wanted. Instead, her gaze shifted to the window. From the look on her face, it seemed as if she just had a sense of something dreadful coming to pass.

That night, Jonah asked Bess to sit out on the porch with him to watch the sunset. She knew he had something on his mind. It was a clear night. They watched the sun dip below the horizon and the sky turn a bruised blue. Then he told her about his mother wanting her to get the blood test. Bess sat on the porch steps, hugging her legs, with her chin leaning on top of her knees as she listened to him.

"I want you to pray about this tonight. I don't want you feeling any pressure to have the test."

Bess turned her head toward him. "You were willing to give Simon your marrow, weren't you?"

Jonah nodded. His heart ached in a sweet way when he saw the earnest look on her face. "I was willing, but that doesn't mean you have to. The blood test is pretty simple, just a prick in your arm. The marrow test is a much more complicated procedure. You'd have to have general anesthesia and stay in the hospital, and it will be a little painful. The chance of you being a match is highly unlikely. I can almost rule it out. It's just that your grandmother . . . well, you know how she can be once she gets an idea in her head."

Bess lifted her eyebrows. "Sie is so schtarrkeppich as an Esel." *She is as stubborn as a mule.*

This time Jonah had no trouble

smiling. "It seems very important to Mammi that we at least rule it out."

Bess shrugged. "I guess I can understand that. Simon is her brother."

"But that doesn't mean you have to do this, Bess. If you'd rather not, I would never make you do it, no matter what Mammi has to say about that."

"But you were willing. To give Simon your bone marrow."

"I was willing."

"And Mammi was willing?"

Jonah nodded again. He knew his daughter's tender heart. "Bess, I don't know if he . . . deserves such mercy." He told her the entire story, all that he knew, about Lainey and her mother and how Simon treated them. He was surprised to realize that Lainey had never mentioned Simon to Bess. He knew the two had grown close this summer. He could see Bess was shocked when she learned Simon was Lainey's stepfather. She grew quiet for a long time. Jonah wondered why Lainey had never told her, but then he decided that she was probably protecting Bess. Knowing what he knew of Lainey, he thought she was trying not to influence Bess one way or the other.

They sat quietly for a long time, watching the stars fill the sky. Finally, Bess lifted her head and gave him a soulful look. "Simon may not deserve our mercy, but Lainey is always telling me God has a different perspective on mercy."

Those words cut into him as real as a sharp knife. That old disquiet filled him again, gripping his chest like an actual pain. He had discovered something about himself this summer— something that shamed him deeply. He had believed in God all of his life, but did he truly believe God was sovereign over all? Did he believe that God's ways were truly merciful?

Fifteen years ago, he would have said yes. But after the accident that killed Rebecca, a part of him had stopped counting on God the way he had before. As if God couldn't entirely be trusted.

And so Jonah had run. He had run from God, the same way he had run from his memories. It was too difficult to remain in Stoney Ridge, driving by the accident site nearly every day where Rebecca had died, constantly reminded of what he had lost.

Lainey had just as many reasons to leave Stoney Ridge as he did, yet here she was. Back, facing the very things that haunted her. She was even willing to face Simon in the hospital. When she had come out of Simon's ward into the hallway, the look on her face nearly sliced his heart in two. It was filled with sorrow, but not for herself.

It was filled with sorrow for Simon's lost soul.

Billy hadn't been planning to go to the gathering tonight. It was Bertha Riehl who pinned him to the wall to go and take Bess along too. That woman had a way of getting what she wanted. She didn't ask directly, she just stared at you until your knees buckled and you caved in.

He wasn't in much of a party mood, and hadn't been, and probably never would be again, since Betsy Mast's departure. He still couldn't believe she had up and gone. He had had so many plans for their future together. As soon as he turned twenty-one, he was going to buy some land to farm. He knew just the kind of house he wanted to build for himself and Betsy: it would have a southern exposure, and a barn on a right angle, and a pond to fish and swim in. A pond that would be safe from polluters.

In his vision, his father and brothers would see what he had done—bought a parcel of fine land, married the most sought-after girl in the district, started a thriving business—and they would treat him with respect, not just as the baby of the family. Der Kaschde. *The runt of the litter*, his brothers called him.

But that dream was gone now. What irked him most was that he thought he knew Betsy. He thought she would want the same things. It still stunned him that she was gone. She had left her family, her church. She had left him for another man.

Bess had told him once that he had

made up the idea of Betsy in his head. Maybe he didn't really know her at all, she pointed out.

He glanced over at his cousin Maggie, talking a mile a minute, and Bess on the other side of her. Bess was in a cranky mood today. The day had started out fine. She had been helping him get some plants ready to sell to a customer this morning, and he told her his latest theories on Betsy's departure. She grew quieter and quieter, like she was getting a headache, and didn't say goodbye to him when her grandmother called her in for lunch. Girls could be like that, he was learning. Moody and unpredictable.

As soon as they reached the yard where the gathering was held, Billy jumped down, tied up the horse, and sauntered off to join his friends at a game of volleyball. He didn't even notice where Maggie and Bess had gone until Andy Yoder pulled him aside.

"Who's that?" Andy pointed across the yard to a tight knot of girls.

"Who?"

"The blond."

"The skinny one? That's Bess. Bertha Riehl's granddaughter."

Andy snorted a laugh. "Maybe you need eyeglasses. She ain't so skinny now. Seems like she's got a different shape up above." He handed the volleyball to Billy and walked across the yard to meet Bess.

Billy watched Andy make his way to sit next to Bess. It occurred to him that Bess was going to be quite a nice-looking girl. It was a thought he'd never had.

After volleyball and dinner, then hymn singing, Billy was ready to go home. When he found Maggie, he told her to go get Bess and he would meet them at his buggy.

"She already left," Maggie told him. "With Andy Yoder."

❧❧

Bess woke up in the morning with a firm resolution: last night was the final time she would cry herself to sleep over Billy. She could feel how swollen her eyes were and wondered if she could sneak out to the garden to snatch a cucumber without Mammi spotting her. She had heard girls talk about putting cucumbers on their eyes as a cure. She tiptoed down into the kitchen and was glad to find it empty. She was just about to open the side door when she spotted Mammi, picking beans and filling up her apron, talking to Billy in the garden. Bess couldn't go out there now.

Maybe pickles would work. She grabbed a jar from the pantry and hurried back upstairs. She opened the pickle jar and lay down on the bed, placing a sliced pickle over each eye. Within seconds, her eyes were stinging from the vinegar. She jumped up and reached for a pitcher of water. What a terrible idea! Her eyes were bloodshot now and even more swollen-looking than before. A sharp scent of dill and vinegar hung in the air.

An hour later, she was in the barn spreading rose petals when Billy came in with a freshly filled basket. "Where do you want them?"

She kept her head low and pointed to an empty tray.

He carefully spread the petals out, single layer, on the screen. "So Andy Yoder took you home last night?"

She shrugged. That was her business and no one else's.

"You could have at least told me. I wasted time looking for you."

Bess looked up, pleased. "You did?"

"Sure." Billy shook out the basket and set it on a shelf with the other baskets. "Last thing I want is to have your grandmother sore at me for not bringing you home."

Charming. "Well, she's not sore at you." She gave him a sideways glance. "She thinks Andy Yoder is a fine fellow."

"Bertha Riehl said that?" he asked, amazed. "Andy isn't very selective about girls. He'll take any female who smiles his way."

She brushed past him to go to the farmhouse.

He sniffed the air as she walked by him. "Strange. I keep getting a whiff of pickles."

※※

Jonah was about to turn off the kerosene lamp in the kitchen and head to bed when a knock on the door surprised him. He opened the door to find Lainey standing there in the moonlight.

"Jonah, I would have come sooner, but I was working late tonight in the bakery for a big order tomorrow. A call came for you today. From the hospital." She bit her lip. "Bess is a perfect match for Simon. Six for six."

Jonah was stunned. "How could that be? How could that possibly be true?"

Lainey looked past him with a hard stare.

Jonah turned to see what she was looking at. His mother was on the bottom stair. It looked as if she had come down, overheard them, and was starting to tiptoe back up.

"Tell him, Bertha," Lainey said in a firm voice.

Bertha stopped in her tracks.

"Tell me what?" Jonah asked, looking from his mother to Lainey and back again.

Lainey and Bertha locked gazes. "If you don't tell him, I will."

"Oh, I'll tell him. I said I would and I will." Bertha scowled at Lainey but sat down at the kitchen table.

The tendon of his mother's jaw was working, so Jonah knew to prepare himself for a revelation.

Bertha looked at him carefully, paused a long while to gather her thoughts, then slapped her palms on the table and turned to Lainey. "Fine. You tell him."

Lainey gave Bertha a look as if she couldn't believe what a coward she was. She dropped her head and let out a deep breath. She pulled out a chair across from Jonah. "This is a story that goes back to that night fifteen years ago when you and Rebecca and . . . your baby . . . were in that horrible accident."

Jonah stiffened.

But Lainey didn't waver. She told him the entire story, she didn't leave anything out. When she was done, she looked directly at him. "I switched those babies, Jonah. Your baby for my little sister."

Jonah was stunned silent. The kitchen

was so quiet that the sound of a fly buzzing against the window echoed through the room. He stared at Lainey as if she had been speaking in a foreign language. The full realization of what she said slowly started to dawn on him. *No. It couldn't be. It couldn't possibly be true.* He had trouble speaking—the words tangled up in his throat, and he had to stop and unravel them before he could say what he needed to say.

In a hoarse voice, he spoke at last. "You were only ten. You must not be remembering clearly. You must have it mixed up."

"I remember it right, Jonah," Lainey said softly. "I'll never forget that night."

"But . . . how? How could you . . . how would you even know if a baby was dead?" He leaned forward in his chair. "Maybe she wasn't. Maybe—"

Lainey shook her head. "She died instantly. I know I was young, but I knew she was gone." Her eyes welled with tears.

In a tight voice he said, "But I was

told my daughter was completely un-
hurt. I was told it was a miracle."

"I put my baby sister in Rebecca's
arms—to bring her comfort—and
waited until I heard the sirens. I just
stayed right by the two of you, telling
you over and over again not to quit.
Not to give up. But by the time the
ambulance arrived, I had made a decision."

Silence fell over the table. Jonah's
mind struggled to grasp what Lainey
was saying. He grabbed hold of the
table, feeling like the victim of a hur-
ricane, his life strewn to pieces. Everything seemed to be floating.

Bess wasn't really his daughter. It
shocked him to the core.

Then he had an even greater shock.
His eyes met his mother's and he real-
ized that she wasn't at all surprised.
She *knew* this. She knew this!

As if Bertha could read his thoughts,
she crossed her arms defensively
against her chest. "Yes, I knew about
this, Jonah. I knew. The night of the accident, I went to the hospital and found
out Rebecca had passed and you were

in bad shape. They said the baby had come through the accident unharmed. A miracle, they called it. They kept her overnight for observation. Then the next day, she was given to me to take home. But she wasn't our Bess. By that time, I had already heard about Lainey's sister's passing and put two and two together. I went to the county morgue, to be sure. I planned on telling you, but it got harder and harder, and then . . ." Her voice drizzled off.

He lifted his eyes to look at his mother. "And now you've finally come clean because of Simon."

Slowly, Bertha nodded. "When Lainey showed up out of the clear blue sky, I knew the time had come."

"How could you do that? How could you lie to me for fifteen years?"

"Some things are just worth a little bit of trouble."

Jonah exploded. He rose to his feet and leaned his palms against the table. "Don't you dare make this sound like something trivial!"

Bertha didn't back down. She looked straight at him. "You needed that baby,

Jonah." She pointed a strong finger on the table. "And she needed you."

Once again, silence covered the room. In a voice so calm he hardly recognized it, he said, "Tomorrow, Bess and I will return to Ohio. This topic is closed. Forever." He stared at Lainey, hard, for a long moment, then reached for his cane and went up the stairs.

⁂

At breakfast, Bess could tell that something had happened between her father and grandmother, but she had no idea what had made her father decide to leave Stoney Ridge so suddenly. It saddened her when he told her at breakfast. She tried to object, but she could read the stubborn look on his face. There was no changing his mind. And Mammi, as usual, wasn't talking.

Bess went up to her room to pack up her belongings. As she folded her dresses and aprons into her small suitcase, she could hardly believe how attached she had grown to Mammi, to Lainey, to Rose Hill Farm. To Billy. It had been only two months, yet she felt as if she belonged here. As if this was her home.

She heard her father call to her to come downstairs. She looked around the room one last time to brand the image on her memory: the pale green walls rimmed with pegs for clothing. The scratched-up wooden floors. The small wooden bed with Mammi's hand-made starburst pattern quilt on top, the nightstand with a glass oil lamp, the windowsill where she sat some nights, watching the moon rise and cast shadows over the rose fields. She sighed and trudged down the steps.

Billy was out front, waiting for them by the buggy. Jonah had asked him to drive them to the bus station to catch the noon bus. She walked up to him and he took the suitcase from her.

"What's going on with your dad?" he whispered. "What's the big rush to leave town?"

Bess shrugged. "Just needs to get back to his business, I guess," she said nonchalantly. Bess felt a small sense of dignity rise up in her. After

all, Billy had disappointed her tremen-
dously. Maybe it was good that she
was leaving. Maybe he would pine for
her. Maybe he'd even write long letters
to her.

"I'll go scrounge up that black cat
of yours," he said, heading over to the
barn.

Blackie! She'd nearly forgotten him.

Mammi and Jonah came out to the
buggy.

"What's keeping Billy?" Jonah asked,
looking anxiously at the barn.

Not a moment later, Billy let out a
large whoop. He came outside, cra-
dling two small kittens in his arms,
with an angry Blackie trailing behind.
"Hey, Bess! So much for your scien-
tific skills! I thought you said your cat
was a boy!" he cried out, laughing.

Bess ran over to see the kittens.
Blackie curled around her legs. She
looked back at her father. "I can't take
them! They're hardly a day or two old!"

"They'll stay," Mammi said deci-
sively. "Their mother stays too. She's a
decent mouser after all."

Bess gave each kitten a kiss and let

Billy take them back to the barn where he found them. She reached down to stroke Blackie, but he . . . she . . . glared at her and hurried after her kittens.

Bess watched them go and turned to say goodbye to Mammi. When their eyes met, Bess felt tears choke in her throat. She ran to her grandmother and threw her arms around her big shoulders. She felt Mammi's arms reach up to pat her on her back. When Bess finally let go, Mammi took off her spectacles, breathed on them, and rubbed them with her apron. Needed polishing, she said.

Jonah offered his mother a stiff handshake. Mammi held onto his hand extra long, Bess noticed, as if she didn't want to let go.

But Jonah was undeterred. He went to the buggy just as a pony and cart pulled up the drive. It was Andy Yoder, carrying a bouquet of wildflowers in his arms.

When he reached the yard, he reined the pony over to the buggy and jumped off the cart. "What's going on?"

"They're heading back to Ohio," Mammi said, glaring at Jonah.

Andy looked horrified. "But why?" When no one answered, he looked to Bess, but she only shrugged. Then he turned to Jonah. "Well, could I at least speak to Bess? Privately?"

Jonah rubbed his forehead as if he had a headache coming on, but he climbed into the buggy. Mammi stayed put.

Andy gave a sideways glance at Mammi before thrusting the wildflowers at Bess. "What would you say if I wrote to you? Would you write back?"

Billy came out of the barn and stopped abruptly when he saw Andy handing the wildflowers to Bess. "We'd better get going if you want to make that noon bus, Jonah," he said in a loud voice. He climbed into the buggy.

"He's right, Bess," Jonah called out.

Andy looked stricken. Bess got into the buggy and sat in the backseat.

"Write to me, Bess!" Andy yelled as Billy slapped the reins to get the horse moving.

Bess leaned a hand out the window

to wave to Mammi and Andy and the rose fields and the house and Blackie.

When Billy turned left onto the road, Bess said to her father, "I want to say goodbye to Lainey."

"No time," Jonah answered, eyes on the road. He spoke sharply but without conviction.

"We're going right past the bakery and it won't take but a minute," she said firmly.

Jonah didn't respond, so Billy pulled the horse to the hitching post. Lainey came out as if she had been expecting them. Bess ran into her outstretched arms.

"I don't know why he's doing this, Lainey!" Bess whispered. "Something's happened to make him upset."

Lainey didn't answer at first. Then she pulled back and held Bess's arms. "Being here . . . it's hard for your father. It brings up a lot of sad memories. Things he'd rather forget about. Give him time. He'll come around." She hugged Bess again and released her.

Jonah came toward them. "Bess,

hop in the buggy. I'll be there in a moment."

Bess went to the buggy to wait with Billy. She kept her eyes on her father. Lainey was saying something to him, but he didn't say anything back. He looked away while she spoke, as if he didn't really want to hear it.

"He'll be in love with a new girl by week's end," Billy said crisply.

Bess's gaze was fixed on her father and Lainey. "I don't think so. I've never seen him like this."

"What do you mean? He's like this all the time."

She turned to Billy. "Who?"

"Andy Yoder. He's girl crazy."

Bess rolled her eyes.

"I'm only looking out for your welfare."

Bess turned back to her father and Lainey. He was saying something to her now, something that made Lainey look hurt. He returned to the buggy and gave a nod to Billy to get going. Bess waved to Lainey, who blew a kiss at her and waved back, slow and sad.

Jonah and Bess's quick departure left Billy with a vague unease, as if he had left the barn door open or forgot to water the new rose graftings. Something just didn't feel right. What was Jonah's big hurry about, anyway? Billy clucked to old Frieda to get her moving faster. This horse moved plenty fast for Bertha but acted like a tired old nag for everybody else.

His thoughts drifted to the way Jonah and Lainey looked—so serious—when they were talking to each other outside the bakery. If he didn't know better, he would say they looked like their hearts were breaking. But that couldn't be right. A straight-up fellow like Jonah Riehl would never get involved with an English girl. Bertha Riehl would have him drawn and quartered.

But what did he know about love? He thought Betsy was straight up, and he sure was wrong about that. *Oh Betsy, Betsy, I thought I knew you,* Billy lamented as the horse plodded along.

He felt himself slipping back into what

Bess called his Betsy funk. He tried to snap out of it by thinking again about Jonah and Bess and Lainey. Bess had been trying to figure out what Jonah and Lainey were saying to each other while he was trying to warn Bess not to count on Andy's devotion for longer than a minute. Bess was awfully innocent about boys, though she didn't seem to appreciate his warning. She had told him to hush.

"They're saying something important," she scolded him, watching Jonah and Lainey. She squinted her eyes, trying to lip-read. "She's asking him if it would have been better to be raised by *that* man. He's telling her that he thinks living with the truth would have been better. No . . . best." She shrugged and blew out a breath. "*What* is going on with those two?"

As Billy turned the horse right into Rose Hill Farm, he felt an odd feeling stir in the pit of his stomach. It surprised him, that feeling. Bess wouldn't be there anymore.

Gone would be their daily challenge: he would give her a math problem to figure out, only to have her give him a vocabulary word that he had to puzzle over. She didn't think she was very smart, but he thought differently. She knew about things he'd never heard of: Latin names of birds that visited the rose fields. She would hold her head in dismay as he butchered the pronunciation. She said he did to Latin what her grandmother did to English. Bess was interested in everything: how to graft a rose, how to gather honeycombs without making the bees mad, even how to track animals. He never knew anyone with such curiosity. He thought about how her eyes always widened when she thought deeply. He would wait and lean in her direction, as a sunflower would follow the sun, for whatever illumination was sure to follow.

He felt a strange ache in his heart, a different kind of ache than Betsy Mast's devastating betrayal. He was going to miss Bess.

9

Bess had never seen her father like this before.

Jonah was carrying a burden, heavy-hearted. He hardly said more than a few words during the long bus ride to Ohio. When they returned to the house late that night, Sallie rushed right over and Bess's heart sank to her knees. Bess fled upstairs to open up the windows, she told Sallie, and let the house cool off. It was so hot and stuffy inside that candles had melted in their holders. She didn't intend to eavesdrop, but Sallie and Jonah were outside on the porch, right below her window.

"My oh my, but you gave me a start!" Sallie was saying. "I was beginning to think you weren't coming back at all! Not at all!" She spoke so quickly that her words blurred together.

Jonah said something so quietly that Bess couldn't make out what he said.

"If you were much later, I was afraid we'd have to wait until December to get married. But November will still work. Not a minute too soon, mind you. We're already way behind schedule. Not to worry, not to worry! It will all get done!" She started listing out all that she had already done—made a list of people to invite, made a list of foods to prepare, decide which house to live in . . . but that could be discussion for another day, she told Jonah. Then Sallie gave up a rare pause. "You do still want to get married, don't you, Jonah?"

There was silence down below. *Oh please, Dad. Please, please say no!*

"Yes," Jonah finally answered, loud and clear. "Of course."

Bess's heart sank. She tiptoed to another room to open the windows and get a cross breeze. She knew when to leave things be.

Maybe, Lainey thought, maybe it was just as well that Jonah had left before anything more serious developed between them. She had a lot of thinking to do about her future, and being around Jonah made her mind a little scrambled. She didn't like feeling scrambled. She liked having plans laid out, even and straight. Not that plans couldn't be changed. They could.

In fact, she was changing her plans this very day.

Earlier today, Lainey had met with the realtor, Ira Gingrich, wanting to have an informal conversation about the purchase of Simon's former house. She had thought long and hard about this. She prayed about it every time she walked past the cottage. She felt as if there was something about that cottage she couldn't ignore—as if it was a metaphor for how she felt about her life. God was in the business of restoring things. People too. The old could be made new.

Ira Gingrich was a plump, easygoing

man with pink skin and white hair, who sat with his hands resting on his belly. The house had been on the market for three years, without a bite, he said sadly. When Lainey made a ridiculously low offer on it as a joke, he squinted at her in confusion. Then a sudden smile creased his face.

"Sold!" he shouted and jumped to his feet, thrusting his hand out to grab Lainey's and pump it up and down.

Stunned speechless, she was suddenly the owner of a dilapidated, run-down, neglected house sorely in need of some love and attention.

That night, in her little room, she went over her finances and felt rather pleased. The money she had saved up for culinary school would suffice as a down payment. She thought she would talk to Billy about doing some renovations for her. She had a lot of confidence in Billy's abilities. She had noticed how carefully he worked at Rose Hill Farm. If he didn't know how to do something, he would find out. She figured out that her bakery hours would cover her mortgage payments . . . just barely. Even still, she didn't regret this turn of events. Not at all. For the first time in her life, she had a home of her own. And she hoped and prayed that Jonah would come to his senses and at least let her be a sister to Bess. She had squelched the hope that was stirring within her heart for Jonah.

It was probably a good thing that he left when he did, she told herself. Over and over and over. After all, she thought, it made things simpler.

Ira Gingrich sped up escrow so Lainey would close on the house by Friday. Bertha observed that nobody had ever seen Ira Gingrich move this fast, not even at quitting time at the bank. She said he was moving that escrow through like a greased sow before Lainey could think twice and change her mind. Lainey started a list of things she would need: a bed, sheets, a table, chairs. She wondered if Bertha might have a few extra pieces of furniture to loan in that big attic at Rose Hill Farm.

By the time Friday dawned, Lainey

woke up more excited than she had
ever felt about anything in all her life.
She wished she could be sharing the
day with Bess and Jonah. Instead of
missing them less, she found she was
missing them more. Especially Jonah.
Every morning when she went to the
bakery, she expected him to be there,
waiting for her. And often at night, as
she had closed up shop, he would happen to stop by to walk her home. She
hadn't even realized how often Jonah
filled her thoughts. It worried her. She
had only known him a month's time.
Was Caleb Zook right? Was she planning to get baptized for Jonah's sake?

No. She had an unwavering cer-
tainty that it was more than that. She
had been longing for something all of
her life . . . and when her VW Beetle
died on Main Street in Stoney Ridge, it
wasn't long before she knew she had
found what she had been looking for.
She wasn't one to think that only the
Amish were Christians . . . she'd been
around too many types of people to
know that God cared about the interior
condition of a person's heart, not their

exterior labels. But for her, she knew she worshiped God best here. What she liked best was that being Amish, to her, meant that every part of her life was a testimony to God.

She had given away her clothes and makeup and was wearing the garb now. Even at the bakery. Mrs. Stroot took one look at her, shook her head, and blamed Bertha Riehl. It took Lainey a few days to feel comfortable, to get used to startled stares. After a while, she decided that the reason the Amish wore Plain clothes was to identify them as belonging to God. So each time she was reminded she was dressing differently from others, it drew her attention to God. She liked that.

As she was dressing this morning for work, it dawned on her that she had an answer to the bishop's nettlesome question: if Jonah Riehl was the reason she was going Amish, that reason was gone. Most likely, he was planning his autumn wedding to that Sallie woman in Ohio whom Bess had mentioned once or twice.

And still, Lainey was determined to become Amish.

※

Bertha Riehl burst into the bakery midafternoon on Friday as Lainey was pulling chocolate chip cookies out of the oven. "Been to see Simon. He's only got a few weeks left. They said we should take him on home. Let him die in peace."

Lainey set the trays on the counter to cool. She took off the mitts. "You're awfully kind to do that, Bertha." She slid a spatula under each cookie to loosen it.

Bertha eyed the cookies. "Do what?"

Lainey put a warm cookie on a plate and handed it to Bertha. "For taking in your brother. For seeing him out."

Bertha took a bite of the cookie. With a full mouth, she said, "I'm doing nothing of the kind."

Lainey looked up, surprised. "Where will he go?"

Bertha kept her head down over her plate with the cookie.

The terrible truth dawned on Lainey.

"Oh Bertha, you can't be thinking I would take him in!"

Bertha snapped her head up. "Why not? You got a house now."

"But . . . but . . . why can't *you* have him?"

There was never a more surprised look on a person's face. "Simon was shunned."

"That was so long ago! The bishop would certainly understand. Simon is dying!"

Bertha nodded. "Mebbe so. But my Samuel wouldn't hear of it. If he were still living, it would give him a cardinal arrest."

That remark didn't surprise Lainey. It was always Bertha who had come visiting, bringing casseroles and tucking money under the sugar bowl. Never Samuel. People often made the mistake of blurring the Amish together, assuming that because they dressed alike and looked alike, their thoughts ran alike. But that assumption was wrong. Bertha and Samuel Riehl were as different as two people could be. She remembered every detail of Samuel:

the clear-rimmed glasses and broad smile, the grandfatherly bald head like a warm, bright lightbulb. He seemed so trustworthy and kind, and he was, as long as it fit inside the Amish box.

Lainey came to herself with a start. While Jonah had his father's warmth, he also had his father's strict observance to rules. How had she not seen this before? Now she understood why Jonah left Stoney Ridge so abruptly after learning Simon was the real father of Bess. He was his father's son.

A combined sigh of impatience and exasperation from Bertha jolted Lainey back to her present dilemma. "Bertha, that house is a disaster. It's not safe! There's no way anyone could live in it . . . for weeks! Maybe months! I don't even take possession of it until the end of today."

"We'll help."

Lainey didn't know what to say. Her stomach twisted up in a firm knot. "I have to think about this, Bertha. You can't just bully me into it."

Bertha lifted her eyebrows as if she couldn't imagine what Lainey was talking about. "Just don't take too long. He's getting ejected from the hospital next Friday," she said at the door.

"What if Simon doesn't agree? Have you thought of that?"

"You leave Simon to me," she said. "He may be a tough caricature, but he's still my baby brother."

Lainey covered her face with her hands. When Bertha Riehl got her mind set on something, you'd just as well prepare to see it through.

❧

Ira Gingrich handed Lainey the keys as soon as he received her cashier's check. She left his office holding those keys so tightly that they made a red indentation in her palm. Ever since Bertha had paid her that visit to the bakery and told her she should take in Simon, she had been filled with doubts about buying this cottage. She had an inner debate with herself. If our possessions belong to the Lord, why is it so hard to share them with others in need? And Simon certainly needed *someone*.

But then she would go back to

wondering why *she* needed to be the one to help him. She began to question if becoming Amish was such a wise thing, after all. If they believed so strongly in community, why would she be left on her own to take care of Simon? Maybe she had glamorized being Amish. Maybe it wasn't any different than so many other Christian churches. Big intentions, little action. A mile wide and an inch deep.

She walked to the cottage and stood outside of it. A small bead of sweat trickled down her back. What had she gotten herself into? And was it too late to get out of it?

She heard a noise, like a very loud woodpecker, coming from inside the house. Slowly, she went up to the porch. The noise was definitely coming from inside. It sounded like a team of woodpeckers. She was just about to push the door when it flew open. There stood Billy with a hammer in his hand and nails in his mouth.

He took the nails out of his mouth and grinned. "Saw you standing out front with a dazed look on your face."

Behind him came Bertha, with a broom in her hands. Past the two of them were a few other men whom Lainey had seen at church. Through the front room, Lainey could see some women scrubbing the kitchen.

"What's going on?" Lainey asked.

"Billy's fixing loose cupboards in the kitchen. Them two men are working on the chimbley. I'm cleaning with them ladies." She spread her big arm out. "It's called a working bee. More are coming tomorrow." She took in Lainey's stunned look. "It's what we do."

Lainey clapped her hands to her cheeks. "I don't know what to say."

"I told you we'd help," Bertha said, starting to sweep the cobwebs out of the ceiling corners.

"But . . . I didn't really expect it. It's just so touching. So . . ."

Billy shrugged. "Amish," he said. As if that explained everything.

Lainey nodded as tears started to well in her eyes.

"It certainly gives a person something to compensate about," Bertha added. She gave up a rare smile.

"It does, Bertha," Lainey said, talking through her tears. "It definitely gives a person something to compensate about." That clinched it for her. Any lingering doubts she had just vanished. She wasn't alone. She would tell Caleb Zook this very weekend that she wanted to be baptized as soon as possible.

Bess watched the clouds float across a sky so bright a blue it shimmered, and her thoughts turned to home. But it wasn't Berlin, Ohio, that she was thinking of. She was thinking of Rose Hill Farm. She felt as unsettled as a yanked-up weed.

This summer, she had grown to love her grandmother. She began to notice how hard Mammi worked and how old she was getting. She wanted to be there with her, helping her grow roses and make jam and tea and rose water and soap. It troubled her to think of Mammi alone on that big farm.

She was worried about her father too. She had thought if she left him be, he would work himself through this sulky mood. But two weeks had passed and he was still moving through each day in slow motion, as if weighed down by something. By contrast, Sallie was moving like a runaway train with their wedding plans.

Tonight, as they finished up another silent dinner, she spoke up. "I got a letter from Lainey today."

Her father didn't respond, didn't even look at her. Bess decided to give him most of the details anyway.

"She said Simon is nearly dead. The hospital, according to Mammi, is ejecting him by week's end." Bess hoped her father would react, reminded of his mother's way of mangling English words.

The ghost of a smile flickered across Jonah's face, but he didn't make a comment. He moved his fork around on his pie plate.

"I'm not sure I should be telling you this, but I'm not sure I shouldn't, either. Lainey is getting baptized this fall. She's becoming Amish."

Jonah stilled, but he kept his eyes downcast. "She is, is she?"

Bess nodded. "All summer long I've been teaching her how to do things without electricity. And I was teaching her Deitsch."

Jonah took that information in silently. He avoided Bess's eyes.

She bit her lip. "Dad, won't you please tell me why we left Stoney Ridge so suddenly?"

Jonah's face set in warning lines. Bess could see the shutters coming down.

He eased back in his chair. "Things are . . . complicated, Bess."

"Maybe if you told me about it, I could help you uncomplicate things."

Jonah gave her a slight smile. "Things happened long ago that you wouldn't understand."

She felt offended. Nothing irked Bess more than when someone inferred she was a child. Usually, that someone was Billy Lapp. "Try me."

"Oh Bess . . . some things are best put away." He dropped his chin to his chest as if he was fighting something inside himself. He was quiet for a long while and Bess let him be. She knew not to push him. He was like Mammi that way. He let his fork drop on his plate. "Your blood test came back as a perfect match for Simon."

She *knew* it! She just knew this had something to do with that blood test. Her father was so protective of her. She looked into his kind, dark eyes and reached out for his hand. She took a deep breath. "Then we need to go back to Stoney Ridge. As soon as possible. I want to give my bone marrow to Simon."

Jonah looked at her, horrified. His voice nearly broke on the words. "Why? Why would you do that? It's a painful procedure. And for a man who . . . a man like him." He raked a hand through his hair, as if he was struggling with how to grapple with this. "Maybe it's just consequences for the life he's led. I'm not at all sure we should interfere. Maybe it's Simon's time to pass. Maybe it's . . . God's will."

Bess's gaze shifted out the window. "I asked Lainey what she remembered about Simon. She said he slept till noon, then took a nap. He could lie as smooth as new cream. And that was on his good days. When he got to drinking spirits, she said he was like another person. So mean he could make angels weep. Once he made her kneel on uncooked rice until she had cuts in her knees." She turned back to Jonah. "I asked Mammi what made him so mean and she said he was just born that way."

She got up out of her seat and went to put the dishes in the sink. "Lainey bought Simon's old house with her cooking school money. She's taking him in. To die." She filled up the sink with hot water and added dish soap. She swirled the water with her hand to make it sudsy. "I guess if Lainey can do that, after how he treated her, if she can forgive him . . . well, if my bone marrow could give him a chance to live and maybe to love God through it . . . then I should at least offer it to him." She wiped her hands on a rag and turned to her father. "I *need* to do this, Dad."

Jonah rubbed his face with his hands for the longest time. Finally, he stood, walked over to her, and put his arms around her. Bess burrowed her face into his shoulder.

"We'll leave in the morning," he finally said in a husky voice.

❧

Jonah looked out the window as the bus drove over the bridge into West Virginia. Bess had drifted off to sleep and was starting to lean her head against his shoulder. He felt such tenderness toward her. She was hardly the same girl he sent off in a bus to visit his mother. He had always thought of Bess as excitable as a hen walking on hot coals, never able to keep still, always jumping up with some further excitement. Yet gentle too. He had worried that others might take advantage of Bess's gentle ways. A part of him felt his mother had taken advantage of her, deciding she was a last-ditch cure for Simon. He felt a hardness toward his mother that plagued him.

But it was starting to dawn on Jonah

that he didn't need to worry about Bess the way he used to. Next to him was a calm, assured young woman who knew her mind. She had grown up, slower than she wanted, faster than he realized.

Bess jolted awake and looked at him as if she hadn't been asleep at all but had been thinking. "Don't you wonder how two people from one family—like Mammi and Simon—could begin their lives at the same point and somehow take turns that would lead them to such very different lives? I mean, are we born who we are, or does life make us that way?"

That is an eternal question, Jonah thought, as he watched Bess drift back to sleep. *Take you and Lainey. You started in the same point, took a turn, and then seem to be ending up leading very similar lives.*

They arrived at Stoney Ridge not long after dawn. Bess wanted to see Lainey first thing, hoping she'd already be at the bakery. Jonah said to go ahead without him. He had an errand of his own. He walked Bess to Main Street, saw the lights on in The Sweet Tooth, and then told her he would meet her later at Rose Hill Farm.

She didn't ask him any questions, but she did put a reassuring hand on his shoulder. "Everything is going to turn out fine, Dad."

When did they switch roles? he wondered as he walked the road that led to Caleb Zook's farmhouse, Beacon Hollow. When did Bess become the parent and he become the child?

Jonah found Caleb in the dairy barn, just as he had expected. The cows had been milked and Caleb was stacking the emptied-out milk cans into the sink to be washed. Jonah stood for a while, watching him work. Caleb had been Jonah's closest childhood friend. They did everything together—hunt and fish, swim, skip school. They stood together as witnesses for each others' weddings. And Caleb was by his side to help him when Rebecca died. When Jonah moved to Ohio, they lost touch. *No,* he corrected himself. *I lost touch.*

With everything and everyone from Stoney Ridge.

Caleb rinsed out the last bucket and hung it upside down on a wall hook to dry. That was when he noticed Jonah. "Well, well. Skin me for a polecat." Caleb looked pleased. He picked up a rag and dried his hands as he walked over to Jonah. "Heard you had returned to Ohio."

"I did," Jonah said. "Now I'm back." He shook Caleb's hand. "Would you have time for a talk?"

"For you, Jonah, I have all the time in the world." Caleb led Jonah down to two lawn chairs that sat under the willow tree, along the creek that ran parallel to the road.

Jonah watched the water make its way around rocks. Caleb didn't press him, and Jonah expected that. Caleb always had a way of knowing how to work with others. When Jonah heard Caleb had become a minister, then a bishop, he knew the Lord had chosen well for the district.

A mother sheep bleated for her lambs, and the two hurried to find her.

The sun was just starting to rise as Jonah took a deep breath. "Caleb, I learned something that has turned my world upside down."

Caleb leaned back in his chair. "Well, my friend, let's see if we can make things right side up again."

Jonah spilled out the entire story, leaving nothing out. Caleb didn't say a word. He just sat there, letting Jonah work through his tangled thoughts and feelings.

"This summer," Jonah said, "it's like I've woken up after a long sleep." There'd been joy this summer, in seeing his mother and Bess grow so close, and in meeting Lainey, he told Caleb. But there was pain too, as he was reminded of Rebecca and the life they should have had together. And now, there was fear. He hadn't been able to tell Bess the whole truth, about Simon being her father. What if he did tell her and she told Simon? If Simon did get well, would he take Bess away from him?

"Lainey was only ten years old and she was trying to give her sister a better life. She was keeping a promise to her mother. I understand that." Jonah looked up at the sky. "But my mother! She knew, yet she didn't tell me the truth." He wiped his eyes with his palms. "How do I forgive her for that, Caleb? How do I forgive my mother for coaxing Bess here this summer to be a bone marrow donor for Simon?"

Caleb took his straw hat off of his head and spun it around in his hands. Finally, he looked over, past Jonah, to the large vegetable garden on the side of the house. "I've been trying something new this summer. I've got a compost pile working just for kitchen scraps."

Jonah looked sideways at him, alarmed. Did Caleb not hear him? What did a compost pile have to do with all that had just spilled out of him?

Caleb leaned forward in his chair. "Composting is a miracle, really. It starts out with carrot scrapings and coffee grinds and banana peels. And then you give it time and the sun warms it and God turns all of that rubbish into something wonderful and useful.

Something we can use and spread in the garden."

Jonah tilted his head. "You're trying to make an analogy of composting to the lie I've been living with for fifteen years?"

"I guess I am." Caleb smiled and set his hat on his knee. "The funny thing about composting is that it ends up benefiting us. Nothing is beyond God's ability to repair. Even kitchen scraps. He is all-powerful."

Jonah glared at him. "So you're saying that I just forgive and forget?" He thrust his fist against his chest. He felt so angry. He felt so cheated. "Something as big as the fact that this child I've been raising isn't really mine?"

"Isn't she?" Caleb asked, holding Jonah's fixed gaze. "Could Bess really be any more your daughter?"

Jonah dropped his eyes to the ground. Caleb was right. Bess *was* his daughter. He had to fight back a lump in his throat.

"Nothing can ever change that, Jonah."

Jonah looked down at the creek.

"You probably want me to tell Bess the whole story."

"I'm not the one to tell you what to say or what not to say. You'll have to pray long and hard about that matter. I do understand that it's heavy information for a child to bear."

"She's not a child any longer. She's grown up years this summer."

Caleb smiled. "There are seasons in our life that are like that."

The sun was up now, filtering through the trees, creating shadows over the creek.

"As far as forgiving your mother," Caleb said, "Peter asked Jesus, how many times should he forgive another? Peter wanted a statistical count. And Jesus responded with a story. 'Not seven times, but, I tell you, seventy-seven times.' Jesus was teaching him that we don't live by careful book-keeping. Through God's mercy, book-keeping has given way to extravagant generosity." He paused for a moment. "So this is your story, my friend."

They spoke no words for a long

while, and yet the silence didn't seem uncompanionable.

Then Caleb placed a hand on Jonah's shoulder and added, "There's someone else you need to think about forgiving."

Jonah looked at him with a question.

"Yourself," he said softly. "For the buggy accident."

Jonah winced. He started to protest, to give the pat answers that he always gave—God was in control. God knew best. God has a purpose in all things. But he couldn't say the words. He stopped and leaned forward, resting his elbows on his knees, holding his head in his hands. "I should have prevented it. I should have been paying closer attention to the road." His voice grew hoarse. "It's hard enough to accept that I could have prevented Rebecca's death . . . now I've learned that my daughter died in that accident too. I was responsible for them." He covered his face with his hands and his shoulders started to shake. Something broke loose inside of him and he began to weep. He couldn't even remember the last time he cried. He didn't even cry when he learned that Rebecca had passed. He just felt numb. But now, this morning, he felt fresh, raw, searing pain, as if the accident had just happened. He was spilling out grief he had stored for fifteen years, his chest heaving and racking with sobs.

Caleb sat quietly until Jonah's tears were spent. Finally, he spoke. "You didn't cause that accident, Jonah. It's hard to understand why God allowed it, but we trust in God's sovereignty. Your wife and baby's lives were complete. And now we trust they are in the presence of our Almighty Lord." The faint clang of a dinner bell floated down to the creek. He rose to his feet. "Breakfast is ready. Jorie's probably wondering where I've disappeared to. I know she'd be pleased to have you join us."

"Thanks, Caleb. Another time."

Jonah started to rise, but Caleb put his hand on his shoulder. "Why don't you stay here awhile and talk this all out with the Lord? I find it's my favorite place to hammer things out with him."

As Jonah eased back down, he asked

Caleb, "So you think Bess should give Simon her bone marrow? A man such as him?" He looked away. "You remember, Caleb, how he treated Lainey and her mother. How the sparkle drained from them." And what life would have been like for his Bess, too, had she been raised by Simon. Lainey had pointed that out to him, but he hadn't listened to her.

Caleb rubbed his forehead. "Are we going to be part of condemning a man? Or are we going to be a part of releasing him from condemnation?" He sat back down again. "Jonah, we want to share in this world, of forgiving and being forgiven. Even such a man as Simon."

It wasn't easy, though. Even for Caleb. Jonah could see this was a temptation for both of them, to let consequences fall as they would. To let Simon pass away without a hand of kindness offered to him. Except for the hand of Bertha. Suddenly, Jonah felt a slight softening toward his mother. He realized how hard this must be for her, what a difficult spot she was in.

Despite everything, Simon was her brother.

Caleb added, "You probably know this, but Lainey O'Toole is planning to be baptized."

"Bess told me," Jonah said.

"When she first came to me a while back, I told her to go without electricity for a week. That usually changes folks' minds right off. They miss their radio and hair dryer and television too much. But she didn't bat an eye. She's been learning our language and choring without modern convenience. Even still, I had to make sure she wasn't doing this on a whim."

He nodded.

"I asked her why, and she told me she truly believes that she can serve and love God best by being Plain." Caleb lifted his eyebrows. "Sure wish some of our members felt that way. Quite a few of them claim to be meditating during church." He raised his eyebrows. "An activity that looks suspiciously similar to dozing." He rose to his feet. "God always has a plan, doesn't he?"

Jonah looked up at Caleb and did his best to offer up a slight smile. He wished he had Caleb's unwavering faith. Ever since Rebecca—and his baby—had died, he had been able to summon only a pale shadow of the faith he once had. For how could a loving God let a twenty-year-old young mother and her newborn baby die in a careless accident? If God was sovereign, then his sovereignty seemed frightening. It was a question Jonah had never been able to work through to a comfortable solution.

Caleb watched him carefully, as if reading his thoughts. "God may allow tragedy, Jonah, just like he allowed his Son to have a tragic death." He leaned closer to Jonah. "But God is a redeemer. Never, ever forget that truth."

❦❦

Once a week, on her day off from the bakery, Lainey traveled to Lebanon to visit Simon. She brought him baked goods and a magazine or a puzzle. He was not looking well. He had become even more pale and thin, with dark circles under his eyes. Today, she found him on the patio, getting some sun. Simon, who had always looked so sure of himself, seemed hollow and fragile.

He opened one eye when he heard her. "What's in the box?" he asked in a gruff voice.

"Doughnuts. Jelly filled. Your favorite, if I remember right."

"I never liked doughnuts." He held out his hand, palm up, for a doughnut.

She opened the box and handed him one. He ate it carefully, as if he had sores in his mouth, and jelly dripped down his chin. She wiped it off with a tissue and he let her. It amazed her to see Simon helpless. "So the nurse said they're going to release you."

He narrowed his eyes. "They just want the bed. Government can't bother themselves with a dying vet. Even one with a purple heart."

Lainey tried not to roll her eyes. She had heard that purple heart line many times before. "It was Bertha who talked them into releasing you. She thought you'd be better off in a home."

"I'm staying right here. I got my rights."

She knew the truth was that he had no place to go. He was a pathetic, lonely old man who was dying. She looked at him with eyes that were not hard or cold. She saw him objectively. "I'd like you to come home with me."

Simon didn't move a muscle. He didn't even blink.

"I bought the old cottage and neighbors helped fix it up. We're going to rent a hospital bed for you and keep it downstairs in the living room, so you feel like you're part of things."

He eyed her suspiciously. "If you're looking for money, I told you I ain't got none."

She smiled. "I don't want your money, Simon, even if you had any."

"Then why would you be bothering with a sick old man?"

That was a question she had asked herself and prayed over ever since Bertha suggested—no, informed her— she should take in Simon. She finally decided the answer was because she was able to make something right in at least one tiny corner of the vast house of wrongs. It was another thing she was learning from the Amish. "Everybody needs somebody in this world to help them through. I guess you're stuck with me." *And I'm stuck with you,* she thought but kindly didn't say.

Simon tucked his chin to his chest. She thought his hands were trembling a little. Maybe not. Then he lifted his head. "I like my coffee strong, and served right at six a.m."

A laugh burst out of Lainey. "Oh, I see you're already giving orders." She stood. "I'll go talk to the nurses about getting you released."

He put his hand on her forearm to stop her. He looked up at her, and for the first time she could remember, he didn't look full of mockery. He looked scared. "Lainey, why?"

She patted his hand, the way she would a child. "Your debt is canceled, Simon. That's why."

Jonah hadn't seen Lainey yet. Nor had Bess. When he returned to Rose

Hill Farm after talking to Caleb, Bess was already there. Apparently, it was Lainey's day off from the bakery and Bess couldn't find her anywhere.

By late afternoon, Jonah drove the buggy down to Lainey's cottage to see if she had returned yet. There was no answer at the door. It amazed him to see that cottage transformed. It had been well worthwhile to fix it up. It was starting to look the way it was probably intended to look, years ago, when it was first built by the original owners. It was a lovely little house, with good bones and a solid foundation. He could still smell the fresh paint. New windowpanes replaced the broken ones.

He sat on the porch steps to wait for her. He had been worried to hear that she was going to live in this house— the one where her mother had died in childbirth. He put a hand to his forehead. She died delivering his Bess! Right here. Another discovery that hadn't occurred to him. How could Lainey live in a house that sheltered so many unhappy memories? He couldn't have done it.

His back was stiff from sitting for so long, so he got up to stretch. He hoped she would return soon. Soon it would be more dark than day. He walked down the pathway and around to the back of the house. He peered inside the window and recognized some furniture and an old rug from Rose Hill Farm's attic. He should have known his mother had a hand in this. He walked all around the perimeter of the house, stopping by a small, newly planted rose garden. He smiled. More evidence of Bertha Riehl. He walked around to the front and then he saw Lainey. She stood by the road, watching him, wearing a Plain dress— lavender that brought out her eyes. Her hands were clasped before her to keep them steady.

"Lainey," Jonah said softly as he approached her.

"You came back," Lainey said. "There's so much I need to explain—"

"Would you take me to see my child's grave?"

She nodded. "We can go right now."

They didn't speak in the buggy as Jonah drove them to the town cemetery. Lainey led him straight to the back where her mother was buried. A small grave marker was next to it. He could see that the two graves had been recently weeded. They looked cared for. By Lainey, no doubt.

"I'll give you some privacy," she said quietly, and went to wait in the buggy.

Jonah knelt in front of his daughter's grave. And for the second time that day, he wept.

❧

As Jonah drove away from her cottage, Lainey stood by the road and watched until his buggy had dipped over the rise and was out of sight. They had stayed at the cemetery and talked for hours. It was as if they were filling each other in on the last fifteen years of their lives. They talked until the shadows got longer and still had more to say to each other. It wasn't until long after the dusk turned to darkness and

the stars came out in the clear sky that
Jonah said he should be getting back
to Rose Hill Farm. But he didn't look at
all as if he wanted to leave.

10

The next morning was a church Sunday. Bess dressed quickly and offered to go down the road to pick up Lainey and come back for her father and grandmother, but Jonah said he wouldn't mind going. He said old Frieda needed a little warming up, but Bess wasn't so sure. Her dad came back late last night, whistling. Even Mammi noticed how happy he seemed. You had to know Mammi pretty well to decipher a difference in expression, but Bess thought she hadn't stopped looking pleased ever since she and Jonah had arrived.

Bess wished her father would hurry old Frieda along. She hadn't seen Billy at Rose Hill Farm yesterday. She knew he would be at church this morning, and so she took extra care with her hair. She even pulled a few strands loose behind her cap and tried to curl them into tight ringlets. She didn't think anyone would see since they sat in the back bench, but she hoped maybe Billy might notice. Betsy Mast often had corkscrew curls slipping under her cap and down her neck. But then, Betsy had thick, curly hair, and Bess's hair was thin and straight.

She spotted Billy by the barn the minute they arrived at the Smuckers'. He was surrounded by a group of friends; they were laughing over some joke. Mammi took her time getting out of the buggy from the backseat, which gave Bess a chance to furtively glance at the boys while pretending to help her down. She saw Andy Yoder spot her with a delighted look on his face. Billy hadn't noticed her yet. He had turned around to talk to someone else. As soon as Bess climbed out of the buggy, Andy was at her elbow.

"Bess! You're back! Hallelujah! You

look . . . wonderful." Andy's admiration was unqualified. "I was just this minute trying to talk Billy into making a trip to Ohio to see you! But he made it sound like we were going to the far side of the moon."

Bess stifled a smile. Andy was the kind of person that sometimes told you unexpected things.

"Don't listen to a word this fellow tells you," Billy said, approaching them from behind.

Bess whirled around to face Billy. "Which words?" Her heart was pounding like an Indian war drum. She was sure Billy could hear it.

Billy looked at her as if he was seeing her for the first time. For a few seconds, he was literally unable to find words. "The second part," he said simply.

Then it was as if the mist had cleared and they went back to their old ways.

"Missed picking rose petals, did you?" he asked.

She grinned and held out her palms. "Especially the thorns. When the last cut healed, I told Dad we needed to return. My hands looked too good."

Billy and Andy peered at her hands as if they were made of fine china.

Jonah handed the reins of the horse to one of the Smucker sons and interrupted them. "Well, boys—"

Bess cringed at the undue emphasis her father placed on the word "boys." Couldn't he see that Billy was a man?

"—it's time we went in to the service." Jonah put a hand protectively on Bess's shoulder to steer her to the house for meeting.

⚜

Around three o'clock, they left the Smuckers' to return to Rose Hill Farm. Bess invited Lainey to join them for supper, and Jonah couldn't hold back a smile. As he turned the buggy into the drive, he felt a jolt. Bess let out a gasp.

There, on the front porch, patiently waiting, was planted Sallie Stutzman, her twin sons, and Mose Weaver.

Jonah swallowed hard. In his haste,

he had completely forgotten to tell
Sallie and Mose that he and Bess were
leaving.

☙❧

Over breakfast on Monday, Bess
asked her grandmother if she would
take her to see Simon in Lebanon as
soon as it was convenient. Mammi
said it was convenient right now and
grabbed her bonnet to head out the
door. Sallie and her boys and Mose
were staying at Rose Hill Farm, and
Sallie's "cheerfulness," Mammi said,
was making her dizzy.

They didn't talk much on the bus
ride. Something was building inside of
Bess, something she had discovered
last night as she watched everyone at
dinner. She was so sure she was right
that she felt as if she might explode.
Finally, she blurted out, "Oh Mammi!
Whatever are we going to do?!"

Mammi had been looking out the
window. She turned to Bess as if she
had forgotten she was there. "About
what?"

About *what*? Wasn't it obvious? "Dad

loves Lainey and Sallie loves Dad and Mose loves Sallie and Lainey loves Dad! If we don't do something quick, the wedding is going to happen because Dad is too honorable to tell Sallie no. That's what!" Sallie hadn't stopped talking about the wedding last night. That dinner was one of the most painful moments of Bess's life. Her father looked stricken, Mose kept looking at Sallie with this terrible longing—Bess knew Mose well enough to know that his mild look held *terrible* longing—and Lainey! Poor Lainey! She hardly said a word. When Jonah offered to drive her home, she refused him, flat out.

Mammi turned back to the window and exhaled. "We let nature take its course. *That's* what." She patted Bess's leg. "That's what we do. Never forget that."

Bess turned that thought over and over in her mind, not at all convinced it was the best plan. Didn't Mammi care? Didn't she want her dad to be happy?

Just before they reached Lebanon,

Mammi asked, "Does that little round gal ever stop talking?"

"No," Bess said glumly. "She never does."

"Them two boys ever stop wiggling?"

Bess shook her head. "Not even in church."

"Does that tall fellow ever say a word?"

Bess scratched her prayer cap. "None that I recall."

"Hoo-boy," Mammi said. "Nature has her work cut out for her."

❧

After they arrived at the hospital, Mammi went in search of a bathroom and Bess knew *that* could be a long wait, so she decided to go ahead to Simon's ward. She tiptoed up to his bed. She could see he had grown much weaker than the other time she had visited. Sweat gleamed on his face, like he was feverish.

"If you're another vampire, go away," Simon muttered without opening an eye. "I don't have any more blood to give."

"But I'm not . . . I'm not a vampire," Bess said. "It's me. It's Bess. Bertha's granddaughter. Jonah's daughter."

"Well, well. It's the holy howler." He groaned. "If Bertha sent you here to get me to confess my sins before I kick the bucket . . . tell her no thanks."

"She didn't," Bess said quietly.

Simon didn't respond.

"Would it be such a bad thing, though, to confess your sins?"

Now he looked at her. "It wouldn't be if I didn't enjoy sinning so much."

Bess had never heard of anyone who enjoyed sinning. She gave him a look of great sadness. "I'll pray for you, for your soul."

"Have at it," Simon said mockingly. "I'm afraid all those childhood lessons in holiness slid off me like hot butter off the griddle." He pointed to the door. "Now go look for where the carpenter made a hole."

She supposed that was his rather impolite way of telling her he wanted her to leave him alone. For a brief moment, she thought about not going through with the bone marrow operation. Simon would never appreciate the gift.

And yet, she wasn't doing it for him. She was doing it for God. And for Mammi. She bit her lip. "I came here today to tell you some good news. It turns out we're a match, you and I. I can give you my bone marrow."

Simon lay very silent, but he was listening, she could tell that.

"So instead of going home with Lainey to d—," Bess gulped back the word, "um, you're going to be getting some medicine to help your body get ready for the transplant. In another week or so, I'll have the procedure. Harvesting the marrow, they call it. Then they'll give it to you and, hopefully, it will cure you right up."

He still didn't look at her. He didn't say a word.

"I guess it won't be that fast," Bess said, rambling now. "Sounds like it will take a while to graft. They called it grafting, which is interesting, because that's what we do with the roses at Rose Hill Farm. We graft them onto better rootstock. Then they're stronger and healthier. I guess that's just what it will be like for you. You'll get stronger and healthier. That's the plan, anyway." She ran out of things to say. "I just wanted to tell you the news myself."

Simon lifted his chin. "I'll have to think on it."

"Well, think a little faster," Mammi said. She had come into the ward and eased into a chair beside Bess.

Simon frowned at his sister. She frowned back at him.

"Well, Bess," he said, "don't expect me to thank you."

Bess lifted her chin a notch. "I don't. I don't expect a thing."

"Good. As long as we're clear on that." But he did look at her, right in the eyes.

Bess held his gaze. "We're clear on that."

"Simon, anybody ever tell you it's hard to put a foot in a shut mouth?" Mammi said, standing to leave.

❧❦

Everything was happening so fast that Jonah didn't know what to do.

Sallie had settled into Rose Hill Farm like she wasn't going to budge. The dining room table was covered with wedding invitations that she was busy addressing. Mose, too, seemed to be in no hurry to leave, and even though the fate of their business troubled Jonah, he was thankful for Mose's presence. Mose acted like a self-appointed shepherd to those boys, and it was a good thing. They *were* little monsters, just as Bess had said. How had he never noticed? The first day, they ran their scooters into his mother's most cherished rugosa and broke the bush at the stem.

His mother went so still it scared him, like the quiet right before an Ohio tornado hit. When she finally spoke, it was in a chilling voice. "Bess, go get Billy Lapp. Tell him we got us an emergency."

The second day, those boys knocked over a shelf of freshly canned rose petal jam in the barn when they were horsing around. The third day, they forgot to latch Frieda's stall and she wandered into the vegetable garden, trampling a row of tomato plants.

And he would never forget the look on Lainey's face when she was introduced to Sallie on Sunday. He had never mentioned Sallie to Lainey . . . it never occurred to him to mention her. But Sallie started right off with wedding talk, and Lainey responded with forced cheer, like daffodils in January. When he offered to give her a ride home—hoping for a chance to explain—she gave him a firm "No."

It made him feel sick to his stomach.

Dear Robin and Ally,

I haven't written in a while because so many changes have been happening so quickly and I didn't know where to begin. First of all, I bought a cottage with my savings. A fixer-upper would be a generous description. It's the home I lived in as a child. And I am going to be taking in my stepfather, Simon Troyer. He's been quite ill. I've told you about

Bess. We've grown as close as . . . well, she's like a sister to me.

And to answer your question about men: no. There are no men of interest in Stoney Ridge. None whatsoever.

Love, Lainey

For the actual bone marrow transplant, Simon had been moved from the Veterans Hospital down to the hospital in Lancaster, where a specialist worked who was skilled at performing the relatively new procedure. Bess would be given a general anesthesia, and the marrow would be removed from her hip bone. She would stay one night, just for observation, and be allowed to go home the next morning.

The night before the operation was scheduled for Bess was one of those hot late-August nights that never cooled off. She had trouble sleeping, so she got up and went outside to get some fresh air. She sat on the porch steps and gazed at the stars. Some-

how, the night sky gave her a sense
of the majesty of God. She seemed
so small and he seemed so big. In the
distance, a horse whinnied and another answered.

"Bess?"

She looked out toward the yard and
saw the silhouette of a person. "Billy!
What are you doing here?"

Billy hesitated. "I forgot my books."
He looked toward the barn. "In the
barn. I forgot my books." He kept his
books in Bertha's barn because his
brothers teased him for being a book-
worm.

"And you couldn't wait until morning
to read?"

"No. I was right in the middle of a
good part. What are you doing out
here?"

"Couldn't sleep."

He walked up to her. "It's a brave
thing you're doing. Giving Simon your
bone marrow."

"I'm not at all brave," she answered
truthfully.

"Are you scared? About tomorrow?"

She squeezed her elbows. "Maybe a little."

"Think it will hurt?"

"I'm not too worried about the pain. They said it's not much more than a bad fall on ice. I've suffered through plenty of those. It's more . . ."

He sat beside her on the porch steps. "What?"

"Well, I've never had general anesthesia before. Where do you go, when you're put to sleep like that? I won't even dream, the nurse said. I mean, where does your soul go?"

Billy didn't answer for a long time. "Caleb Zook said once that our great hope is when we're absent from the body, we're present with the Lord." He looked over at her.

She thought about that for a while in the quiet of the night. That answer satisfied her. It gave her peace. "Thank you, Billy."

"Bess?" Billy asked, husky-voiced.

She turned her face to him to see what he wanted. He held her face in both his hands and kissed her very softly on the lips. Then he drew away.

She could hardly breathe, so stunned by the kiss.

He tucked a loose strand of hair under her cap, and then gently grazed her cheek with the back of his hand. "Good night." He stood and took a few steps down the walkway before turning slightly. "I'll see you in the morning. I'm going to the hospital."

His tone was so sweet that it made her heart flutter. She was just about to tell him that he forgot his books again, but then she realized that he hadn't come over for the books at all. Billy had come over this night because he was worried about her. It gave her the shivers, even on a hot night like this.

It was the longest day Jonah had ever known. As soon as Bess arrived at the admitting office, the hospital machinery moved into action. She was whisked away in a wheelchair with barely time enough to wave goodbye to everyone who had come with her that morning: Bertha, Billy, Sallie and her boys, Mose. And Lainey, who was keeping a considerable distance from Jonah.

Jonah waited with Bess in the pre-op room. Machines hummed softly and white-soled shoes whispered up and down the halls. A nurse came into the room. "We just got word that the doctor is getting prepped." After she left, Jonah and Bess sat in silence. Suddenly, this was real.

Jonah leaned down to smooth her hair from her face. "You," he pronounced, "will wake up and still be the same girl who cannot be bothered to study for a math test and vanishes when there are chores to do and goes to sleep reading with the light on." But all he heard himself say was the first part of the sentence: "You will wake up and be the same girl . . ." That's all he was praying for.

The anesthesiologist came in and put the mask over Bess's mouth and nose. He told Jonah to count aloud to Bess, but instead, Jonah recited the Lord's Prayer in Deitsch. It was Caleb Zook's suggestion. He recommended having Bess hear the words "Thy will be done" before she fell asleep. When her eyes drifted shut, the nurse ushered him out to the waiting room.

Lainey looked so worried that Jonah wanted to take her in his arms and tell her everything would be all right. But of course he couldn't.

And there was part of him that wasn't sure everything would be all right. A terrible fear came over Jonah, a feeling he struggled to disown. He knew he must yield absolutely to God's will and trust in his ultimate mercy. "Not my will but Thine be done," he had told Bess before she slipped into unconsciousness. He had spent a lifetime reciting that prayer and wanted to believe it. But the fear of God's will was there, nonetheless. He still struggled against yielding to God's will, and he prayed desperately that God would bring Bess back to him, whole and well.

He looked over at his mother, sitting in a plastic chair with her head tucked down and her hands clasped together in her lap. He wondered if she felt worried too. She was more a woman of action than of words and worry. Her eyes were closed, either praying or meditating or . . . she let out a loud snore. A laugh burst out of him, Lainey too. He looked at her then; his brown eyes met hers, and they shared a smile. Sallie had been telling Mose something and caught the look that passed between Lainey and Jonah.

She stopped talking. Sallie Stutzman stopped talking. Her eyes darted back and forth between the two of them.

Jonah felt like he was a boy caught with his hand in the cookie jar. Guilt washed over him and he made sure he didn't look in Lainey's direction again.

It seemed like an eternity, but it was really less than an hour before the doctor came to the waiting room, searching out Jonah. The doctor seemed a little startled to find a large group of Amish jump to their feet, eyes fixed on him.

"She's fine," the doctor reassured everyone. "Bess is awake now. We're just going to observe her for a while, make sure no complications develop, and then we'll put her in a regular room for the night."

"Can I see her?" Billy asked.

Jonah turned to Billy with an eyebrow raised.

"Uh, I mean, can her father see her?" Billy stumbled.

"In a little while," the doctor explained.

"What about Simon?" Bertha asked. "When will he be getting Bess's marrow?" Simon had been in isolation for over a week and hadn't been allowed any visitors because of risk of infection.

Jonah felt shamed. He hadn't even given a passing thought to Simon. *Forgive me, Lord*, he prayed quickly.

"It's actually easier for him to receive the marrow than it was for Bess to give it," the doctor said. "A needle is inserted into the cavity of the rear hip bone where a large quantity of bone marrow is located."

The doctor became quite animated with such a rapt audience. "We harvested about one to two quarts of marrow and blood. Bone marrow is actually a spongey material, found inside the bones. While this may sound like a lot, it really represents only about 2 percent of a person's bone marrow, which the body replaces in four weeks."

Billy looked as white as a sheet. Bertha told him to go sit down and put his head between his knees so he wouldn't faint.

"Men don't faint," he said in a weak and pale voice, but he let her help him to a chair. "They might pass out, but they don't faint."

"Whatever handle you want to call it by, you look like you're just about to do it," Bertha told him.

"Everything's getting ready for Simon now, and I'm going to head in and take care of that." The doctor clapped his hands together. "Hopefully, the donation will 'take' and make its way into the central shaft of larger bones to restore stem cell function."

Billy groaned, then stood abruptly and hurried down the hall, in need of a men's room.

Bertha watched him weave down the

hall and shook her head. "That poor boy's going off his feed again."

※

Early the next morning, Billy went over to Rose Hill Farm to finish chores as fast as he could. Billy had told Bertha he would take her to the hospital to meet everyone for Bess's release this afternoon. For the last two days, he had felt an odd anxiety and he hadn't been sleeping well, as if something wasn't quite right and he didn't know what.

He was walking up the tree-lined drive when he heard Boomer barking up a fury in the rose fields. He glanced at the house and was surprised there was no buttery glow from a lantern light in the kitchen. Usually, he could see Bertha at the stove and smell something delicious frying. Even though he had just eaten a full breakfast at home, his stomach would begin to rumble in happy anticipation. Not today, though. The farmhouse looked dark and cold.

He jogged over to see what Boomer's ruckus was about, then slowed as he approached him. A chill ran down his spine when he saw the frantic, wild-eyed look in the dog's eyes.

Then he discovered what Boomer was troubled about. Bertha Riehl was lying on her side, as if she had laid down to take a nap among her roses. Billy rushed to her and rolled her on her back. Her eyes were closed, her lips were blue, her face was white, and he could see she wasn't breathing. She'd been gone for a while. She had been out spraying Coca-Cola on her roses when she passed. She looked utterly at peace. He held her hand for a while, tears streaming down his face, unsure of what to do next. Boomer rested his big woolly head on Billy's shoulder.

Billy took a few deep breaths, trying to steady himself, and went up to the farmhouse. He was looking for Jonah, before he remembered Jonah was spending the night at the hospital with Bess. It looked like their company— Sallie and her boys and that Mose— were gone too. Probably at the hospi-tal, Billy figured. Billy rubbed his face with his hands. His father would know what to do. He hated leaving Bertha like this, but he couldn't move her on his own. Boomer was standing guard by her. He bolted down the drive and ran home to fetch his father.

Billy knew word would trickle quickly through the community about the passing of Bertha Riehl. He had to act fast to get to the hospital in Lancaster as quickly as he could. His father tried to insist they get Caleb Zook to tell Jonah and Bess the news about Bertha. "That's what bishops are for," he told Billy. "They know best how to say these things."

Billy was tempted, but he knew, deep down, he needed to be the one to go. Part of being a man was not avoiding hard things. He changed clothes and his father drove him into town to catch the bus to Lancaster.

"Maybe I should go with you," he told Billy.

"No, I need to do this myself." Billy wasn't sure how he was going to break the news to Jonah about Bertha's passing. But he had to get to them before they returned to Rose Hill Farm and found a group of women gathered, preparing the house for the viewing.

Just before he hopped on the bus, his father stopped him by placing a hand on his shoulder. Billy turned to him, and his father didn't say anything, but there was something in his eyes— a look that said he was pleased with him. He couldn't remember ever seeing that look from his father before.

Not an hour later, Billy arrived at the hospital and found Jonah and Lainey and everyone else sitting in the waiting room.

"Billy!" Lainey said when she spotted him. Then she grew solemn, sensing from the look on his face that something had happened. "What's wrong?"

Billy sat near them, struggling to speak. Lainey took hold of his hand to give him strength. "It's Bertha," Billy started, then tears filled his eyes. "She's gone." He had to stop and wipe his eyes with the back of his sleeve. "I found her in the roses." He covered his face then, unable to continue.

Jonah heard the words come out of Billy's mouth, but he couldn't understand them. It was as if everything had stopped. The sound of the nurses' shoes as they hurried up the hallways, the clocks ticking, the elevator opening and shutting. He looked at Billy and felt pity for him. Poor Billy. He was suffering. And then he looked at Lainey, with tears running down her cheeks. Sallie started to tell Mose a list of things they needed to do for the funeral. It was like Jonah's mind had shut down and he wasn't able to process the meaning behind the sentence, "She's gone."

His mother had passed? She was dead?

Like a fog lifting, the full meaning behind those words started to sink in to him. Then the pain rushed at him, as real as an ocean wave, and he felt the tears come. Billy crouched down beside him and Jonah put his hand on Billy's head. They sat there for a long while, until a nurse came and timidly interrupted to let them know Bess was ready to go now.

Jonah nodded and wiped his face

with his handkerchief. "I need to tell her."

"I'll go with you," Lainey offered.

"*I* should go," Sallie said as she rose to her feet.

"No," Lainey said, giving Sallie a firm look. "No. I'll go."

Sallie looked confused, then hurt, but Mose put a gentle hand on her arm. Jonah didn't have the presence of mind to do anything more.

Before walking into Bess's room, Jonah took a deep breath and prayed for God's strength. Bess had grown so close to his mother this summer. More and more, she was acting like her too. She even cooked like his mother. He opened the door a crack and saw her waiting by the window, dressed and ready to go.

"How are you feeling?" Lainey asked her.

"Not too bad," Bess said. "A little sore. They won't let me see Simon, but they did tell me it went well for him."

Jonah nodded. "So I heard."

Bess picked up her bonnet and cape. "Let's go home."

Jonah pulled up a chair for Lainey to sit in. "Bess, something has happened."

Bess looked curiously at her father. Then she gasped. "It's Simon. He's dead, isn't he? All this effort, and he's dead."

"No. Simon is fine." In a twist of irony, Simon *was* fine and his mother was dead. Jonah pulled the curtain around her bed to give them privacy from the other patients. Then he leaned a hip against the bed frame, crossed his arms against his chest, and lifted his face to Bess. Gently, he told her that her grandmother had passed this morning while she was out tending the roses. He waited, expecting her to break down.

Bess turned to face the window. She hugged her elbows as if she was holding herself together.

Lainey walked up to Bess and put her hands on her shoulders. Softly she said, "It was your grandmother's time. She'd done everything she needed to do. She brought Simon back to his family. She brought you and your dad back to Stoney Ridge." Lainey turned Bess around to look at her. Bess was dry-eyed. "God's timing is always perfect. You see that, don't you? Her life was complete." She spoke with conviction.

Jonah remained silent as Lainey said those words. He was amazed by her, nearly in awe. But it distressed him to see Bess so quiet. It wasn't like her. Two years ago, when their pet dog had been hit by a car, she had cried for two days straight. "Are you all right, Bess?"

Bess nodded but didn't say a word.

"When you're ready," Jonah said, "Billy is waiting for us in the hallway."

"I'm ready now," was all Bess said in a voice unfamiliar to him.

It was afternoon by the time they returned to Rose Hill Farm. The hardest moment of all came as the taxi drove up the driveway. Knowing Mammi wasn't there—and wouldn't be there ever again—made Bess feel an unbearable pain in her chest, as real as if she had been stabbed.

Everyone in the taxi was aware of Mammi's absence. She saw the tight set of her father's jaw. Billy kept his chin tucked to his chest, Lainey just went ahead and let the tears flow. Sallie was quiet, which was a great blessing. Even her boys seemed to know they needed to be calm and still, but it helped to have Mose sit between them in the back of the station wagon.

Rose Hill Farm wasn't empty. The news had spread quickly throughout Stoney Ridge. Friends and neighbors were in and around the farmhouse, cleaning it from top to bottom in preparation for the viewing and the funeral. The women fussed over Bess, but all she wanted was to go upstairs and lie down on her bed. She was stiff and exhausted after an uncomfortable night. Her hip felt sore and so did her heart—aching for her grandmother. It was the bitterest kind of heartache she had ever felt—an ache that burned and gnawed. She hoped that tears would come in solitude and help wash away the pain. It seemed a terrible thing that she couldn't shed a tear for Mammi. She had loved her grandmother more than she had even realized. She knelt by her window and looked out over the rose fields, wondering where it was that her grandmother had lay down and died. But still no tears came, only the same horrible ache of grief.

When she finally went downstairs, she learned that the undertaker had returned her grandmother's body. The women had dressed Mammi in burial clothes and laid her out in the front room. One had stopped all of the clocks in the house at the early morning hour they assumed Bertha had died. They would be restarted after the burial.

Bess walked slowly into the front room. Mammi didn't look like Mammi, she thought as she stood next to her grandmother's still body, lying on the dining room table. Jonah came up behind her and put his hands on her shoulders.

"She's really gone," Bess whispered. "You can tell. Whatever it was that made her Mammi is gone."

"Gone from us, but gone to God," Jonah told her.

❧

At first, Boomer seemed to be in everyone's way, all the time. Bess knew he was looking for Mammi, and it nearly broke her heart. She knew what he was thinking: almost everyone else in Stoney Ridge seemed to be in and out of Rose Hill Farm, doing errands of kindness, but there was no sign of his mistress.

Later that day, Boomer went missing. Bess called for him and put food and water out on the porch, hoping he would return. He seemed to have disappeared.

❧

It was a muggy, rainy day when Bertha Riehl was buried, three days after she passed. Jonah and Bess stood by Bertha's graveside and viewed her for the last time in the large, plain pine coffin.

Jonah stood looking down at his mother. Her face was relaxed and serene, but Bess was right—whatever it was that made her Bertha—her soul? her pneuma?—it was gone. *Our bodies are just a shell, a house, for our eternal souls.*

How differently he would have done things if he'd known his mother was slated for death this summer. How much time he had wasted. He felt moved with a deep grief for the years lost between them. And yet, on its heels came a quiet joy. Coming back to Stoney Ridge last week had been no accident. He and his mother, in the end, they made their peace. Just in time.

He saw Billy lean close to Bess and whisper, "Are you okay?"

Bess nodded without looking up. She was calmer than Jonah would have thought possible, considering. His mother would be proud of her.

The lid of the coffin was nailed shut and lowered into the ground; the young men—Billy was one of them—picked up their shovels to heave dirt. When the first loud clump of dirt hit the coffin, Bess broke down with a loud sob.

Jonah took a step toward her, but Billy had already handed his shovel to another boy and was at Bess's side. He patted her on the back to comfort her, handed her his handkerchief, then as her weeping grew worse, he steered her by the shoulders to lead her to his buggy.

On the drive back to Rose Hill Farm, Billy couldn't find any good words to ease Bess's sorrow. Several times he almost had the right thing. But always he stopped. He couldn't bear it any longer. He turned the buggy down a side road and pulled the horse to a full stop. "Go ahead, Bess," he said as he put his arms around her. "Cry it all out. I'm here. No one's here to see. Have a good cry."

And so she clung to him and wept and wept until he thought that her body would never stop shaking with the sobs and the grief. He didn't think a body could have so many tears to cry, but maybe girls were made with more tear ducts. It was good, though,

to have her finally show some emotion. It worried him to see her tearless.
It just didn't seem like Bess.

"It's not that I'm crying for Mammi,
Billy," she said between sobs. "I know
she's in a better place. And she's with
Daadi now. I'm crying for me. What
will I do without her?"

Finally, the wave of sorrow subsided
and Bess's sobs turned to sniffles.
When he thought she seemed all wrung
out, with not another tear left to shed,
he wiped her face with his sleeve and
took her home.

❧❧

As soon as the house had emptied
out that evening, Jonah went outside
to get some fresh air. He checked
that Frieda had water and alfalfa hay,
then lingered in the barn for a while.
He swept the floor of rose petals and
knocked down a few spiderwebs. He
just didn't want to go inside. Sallie
would be waiting for him and he
couldn't face her. He couldn't deny that
she had been a wonderful help these
last few days. She seemed to know

how to get things done in a matter-of-fact, efficient way.

But all he could think about was how much he wanted to be with Lainey. To talk to her about his mother. About Bess. About Simon. About everything. She had participated in every part of the viewing and the funeral, was accepted by the community as nearly one of them—he noticed that folks weren't switching to English anymore when she came in a room. And he would be forever grateful for the support she had provided to his Bess.

But Lainey continued to avoid him. He couldn't blame her at all, but he didn't think he could abide much more of it.

Jonah hung up the broom and slid the door open to find Sallie walking toward the barn in the dusk. "Shall we walk awhile?" she asked him.

They headed down the drive to the road without saying a word to each other. The strange thing, he realized, was not that he wasn't talking. It was that Sallie wasn't talking. In fact, now that he thought about it, she hadn't

said much at all lately. She was as silent as a Sunday afternoon. Then, with
a start, he realized why.

She knew.

"Sallie," he started.

She held up a hand to stop him from
continuing. "Tomorrow, Mose and I
and the boys, we're heading back to
Ohio. School starts soon for my boys
and I don't want any trouble with that
terrible truant officer. And Mose is awfully worried about the business."

Jonah knew that wasn't true. Mose
didn't worry about a thing. Sallie was
only being kind.

"Sallie," he started again.

She held up another hand. "I'm sorry,
Jonah. I just don't think things are going to work out for us. I need a man
who . . ."

*Who wants to be married to you?
Who wants to be a father to your boys?
Or maybe,* Jonah thought, cheeks
burning, *who isn't in love with someone else?*

". . . who isn't quite as complicated."

Jonah stopped short. A laugh burst
out of him, the first laugh in a very

long time. It surprised him, that laugh. He felt as if a tremendous burden had lifted. "You're right, Sallie. You deserve someone who isn't as complicated as me." He *was* complicated. He spent fifteen years grieving, then finally fell in love with someone new—a woman who wasn't even Amish. Not yet, anyway.

Sallie smiled at him then, a genuine smile. All was well. As they headed back to Rose Hill Farm, she started to tell him about something cute one of her boys had said today. And she didn't stop talking all the way up the drive. Jonah found that he didn't mind a bit.

11

At Billy and Maggie's urging, Bess went to the youth gathering on Saturday evening, a few days after Mammi had been buried. She wasn't in much of a mood for socializing—though her spirits had risen temporarily after Sallie left for Ohio and she learned that the wedding was off for good. Her father had seemed anxious to have her go out tonight. He said it would do her good to get out of the house. She couldn't deny that she always enjoyed watching Billy play volleyball. He was such a good athlete. He had been so kind and attentive to her this last week. It made the upheaval of the last week more bearable. She still struggled with the reality of Mammi's passing, and she missed her dearly. She kept repeating to herself Lainey's reminder: her grandmother's life was complete. This was God's time to call Mammi home.

Bess sat on a rock in the shade by herself, content to be left alone, half paying attention to the game until it came to an abrupt halt. Billy held the ball in his hands, as if frozen. His eyes were glued on a buggy that had just pulled into the yard. Bess's gaze shifted from Billy to the buggy. A clump of girls had arrived and spilled out of the buggy, one by one. The last girl climbed out, scanned the yard, then flashed a dazzling smile when her eyes rested on Billy. It was an awful, heart-stopping moment for Bess as she recognized Betsy Mast, looking fresh and lovely in a pink dress.

Billy dropped the ball and made his way over to Betsy. His back was to Bess and she couldn't imagine what he was saying to her, but she could see Betsy's face clearly. Betsy's eyes sparkled as she laughed and joked with him. Bess's heart sank.

Everyone at the youth gathering learned about Betsy's return in record time, though what they heard bore little relation to the facts. Maggie said that the English boy had refused to marry Betsy and dumped her back at her parents' farm. Andy heard that Betsy tired of the English life and wanted to return to her Amish roots. Someone else said that Betsy heard Billy Lapp had made clear his feelings for Bess at her grandmother's funeral—and hightailed it back to stake her claim on him.

Bess spent the rest of the evening doing her very best to appear at ease, but she kept one eye on Billy and Betsy. At first, she noticed that Betsy was her usual flirtatious self, tilting her head, looking up at Billy from the corner of her eyes, playfully striking him in mock punishment for something he said. As the sun went down, they stood off by themselves. Betsy became serious, speaking to him insistently while he seemed to protest innocence. They both looked at Bess, and she guessed they were talking about her.

Was that good? she wondered. *Probably not.*

❦

Betsy could see that Billy's mind was on other things. They were in his buggy after the youth gathering, parked by the shoreline of Blue Lake Pond. Andy had offered to take Maggie and Bess home, and he was grateful for it. Billy needed time to talk to Betsy alone. His mind was darting in a hundred different directions, like a moth to a flame. Betsy shifted a little closer to him on the buggy seat as she tried to explain again why she had left suddenly and why she had returned.

"What about that English fellow?" he asked her. He'd asked her twice before, but she kept changing the subject, turning it around to accuse him of flirting with Bess.

"You're not going to listen to rumors, are you?" She sidled a little closer to him. "He just gave me a ride to see a friend." She put a hand on his forearm. "I needed to see the other side, Billy.

Just to see, before bending at the knee. You understand, don't you?"

She batted her long eyelashes at him, and he knew he couldn't stay mad for long. She really was a beautiful girl. He saw her familiar features as if for the first time, and he was enchanted again by her sparkling green eyes, her dainty nose, and the determined set of her jaw. Her mouth, he realized, did not quite fit the rest of her face: those lips were too full. It was a mouth made for kissing, and the thought that he might never kiss it again filled him with despair.

Maybe he could understand why she left, after all. Everybody had doubts. Wasn't it better to work that all through before getting baptized? That was what the ministers had told him before he was baptized. Better to not take the vow than to take it and break it. "So are you planning, then, to join the church this fall?"

Betsy was looking up at Billy with her red lips in a big *O* of surprise. "Why do you ask, Billy?" Then she leaned up against him and put her lips on his and he felt his mind start to spin. Kissing Betsy always had that effect on him.

Later, after he dropped her at home and was driving the buggy back to his farm, he realized that she had answered his question with a question and given him no answer at all.

As soon as Bess had left with Billy and Maggie to go to the youth gathering, Jonah hurried to Lainey's cottage. Yesterday, he had said goodbye to Sallie and her boys and Mose, and he wanted to be the one to tell Lainey the news of their departure, before Bess had a chance to tell her at church tomorrow. He found her in the backyard of her cottage, trying to turn sod over with a shovel.

"What are you doing?" he asked.

She looked up, surprised to see him, and wiped her forehead with her sleeve. "Making a space for a vegetable garden." Then she turned her attention back to the sod.

It was hard work, what she was doing. But that wouldn't stop Lainey, he realized as he watched her huff and puff. If she made up her mind to do something, she would see it through.

"Maybe I could help," he offered.

She gave him a sideways glance. "No, thank you." Her tone was crisp.

He came closer and put a hand on the shovel's handle. "The place you've chosen gets too much afternoon shade. A vegetable garden needs at least six hours of sunlight a day." He scanned the yard. "Over there, away from the cottage, would be better."

She blew air out of her mouth, exasperated. "You're right."

She released her grip on the shovel and sat down on the porch steps. He set the shovel against the house and sat down next to her.

"I'll dig the sod for you. This week. Right now, even."

"I can get Billy to do it. You've got your . . . houseguests . . . to tend to."

He glanced at her. "Lainey, she . . . they . . . they're gone. Sallie and Mose and her boys . . . they went back to Ohio." He dropped his cane, leaned back against his elbows, and stretched out his legs, crossing one ankle over the other. "Autumn is coming, and Sallie's boys need to start school and Mose needs to tend the business. I need to stay here and see to my mother's estate." He lifted his head. "Sallie and I . . . we had a talk the other night. There isn't any Understanding between us . . . not anymore."

Lainey stared at her balled fists in her lap.

"It's for the best," Jonah continued, his voice steady and strong. "We have different . . . ideas of marriage. We want different . . ." We want different people, he wanted to say, but he didn't finish the sentence. He glanced at her between sentences, wondering what she was thinking. Unlike Bess, whose every thought revealed itself on her face, Lainey was hard to read. She was cautious and careful about her feelings. He watched her intently, waiting for a response.

Lainey lifted her head and looked at the area Jonah had pointed out as a good spot for a vegetable garden.

"Maybe . . . maybe that might be a better spot for the garden."

"It's important to start with the right spot," Jonah added with a smile, not at all sure they were talking about a garden plot. He rose to his feet and reached for the shovel. "The right spot makes all the difference."

He took off his jacket and threw it on the ground, then marked out the space for the garden before he began to dig. Lainey found a spade and worked alongside him, breaking up clumps of grass.

Jonah felt happy and whole for the first time in what felt like forever. The deep calm had been missing before, but not now. Not anymore.

※

Yesterday afternoon, Lainey had been stunned when Jonah told her that Cheerful Sallie had returned to Ohio. As he spoke, she kept thinking this was a moment when people pinch themselves in case they're dreaming. She kept her hands in a tight ball and pinched the inside of her palms, just to make sure. And it hurt! she found, relieved.

He had dug up a patch of earth for her to make a garden and agreed to stay for dinner in lieu of payment, and soon everything slipped back to normal between them. He stayed after dinner and helped her with dishes, leaving only when he thought Bess might be due in from the gathering. She could tell he didn't want to leave, and knowing that made her heart sing.

And today, Jonah said he wanted to go with her to the hospital to learn about all of the postoperative treatment that Simon's convalescence would require. She was pretty sure Jonah must think she was crazy to take him in, but he didn't say so. Instead, he helped her think through the details she would need for Simon, such as ordering a hospital bed. And then he listened endlessly as she described her plan to start a pie-baking business. She wouldn't be able to work at the bakery anymore because she needed to be available for Simon. Mrs. Stroot crumbled when she had told her this morning that she was quitting the bakery. She crumbled even more when Lainey told her she planned to bake pies from her home.

"You'll run me clean out of business!" Mrs. Stroot had wailed.

"I'd never do that to you, Mrs. Stroot! Never! How could I possibly hurt a person who has been so good to me? I thought I'd only make pies on days when the bakery is closed. I just need enough money to cover the mortgage."

Mrs. Stroot shook her head and wiped her tears. She gave Lainey a satisfied smile. "I have a better idea. I'll buy your pies and sell them here. Fifty-fifty."

They shook on the arrangement, and Lainey had her first customer.

Lainey could hardly wait to tell Jonah about the conversation with Mrs. Stroot. He had barely lighted from the buggy when she rushed to meet him with her news. "She wants me to bake pies for her every week! She said I could vary the fillings by what's in season. And we even talked about down the road. That's what she called it. 'If this works out, Lainey, down the road, we can think about adding your signature cinnamon rolls.'" She looked at him with her black eyebrows raised in delight above her wide blue eyes.

The brackets around Jonah's mouth deepened ever so slightly, and his eyes tightened at the corners. Quietly he said, "Well then, perhaps we should see about getting you an oven."

Her face fell. She hadn't thought about such practicalities. It was so like her, to jump into a lake before she learned to swim. Her enthusiasm for her plans always did carry her away. Of course she would need an oven! And a refrigerator. And a stove top. Her kitchen was sparse, only a table and two chairs, provided by Bertha. "I'll have to go to Lancaster for that."

Jonah tilted his head. "Are you thinking you'll use electricity? The cottage isn't set up." Then his gaze shifted beyond her.

She knew what was behind that question. She had planned to be baptized this fall, but that had to be postponed because of Simon. If she were baptized, she would have to shun Simon. She would wait.

Jonah had never asked her about joining the church. She was getting to know him well enough to know that he was watching and waiting, letting time provide the answer. "No. Not electricity. Bess has been teaching me how to cook on a propane stove top. And how to use a woodstove too."

Jonah looked back at her. "You could get those things, used, at an auction."

She nodded. "Then I'll go to an auction."

Jonah stifled a patronizing smile. "Make out a list and I'll get what you need."

"I can take care of these things." *I can take care of myself*, was what she meant.

Jonah gave a short laugh. "Might be a little hard to purchase items at an Amish auction, Lainey. You don't speak Deitsch."

Now her spine stiffened. "I'm learning." But she was a long, long way from being fluent.

He walked up to her. "I'm offering to help. Would it be so hard to accept it?" He searched her eyes.

Yes, she thought, suddenly shy. *More than you could imagine.* She'd always had a hard time accepting help from others. Depending on others. Trusting others.

But she was trying to get past that obstacle. It was part of what she was learning this summer. How could she become Amish if she didn't learn how to rely on her community? It would be like missing the forest for the trees.

She wiped her hand on her apron and held it out to him to shake. "Then I accept your help."

Jonah looked at her extended hand, then took her hand in his. They remained that way for only the briefest moment, touching palm to palm; she was the one to pull away.

She gave him a shy smile. "Thank you."

❊❊

Dear Robin and Ally,

Isn't the start of autumn wonderful? The air is getting crisp in the morning and evening, and apples are falling off the trees! Don't you just love autumn?

So . . . perhaps there is a man of interest in Lancaster County after all.

Love,
Lainey

P.S. By the way, did I happen to mention that I'm becoming Amish?

Jonah took the time to find out what the state requirements would be to get permits and a license for a commercial kitchen. Then he drove a wagon to an auction and purchased a used propane refrigerator and stovetop oven, delivered them to Lainey's cottage one hazy and humid September afternoon, and hooked them up for her. The sky had begun to cloud over and the kitchen grew dim, so Lainey held a lamp over

his head while he worked. She studied his face in the shifting light of the
flame. Once, he caught her eye and
smiled. She considered how attractive
he was—the type of man who was
clearly comfortable in his own skin and
had grown up unaffected by his good
looks.

When he finished, he stood and
turned on the gas to the stove. When
she saw the pilot light fire up, she
clapped her hands together and said,
"How can I ever thank you?"

Jonah looked down at her. He was
quite a bit taller than she was. "I should
be thanking you, Lainey."

She wanted to ask why but could
see he had something on his mind. He
seemed to be carefully arranging his
thoughts, so she remained quiet.

"There's something I've been meaning to tell you. The night of that accident, when you stayed by the buggy
until the ambulance arrived. You kept
saying not to give up . . ." He swallowed hard. "I remember. I remember hearing your voice and I held on
to those words. They helped me stay

alive." His eyes became glassy with tears and he wiped them away with a laugh. "I can't stop tearing up this summer. It's like I'm shedding a lifetime of bottled tears."

They locked eyes for a long moment, then she leaned toward him. She stroked his face softly. He caught her hand and held it to his lips. He kissed it with his head bent over it so that she couldn't see his eyes.

❧

A month had passed since Simon's bone marrow transplant. Jonah and Lainey were seated in hard plastic chairs in an office as a nurse explained what to expect after Simon was discharged. His blood counts were returning to safe levels, the nurse said.

"Does that mean the bone marrow transplant worked?" Jonah asked.

"The transplanted marrow seems to be engrafting," the nurse said. "We're cautiously optimistic. But I have to warn you that recovery can be like a roller-coaster ride. The patient may be irritable and unpleasant with the caregiver. Helplessness is also a common feeling among bone marrow transplant patients, which can breed further feelings of anger or resentment."

"Even more than usual?" Lainey asked.

"One day a patient may feel much better, only to awake the next day feeling as sick as ever." She gave Lainey a bright smile. "So if his daily blood samples continue to show that he's producing normal red blood cells, he can go home by the end of this week."

"So soon?" Lainey asked in a dull, polite way.

"By the end of this week," the nurse repeated cheerfully.

Jonah had a funny feeling the staff was eager to have Simon leave.

"In the first several weeks," the nurse continued, "he'll be weak and tired and will want to sleep and rest frequently. He'll need to return to the hospital for frequent follow-up visits for medication, blood transfusions, and monitoring."

"And then?" Jonah asked. "How long until he can take care of himself?"

"Recovery from a bone marrow transplant is lengthy and can take up to six months to resume normal activities, including returning to full-time work."

Jonah and Lainey exchanged a look of shock. Six months!

"During the first three months after the transplant, he'll be vulnerable to complications due to the fact that his white blood cell counts will be very low and incapable of providing normal protection against everyday viruses and bacteria. So he'll have to avoid crowded public places such as movie theatres and grocery stores to avoid contact with potential infection." The nurse clapped the file shut. "And he really shouldn't have any friends visiting for a while."

Jonah's eyebrows shot up. "Well, *that* shouldn't be a problem. Simon has no friends."

That made the nurse burst out with a laugh. "Will wonders never cease?"

❧

The first morning after Simon was released from the hospital and moved into Lainey's house, he rang a bell at five in the morning to wake her to help him find the bathroom. At six, he rang it again for coffee. At seven, he complained that the eggs she had scrambled for him were cold.

Bess came by in the early afternoon to see if Lainey needed any help. Stoney Ridge was experiencing an Indian summer, and it was too hot to pick rose blooms. Jonah wanted to keep the rose petal harvest going, though he still hadn't decided what to do about Rose Hill Farm or their home in Ohio, either. The roses were in their second bloom, and they had to work quickly in this heat to get those roses picked and dried. Lainey smiled to see the Band-Aids covering Bess's hands.

Lainey made Simon lunch, went back to the kitchen to clean up, only to have Simon ring the bell again. "I don't like crust on my sandwiches," he complained to her. "I don't like crunchy peanut butter, only smooth. I asked for a Coke, not milk. Do you think I'm a six-year-old?"

Lainey took his plate back to the

kitchen and cut the crust off of his sandwich, then took it back to him with a Coke.

Bess sat in the front room and watched this ongoing interaction. The third time Simon rang the bell to complain, Bess stood abruptly and held a hand in the air to stop Lainey from taking his plate back to the kitchen. "So, you don't like your lunch?" Bess's voice was dangerously calm.

"Dang right I don't like that lunch. Didn't like breakfast, neither." Simon turned to Lainey. "And I didn't like the coffee. I told you I want it strong."

Bess picked up the bell, walked to the door, opened it, threw the bell outside, and closed the door.

Simon did not make any further comments through the rest of lunch. He didn't thank Lainey for it, but he didn't complain about it, either.

For the next few hours, Bess helped Lainey roll out pie crusts in the kitchen, and they talked quietly to each other as they worked, while Simon rested. Finally, sounding hurt that he was being left out of the conversation, Simon called to them to ask what kind of pies they were baking. Bess had just taken a pie out of the oven and stood at the door, holding it in her hands with hot mitts. "Apple and pumpkin."

Lainey pulled out a rack for Bess to set the pies on and asked Simon what his favorite pie was.

He scowled at her. "I only like two kinds of pie: hot and cold."

Bess and Lainey laughed at that, genuinely laughed, and Simon's mournful, hound-dog face brightened a bit.

❧

Not much later, Lainey and Bess were cleaning up the mess they'd made in the kitchen when an ear-busting woof came from the front of the cottage. Bess dropped the wet dishrag and hurried to open the front door.

"Don't open that door!" Simon hollered from his bed. "We're getting bombed!"

"That's no bomb! That's Boomer!" Bess said, clapping her hands in delight. She threw open the door and in charged Boomer, looking a little thinner and smelling pretty bad. He jumped up on Bess, then Lainey, then put his dirty front paws on Simon's bed.

"Get that mutt out of here," Simon yelled. "He smells like he was on the wrong end of a fight with a polecat!"

"This is Mammi's dog, Simon," Bess said. "His name is Boomer. He's been out mourning for Mammi. But now he's back. We'll give him a bath and he'll be as good as new."

"Fat chance of that," Simon muttered.

※

"If you wouldn't mind keeping Simon company for a few minutes," Lainey told Bess after they gave Boomer a bath, "I've got some laundry hanging that I need to take down." She picked up an empty laundry basket and went to the backyard. Having a house of one's own took getting used to, Lainey had quickly realized. There was always some little thing to be done. It wasn't a big house, but there were plenty of chores.

She took her time taking the dry

clothes off the line. Hanging laundry was something she found she enjoyed doing. Pinning clothes up and letting the sun permeate them with its warmth was so much better than sitting in a dark Laundromat guarding a machine. Bess had told her once that working is a form of prayer. At first, Lainey had trouble understanding that. But now, she could see it. She thought it meant the kind of work that came from caring for others.

When Lainey came back inside, she found Bess helping Simon drink from a glass of water. It was touching to see Bess, this child who had grown up with another life and another father, reaching out to this man. When Bess tossed that bell out the front door, it was like Lainey was watching some other girl entirely. Bess was so confident and clear about how to handle Simon. She handled him better than Lainey ever did. In fact, it just occurred to Lainey, she handled him the way Bertha used to. Bertha never stood for any of Simon's bluster.

Lainey tiptoed to the bedroom to

fold the clothes. When she came back out, she found Simon had drifted off, and Bess was curled up in a corner of the couch, sound asleep. Boomer was on the foot of Simon's bed, snoring.

❀❀

Later that week, Bess stood on the porch at Rose Hill Farm and waved goodbye to Andy Yoder after he had dropped off a bushel of ripe apples from his family's orchard. Before turning onto the road, Andy looked back and yanked off his straw hat. He stood on the wagon seat, holding the horse's reins in one hand, waving his hat in a big arc with the other.

The thing about Andy Yoder, Bess was finding, was that you just couldn't put him off. He was cheerful and funny and full of life, and totally convinced that she loved him. Which of course she didn't. It wasn't that she was immune to Andy's charms; it felt nice to be admired. He told her today that he thought she looked like an angel: smooth skin with large, bright eyes and a mouth shaped like a bow. He stared at her mouth when he said it, and it made her stomach do a flip-flop. Andy was like that: chock-full of sweet words and lingering gazes and always willing to share every thought.

But as fun as Andy was, Bess knew her heart belonged to Billy. Each day, they worked in the rose fields or in the greenhouse and talked about all kinds of things. Conversation was so easy between them, even their good-natured arguments. Sometimes, when he was in a professorial mood, she couldn't understand half of what he said. Her thoughts often wandered to imagining that this would be their life: the two of them living side by side, day by day, for always.

Esther Swartzentruber told her at church that Billy was spending a lot of time with Betsy Mast, but Bess knew it couldn't be so. Not after that week when she had the surgery and he had kissed her, ever so gently, and had been worried for her. Not after he had comforted her when her grandmother died. Even Mammi had said Billy Lapp was no fool. Surely, Esther was just spreading rumors.

Bess reached down and hoisted the basket of apples onto her hip. Mammi also used to say that a rumor was "something with truth on the trail," and a flicker of fear ran through her.

❈

Billy Lapp wiped his brow. He had worked a few hours at Rose Hill Farm, teaching Jonah about Bertha's rose business, then spent another hour replacing shingles on Lainey O'Toole's roof. He still needed to get home and help his brothers with the oat shocks. Threshing day was tomorrow, and they needed to knock the shocks down to ready the rows for pitching. Billy had done some research to calculate the best time to harvest the oats. He'd recommended this week to schedule their farm for the community's threshing rotation, and for the first time ever, his father had listened to him. The weather cooperated, and this oat harvest looked to be one of the best they'd had in years. Just this morning, his father was discussing tomorrow's pitching and had given him a nod of approval in front of everyone. That was no small thing.

Billy hopped down from the roof and packed up his tools. Then he told Lainey he was heading home, and she handed him a slab of blueberry peach pie she had just pulled from the oven. It was a recipe of her mother's, she said, and she was trying to improve it.

Billy looked up at the sky and was relieved to see the clouds didn't look as threatening as they had an hour ago. If they worked fast, they might be able to get the north field finished before it got too dark. And wouldn't his dad be pleased with that?

He took a bite of Lainey's blueberry peach pie, then another. It was delicious, that pie. It struck him that Bertha had done the same thing with her roses: took something old and made it new. Maybe that's what life was all about—taking the lot you were given and making it better, he thought, finishing off the rest of that pie slab in two bites as he hurried down the road.

The nurse had been right about the roller coaster of emotions Simon would experience, yet that was nothing new to anyone who had dealings with him. At times, Lainey could see that he was making an effort to be pleasant. Or at least, not unpleasant. And then, hours later, it was as if he used up all of the niceness he had, which wasn't in great supply to begin with. He would slip back to constant complaining, mostly about her cooking. Lainey could brush off most of Simon's insults but not those about her cooking. That area was off-limits. She told him that he was welcome to cook for himself.

He gave her a hard look. "You're in no position to be giving me lectures."

There was a moment's silence.

Lainey thought of what Bess would say. She pulled up a highback chair and sat next to him. "The truth of it is that I am in a position to be giving you a lecture. The way I see it, you have two choices. You can stay here, but only if you stop complaining about every little thing. Or . . ."

He narrowed his eyes.

"Or you are free to leave." Lainey was firm.

She had him there. He had no place to go.

He glared angrily at her. "Women are the devil." He said it at least three times a day.

⁂

And yet it was Jonah who had the most difficulty tolerating Simon. He dropped by the cottage often, to help Lainey with house repairs or to take her on an errand to town. But he was cool to Simon and had little patience for him. If Simon dared make a vague complaint against Lainey, Jonah would put up a hand to cut him off. In turn, Simon acted cautious around Jonah, as if he knew not to cross him.

As Simon's health improved, he liked to talk. While Lainey worked in the kitchen, he would tell her stories about all of the near riches he'd had in his business dealings. Since she was in the other room and working on her pies, she was able to only half listen. But Jonah didn't want to hear the stories, even if he was working on a house repair in another room and Simon was in the front room. He never said a word, but he would quietly get up and go outside.

One afternoon, Lainey followed Jonah outside to the vegetable garden. He had given her some spinach seedlings to get in the ground, but she hadn't had a chance yet. He picked up a hoe and raked a neat furrow. She put a hand on his shoulder and he stopped digging.

"I just can't listen to him, Lainey. This chasing after rainbows and borrowing money from people—never paying anyone back. Simon's spent a lifetime living on the near brink of disaster. It just sickens me to think this would have been the life my Bess would have had."

"But she didn't," Lainey said quietly. "She grew up with you. The life she's had with you is the only life she's ever known."

He finished marking the row. "I can't seem to find a way to tell Bess. I can't see what good would be served if she were to know Simon was her father."

"Is that what you're concerned about? Whether it would be good for Bess to know?"

"I don't want her to be hurt. Or confused."

Lainey sat down on the back step and patted the step in silent invitation for Jonah to sit beside her. He lay the hoe on the ground and sat down. "I'm not sure it's up to us to decide whether truth is good for us or not. Truth is just . . . truth. I guess it's how we respond to it that makes it good or bad."

Jonah looked away. "Lainey, why are you doing this?" He took off his black hat and raked a hand through his hair. "I have an easier time forgiving the truck driver—a stranger—who caused the accident that killed Rebecca and our baby, than I do Simon, for abandoning you and Bess like he did."

Lainey didn't answer for a while. "That truck driver was remorseful. Forgiveness comes a little easier when a person asks to be forgiven."

"Maybe. But that doesn't explain you. You're not even Amish, yet you're able to give Simon something I—who lived my whole life in the Amish church— can't." He turned to her. "Why?"

Lainey lifted her head to the sky. "For a long time, I felt abandoned. And so lonely. I still do, at times. I think it will always be my Achilles heel. But a few years ago, I went to a church service and the pastor happened to be preaching on the difference between divine forgiveness and human forgiveness. I knew I couldn't forgive others without God's help. He said that we fail in the work of grace and love when there is too much of us and not enough of God. That thought stayed with me. Too much of me and not enough of God. Once I understood that and asked for God's help, I was able to forgive Simon and stop condemning him." They sat together there for a long time before Lainey added, "I learned how to love from watching your mother. I know she could scare a body half to death, but a person knew she could fail and still be loved. I think even Simon knew that about your mother. I think that's why he never left Stoney Ridge. She might have been the only person who really loved him."

Jonah tucked his chin. "Rebecca was always frightened by my mother."

Jonah was bringing up Rebecca's name more and more and it made Lainey glad. She wanted him to feel comfortable talking about her. She didn't want him to feel as if he had to forget her.

He glanced at her. "You never were frightened by my mother, were you? Even as a young girl."

"I always knew there was a tender heart inside that gruff exterior."

Lainey smiled at him, and Jonah smiled back at her.

She reached out and jostled his knee. "Listen. Simon's still telling the story."

Sure enough, they could hear Simon's voice through the window, carrying on as if they were still in the kitchen. Jonah gave a short laugh. "Are you seeing much improvement in him?

Other than his talking voice is back in working order?"

"Little by little. He's not needing as much sleep. He took a walk to the end of the road yesterday."

Jonah tucked a curl behind her ear and stood to leave. "Good. Maybe there is an end in sight."

And then what? Lainey wondered, watching Jonah head out to the street toward Rose Hill Farm.

❧

Caleb Zook made a point of stopping by to see Simon every Sunday afternoon. Lainey was amazed. Caleb had no responsibility for Simon since he had been shunned. But Jonah said Caleb was like that. He said Caleb had always managed to be sincere about his faith without becoming legalistic. It wasn't that rules were optional to Caleb. She noticed that he didn't entirely ignore Simon's shunning: he didn't sit at their table for a meal with Simon. Once she offered a plate of cookies to the two of them while they were talking in the living room, but Caleb politely

turned her down. Jonah told her later
that Caleb shouldn't be offered food
from the same plate that had been
handed to Simon. And Caleb didn't
touch Simon, not even a handshake.
But he still showed genuine concern
and interest in him. He seemed to believe that there was something to re-
deem in Simon.

All men of God should be like Caleb
Zook, Lainey thought more than once.

"Do you really believe Simon can
change?" Lainey asked him one Sunday as she walked with him out to
his buggy after he had paid a call on
Simon. "Or are you just saying that
because you're the bishop and that's
what you're supposed to think?"

Caleb laughed at her candor. "Simon
always was chock-full of brag and
fight." He put on his hat. "But, yes,
I think he can change if he wants to.
God wants all men to come to him."

Lainey wanted to ask him more but
waited to see if he was in a hurry to
leave. When he didn't get in the buggy
right away, she blurted out, "What
made Simon the way he is?" It was

a question Lainey had often wondered and wished she had asked Bertha. She did ask Jonah once, but he had no idea. As long as he could remember, Simon was just thought of as the black sheep.

Caleb leaned against the buggy, one long leg crossed over the other, his arms crossed against his chest, that black hat still shadowing his face. "I'm not sure there's an easy answer to that question. I don't think there's one event. But I do recall my mother saying that Simon's mother died bringing him into the world, and his father was a hard man to please." He stopped as a thought seemed to come to him. "A little like Billy's father. Always wondered if that might be why Bertha took such an interest in Billy." He stared down the road for a moment, then turned back to Lainey. "Simon was the last child and only boy in a string of females, and life seemed to be a little more difficult for him—learning in school, getting along with others, learning a trade. He grew up being told he couldn't do anything right. Maybe there came a point when he believed it. It became a way of life for him. A habit. Maybe it was easier to just go ahead and disappoint people in advance. Maybe that's how he has felt about God." He unknotted the buggy reins from the fence. "He's softening, though. Little by little. Bertha would say, 'En Baam fallt net uff der eracht Hack.' *One stroke fells not an oak.*"

Lainey frowned. "Bertha also said, 'You can't make good hay from poor grass.'"

Caleb grinned. "Now, now. How could a man be at death's doorstep and not have some change in his heart?"

Lainey was unconvinced. To her, Simon didn't seem capable of change.

Caleb caught the look on her face. "Let me put it another way. Before Simon's body could accept Bess's bone marrow, the doctors had to kill off his own marrow. Only then would his body be able to accept the new marrow, Bess's sacrifice. There's a spiritual part of this. The way I see it, he's a new man. It's just taking awhile to break those old habits, to kill off that old marrow. That old way of life."

That was a new thought to her.

"But," Caleb warned, "it might take time." He shrugged. "No matter. God has plenty of time. It's one thing he's never short of."

Lainey rolled her eyes. "God might have time, but I'm running out of it. Patience too. It's like trying to take care of a bear with a toothache."

Caleb laughed. "Lainey, now that Simon is getting more energy, maybe you should think about putting him to work for you." He climbed into the buggy. "Work does a soul good. Even a tough old codger like Simon."

As she watched his buggy drive down the road, she wondered if what Caleb said could possibly be true. Could Bess's sacrifice to Simon be changing him, inside out?

She heard Simon's voice yelling for her to hurry his dinner. *Fat chance.*

12

Jonah and Lainey were heading back to the cottage from buying supplies in town. They were on the top of the rise when Rose Hill Farm came into view. This was Lainey's favorite vantage point. She could barely make out the rooftop of her cottage down below, hidden by trees, but it gave her comfort to realize how close their homes were. Suddenly a car honked loudly and careened around the buggy, upsetting the horse so that Jonah pulled quickly over to the side of the road and stopped.

"Dutt's weh?" he asked Lainey. *Does anything hurt?*

"A little scared but not hurt," she said.

He raised his eyebrows. "You understood?"

She lifted her chin. "I understand a lot more than you might think."

He grinned at her. "I'm sure you do." He looked back at the horse. "I haven't known Frieda to rear before."

Lainey looked up the road at the small speck of a black car, now far up the road. "It wasn't Frieda's fault. It was that car's."

Jonah got out of the buggy to calm the horse down. When they arrived at the cottage, they found that little black car parked out front.

"Oh no," Lainey said, worried. She hopped out of the buggy and hurried inside while Jonah hitched the horse to the fence.

There in the living room were her English friends, Robin and Ally. Simon, looking delighted to be in the company of two young women, was entertaining them with stories.

It was Robin who recognized Lainey first. Robin was not quite beautiful,

and certainly not pretty, but men had
always been attracted to her. She had
a straight nose and a strong jaw, and
her green eyes were large and clear.
She was not smiling when she saw her
friend; in fact, she wore a slight frown.
She was studying Lainey, her gaze
moving slowly over her prayer cap, her
blue Plain dress and white apron, then
back up to her starched white cap
again. "You look so . . ."

"Plain?" Lainey offered.

"Then it's true," Robin said. "What
you wrote to us. We thought you
were joking. They've got you in their
clutches. It's a cult, just like he said."

"*Who* said such a thing?" Lainey
asked.

"Him," Ally answered, pointing to
Simon. Ally was round and pleasant
looking. There was something friendly
and understanding about her face.

Lainey glared at Simon. "Don't listen to him. He's always saying crazy
things. Being Amish is not a cult."

"It's a cult of the worst sort!" Simon
said. "Seems all sweet and rosy as
long as a fellow toes the Amish line.

But just put a toe over the line a very little bit and folks will come down on you like a wolf on the fold." He folded his arms across his chest. "If that's not a cult, I don't know what is."

Ally was staring out the front window at Jonah, who was looking over the black car. "Who's he?"

"That's her boyfriend!" Simon called out. "He's been bringing twigs and leaves and starting to build a love nest, just like a couple of doves in springtime." He made a sweeping gesture with his hand. "She's getting baptized just so she can throw me out on the streets. Shunning me just like the rest of 'em."

Lainey lifted her palms and looked at Simon. "Why do you say these things?" She had told him once that she would postpone her baptism until he recovered and could live on his own, just to avoid any complications of his shunning. How had he twisted that around?

Robin walked up to the window and stood next to Ally to peer at Jonah. Lainey looked over their shoulders.

Seeing him at a distance the way a stranger might see him, she felt a surge of tenderness for him. He was such a fine-looking man.

"Oh sheesh," Robin said. "She's gone off the deep end for sure. It's worse than we thought."

Jonah had a pretty good idea to whom the black car belonged. Lainey had told him about her two English friends she used to live with, that they were good-hearted but ran a little wild. He saw the two of them watching him from the window. He took his time getting the horse some water, stalling, trying to settle his unease. Would Lainey be tempted by her friends to return to the world?

Maybe this was good, he tried telling himself as he emptied the water bucket. Now was the time for Lainey to find out if an Amish life was what she truly wanted. To be sure she was hearing God's guidance correctly. And before his feelings for her were at the point of no return, he had to admit, hoping he hadn't already passed it. Cautiously, he approached the cottage porch.

Lainey met him outside. "My friends are here." She had an uncomfortable look on her face. "They think I've gone crazy."

Jonah looked down at her earnest face and tried to hold back a grin. "Have you?"

Her face relaxed into a smile. "No more than usual."

When she smiled like that, with her full-lipped mouth, it always made Jonah think of kissing her. He was seized by an urge to take her in his arms, but instead he reined in those stray thoughts and said, "Then let them see that. They're here because they care about you. Let them see you're still you."

Lainey nodded and turned to go into the house. She stopped and whirled back around. "I just . . . apologize in advance for anything they say that might be considered . . . offensive."

Jonah gave her a reassuring smile and followed behind her into the house.

Lainey gestured toward Jonah. "Robin, Ally, this is my friend Jonah Riehl."

There was an awkward silence as the two women looked him up and down. Then the taller of the two, the woman whose mouth was pursed tightly— Robin—took a few strides forward to shake his hand. The gesture struck him as insincere; he could see a mocking intelligence in her eyes. He turned to the other woman to shake her hand. Ally had a small, round face on top of a small, round body. The image of a sparrow following behind a raptor flickered through his mind.

"I noticed one of your car tires is nearly flat," Jonah said.

"We've been running on three tires since we hit Lancaster," Robin said, as if it didn't seem to matter.

"If you have a spare, I could change it out for you," he offered.

Robin exchanged a curious glance with Ally. "I thought you Amish folks didn't want anything to do with cars."

Now it was Jonah's turn to exchange a glance with Lainey. "Knowing about

something and using it are two different matters." He took off his coat and
tossed it on a chair, then rolled up his
sleeves and went out to the car.

❧

After Jonah went outside, Ally turned
to Lainey. "That sweet old man was
just about to rustle something up for
us in the kitchen. We're starving!"

Sweet old man? Simon? Lainey
heard a curse fly out of the kitchen and
hurried in to find Simon in the middle
of frying up a loaf of scrapple. He was
rubbing butter on his hand. A curl of
black smoke was rising up from the
frying pan. Lainey grabbed a dishcloth
and pulled the heavy cast iron pan off
of the burner.

"Scrapple?" she asked Simon as she
put his hand under cool water. "Why
would you offer scrapple to my friends
at this time of day?" She cracked the
window open to fan out the smoke.

"They wanted something Penn
Dutch," he said, carefully examining
his hand.

"Fine," Lainey said, pulling forks out

of a drawer. "If that's what they wanted, then that's what they'll get." She had just bought a loaf of scrapple in town because Simon had pestered her to get some for breakfast.

It irked her to see Simon bend over backward, acting as charming as could be toward her two friends. To her, he always sounded quarrelsome, even if he wasn't. Why, he had never even cooked before! She pulled plates from the cupboard and napkins and took them to the table. By the time she got everyone something to drink, Jonah had returned from changing the tire. He took one look at the burnt scrapple and said he should be leaving.

"Please, Jonah. Don't go. Sit down and visit." She wanted him to get to know her friends and for them to get to know him. Plus, Simon was on better behavior when Jonah was around. She pointed to the place she had set for him at the table.

Too late, Lainey remembered that Jonah couldn't sit at the same table with Simon. He hesitated, an uncomfortable look passed over his face, until she jumped up and offered him a glass of iced tea. Then, instead of sitting down, she nonchalantly leaned against the kitchen counter and he followed her lead. She had seen Caleb do the same thing once. Still respecting the rules of the church, but without making a scene or being rude to others.

Jonah took a sip of iced tea. "So, what is it you two do in Harrisburg?"

"We're cosmetologists," Ally said.

"They study the stars," Simon said to Jonah, thumping the bottom of the ketchup bottle over his plate.

Robin snorted and Lainey exchanged an amused glance with Jonah. "That would be cosmology," Lainey whispered to Simon.

"Same thing," Simon said.

"Not hardly," Robin said. "We work at a beauty salon."

"Ha!" Simon said. "It is the same thing. You're turning coal into diamonds!" He grinned at his own joke.

For some reason, it irritated Lainey even more that Simon could laugh

off Robin's correction. If she had corrected him, he would have barked at
her.

Ally poked carefully at the scrapple
with her fork. "What's in this?"

"Offal," Simon said, sawing a piece
of scrapple with his fork.

Ally looked up. "Awful?"

"Yup," Simon said. "Hog offal. Heads,
heart, liver, and other scraps. All mixed
together with cornmeal and flour." He
took a bite and chewed it. "Guess
that's why they call it scrapple."

Robin made a face. "It sounds awful!"

"Yup," Simon said. "That's what I've
been telling you. Offal."

Lainey gave a sideways glance with
a smile to Jonah, and Jonah smiled
back at her. An intimacy passed between them that shut everybody else
out. It only lasted a moment, but no
one at the table missed it.

After Jonah left, Lainey showed Robin
and Ally upstairs to the spare bedroom.
She felt as if she should brace herself,
now that they were alone.

"Why, this room is as bare looking as the downstairs!" Robin said, walking into it. There were two twin beds covered with handmade quilts, and a simple nightstand between them. No curtains on the windows, no rugs on the floor, no pictures or posters on the wall. It was a Plain room.

Lainey looked around the room as Robin and Ally did, then her gaze came back to her friends. As they stared at each other, the air seemed to acquire a prickly tension but the silence dragged out.

Finally Robin let out an exaggerated sigh. "You can't actually be thinking of wanting to marry that simple farmer, can you?" she asked, flopping on the twin bed. "Why, he even smells like a farm!"

Lainey liked the way Jonah smelled— of hard-work sweat. It blended with the other scents of summer, of sweet clover and mown hay. He had spent the morning helping a neighbor thresh in his fields.

"Simon told us that Jonah's house

doesn't have toilets," Ally said, eyes as big as saucers. "Or running water."

Lainey winced. "Rose Hill Farm belonged to his mother and she died recently. He's installing indoor plumbing right now." It was the very first project Jonah started work on after his mother had passed, and Bess couldn't have been happier.

Ally sat down on the other bed. "Has he told you he loves you?"

"Not in so many words," Lainey said, handing them towels. "The Amish don't use terms of endearment the way we—you—do. They show how they feel about someone by example." Like the time Jonah cut a cord of wood for her and stacked it neatly into a pile by her front door. She thought of him preparing the vegetable garden for her, then helping her to plant. Or accompanying her on medical appointments for Simon. Even changing her friends' tire today, without being given a word of thanks. Were those things not evidence of love? She knew her thoughts showed on her face, and her cheeks grew warm. "Jonah Riehl will make someone a fine husband," she added. She wasn't sure why she felt as if she needed to defend him.

"Oh, will he really?" Robin asked in mock amazement. "I'll grant you this . . . if he shaved off that beard and took a shower and got a haircut and wore a T-shirt and blue jeans, he could be a looker. But what about that cane? And his limp? How old is this guy, anyway?"

"Not old at all," Lainey said in a crisp tone. She thought Jonah was quite marvelous just the way he was: wise and kind and wonderful.

Robin stood and pointed a finger at Lainey. "And you? You always told us you weren't the marrying kind. Not Lainey O'Toole!"

Robin's words rankled Lainey. It was true, she had said many times marriage wasn't for her. Hadn't she thought this whole thing through a hundred thousand times before? But that was before she met Jonah and grew to care for him. It was a frightening thing—to realize that you wanted to love and be loved more than you could have ever imagined.

"Do you actually think he's going to marry you?" Ally asked. "Wouldn't he be driven off for marrying someone out of his commune?"

Lainey stiffened. "No one ever said anything about getting married." That was the truth. Jonah had never hinted at marriage in any way, shape, or form. He seemed to carefully avoid any discussion of their future. She didn't know if he was planning to return to Ohio or stay here in Stoney Ridge. All she knew for sure was that Sallie Stutzman had married his business partner, Mose, and he didn't seem bothered by the news. Lainey often wondered if Jonah even thought about marrying her at all; she thought about it all the time. "And the Amish do not live in communes. Nor is it a cult."

"But what about culinary school?" Ally asked. "You scrimped and saved for years! It was your dream!"

Lainey shrugged. "I've learned more about cooking in the last few months here than I ever could in a formal school.

Here, food means more than nourishing a body. Sharing a meal nourishes a community. It's like women are feeding a big family."

"That's another thing Simon told us about," Ally said. "Amish women are oppressed. They're always serving the men and the men are controlling and mean-spirited. The women can't speak their mind and they have to do whatever their husband tells them to and they have no self-esteem and they have at least a dozen babies—"

"And you . . . Miss Independent!" Robin interrupted. "How many times have you given us a lecture about respecting ourselves and not falling in love with every guy that looks our way? About how we should have goals and plans? And how a man would only derail our dreams?"

Ally nodded in silent agreement.

Robin lifted her hands in the air. "But along comes a guy in a beard and a buggy—who walks with a cane and has a teenaged daughter, no less— and Lainey falls for him, hook, line, and sinker." She looked back at Ally as if to say "what is the world coming to?" then turned to face Lainey. "Well, honey, if you're not derailed, I don't know what is."

Lainey sat down on the bed. "Listen, you two. I'm *going* to become Amish. Not *because* of Jonah. This has nothing to do with Jonah."

Robin and Ally exchanged a doubtful glance.

"I'm becoming Amish because that's what I think God wants me to do." Once she said it aloud, she realized that was exactly what it was. She truly believed God was leading her in this direction.

Robin put her hands on her temples, as if she had a headache. "I'd like to think your bonnet is on too tight, but you always did go a little overboard with the God stuff. I never imagined you'd go this far."

Stung, Lainey felt no need to reply. Without a word, she rose to leave and went downstairs to start dinner. Still upset, she decided to go sit on the porch steps for a few minutes of solitude and watch the sunset. Why did it seem that when a person really started listening to God, others assumed that person had gone off the deep end? Maybe because God does lead us into unusual places. She looked up at the streaks of red that blazed out from the dying sun. What was it Jonah said? Red sky at night is a farmer's delight. Red sky at morning, a farmer takes warning.

The wind unfurled strands of her loosely pinned hair and pressed her dress to her legs. She smoothed out the apron over the blue dress Bess had made for her. Maybe she shouldn't be so hard on Robin and Ally for their concern. If someone had told her six months ago that she'd be dressing in simple garb and living a Plain life, falling in love with a Plain man, making a life in Stoney Ridge, she would have laughed out loud.

But she was here and so very glad to be . . . where life was simple, where people cared for each others' needs, where faith in God and life blended together as one. This was where she belonged.

She noticed the first star appear on the horizon. Looking up at the bruised blue of the evening sky for a few minutes—at the vast and empty sky—always cut human problems down to size. A short laugh burst out of her as she rose to her feet. *Maybe it is a little crazy.* But it was a crazy that suited her.

❧❦

All through dinner and into the evening, Robin and Ally tried to convince Lainey to return to Harrisburg with them, but she wouldn't budge. She tried to explain her feelings, but they couldn't see her point of view.

"Can't you just be happy for me?" Lainey asked them at last. "I'm still me. I might be wearing a Plain dress and living without modern conveniences—"

"I'll say," Robin interrupted with a sneer.

"—but I'm really, truly happy." Lainey could tell that they still didn't believe her, and it hurt her. The three of them had been friends since high school; Robin and Ally were the closest thing to a family that she'd ever had. The way they looked at her—especially Robin, but Ally always followed Robin's lead—was almost as if she had to choose one or the other, the Amish life or her old friends. Why did it have to be that way?

She would have thought it to be the other way around, that Jonah might frown on her English friends. She knew there were some Amish who avoided the English as much as possible, as if they might be corroded by worldly rust. Jonah didn't seem to share that belief. As he left her cottage yesterday afternoon, he had quietly suggested to her that she might bring them to Rose Hill Farm tomorrow afternoon. He said he wanted them to meet Bess.

On Sunday morning, Lainey tiptoed into their room at seven to ask if they would join her for church. She thought that maybe, if they could see the gathering for themselves, if they could see the kindness and the sincerity of the people, then they would understand why she felt so drawn to this community. If they could only see what a wonderful father Jonah was to Bess, then maybe they could see why she cared for him. And if they could meet Bess, they would understand why Lainey wanted to be close to her. She wanted Robin and Ally to come to her church because it was becoming so much a part of her, the backbone of her life.

Robin opened one eye and said emphatically, "No. Way."

❧❧

Bess couldn't wait to meet Lainey's English friends. Her father had told her what he knew about them, but it wasn't much. Lainey had mentioned their names to Bess once or twice, but then she would change the subject, as if she just wasn't sure how to combine her past with her present. Bess was curious about them. She knew they were important to Lainey, and she was eager to know everything she could about her. Lainey fascinated Bess.

After a light lunch that followed church, Bess, Jonah, and Lainey returned to the cottage. As Jonah hitched the horse's reins to the fence post, they heard Simon singing. It sounded slurry and strange and off-key. And loud. Very, very loud. Jonah motioned for the two to stay put while he went inside. He opened the door carefully, then pushed it wide.

He looked back at Lainey with a look of sheer disgust. "Er is gsoffe." *He is drunk.* Jonah's patience for Simon hung by a thread.

Lainey and Bess went to the door. A near empty bottle of an amber-colored liquid was on the floor and Simon was sprawled on the couch, singing at the top of his lungs. The smell of alcohol oozed from him, sour as old sweat. His eyes shone too brightly.

Lainey stomped over to him and picked up the bottle. "Where did you get this?"

Simon's chest heaved as he drew in a ragged breath. "Don't even think about sharing," he said, slurring his sibilants.

"Your English friends is my guess," Jonah said. He took the bottle from Lainey and poured it out on the grass.

"Did Robin and Ally give that to you?" Lainey asked.

"They . . . might have . . . left it behind," Simon said. "They went into town to get a new tire, then came back and waited for you, but you took too long. They had to get to Philly by nightfall for a rock concert. Said to say goodbye." He waved his hand carelessly in the air.

Silence covered the room. Bess saw the disappointed look on Lainey's face. Jonah saw it too. How could her friends leave like that?

But then Lainey stiffened her spine. "Did you ask them to buy you that booze?" she asked.

"All of you, quit looking down your noses at me!" Simon snapped. "People been looking down their pointy little judgmental noses at me for as long as I can remember. Nobody believes in me! Nobody has ever been in my corner!"

Eventually his voice grew slower, his hand movements less exaggerated. His arms fell to his sides, and soon his head began to hang as if it were

a great weight. Then he stopped altogether. His face was white, but he was
not going to ask for mercy, or understanding, or a second chance.

Bess felt a surge of pity for him.
She took in his thin, greasy hair and
his long, white narrow face. There was
some sincerity in the way he spoke.
If this was his version of his life, then
this was his life.

"Very well, then," Lainey said. Something in her tone made them all look at
her. "You should leave now, Simon. If
that's how you feel, if that's what you
think—after all Bertha went through to
bring Jonah and Bess here, and after all
Bess went through to donate her bone
marrow, and after all I've been doing
just to get your sorry hide healthy—if
that's how you feel, you should leave
this afternoon."

It was more decisive even than Bess
would have been. She looked at Lainey
in admiration. So did Jonah. There was
no hate, no revenge in her tone. Just
a simple statement of the position. It
startled Simon just as much.

Something clicked then. Simon knew

she meant it. He looked at them, one by one, as if he had never seen any of them before. Defeated, he retreated.

⁂

Simon turned a corner after Robin and Ally's visit. He grew noticeably stronger and healthier. He stayed in the spare bedroom now and cheered when the truck drove away with the rented hospital bed. He still napped quite a bit, but his face gained color and he was filling out some.

But Lainey's determination to become Amish felt tangled up after her friends' visit. It was the seeds of doubt about Jonah they had planted that ate at her. They were shocked that he had never said he loved her nor hinted at a life together. Ever since, it had bothered her too.

She knew it was silly to think that words alone would reveal if a man loved a woman. How many times had she mopped up her friends' messes after they had their hearts broken by a man who had professed love? Too many times to count. Words were cheap, she knew that.

But there was a part of her that longed to know how Jonah truly felt about her. Did he care about her the way she cared for him? She knew he had a lot to do to sort out Rose Hill Farm, but she wondered if he was planning to return to Ohio soon. What about his business there?

Would he ever tell her he loved her? Did he need to?

She felt as if she was staring at a fork in a road. One way of thinking was the English way: that words expressed how a person felt.

The other road was the Amish way: that action took the place of words.

It was her friends' visit that showed her how truly English she was. Becoming Amish was so much more than learning their language and their ways. It was changing how she perceived things, even small things. Things like terms of endearment.

If she felt this way about hearing the words "I love you," how many more things were there that she didn't even understand yet? Like being submissive to a husband. What if a husband made wrong decisions? And Robin was right about one thing: Amish women always served the men first. She'd seen Amish women out in the fields, working side by side with their husbands, but she'd never seen an Amish man in the kitchen. Why did Amish men seem to have a complete pass on domestic duties? And what about her little pie business? She loved to bake. How could she keep her business if she had a dozen babies?

She kept these internal musings to herself, but whenever she was alone, the doubts slipped back, as persistent as a buzzing fly that needed shooing away.

Maybe this path wasn't right for her, after all. Maybe becoming Amish was really impossible for an English person. Maybe it wasn't too late for her to leave and return to her original plan—to attend culinary school.

And have a life of independence. Unencumbered.

Alone.

After Sallie had left for Ohio, Jonah told Bess that they needed to stay for a while to clean out Rose Hill Farm and straighten out Mammi's affairs. Bess was thrilled. She loved Stoney Ridge. She adored Lainey. She was hopelessly in love with Billy. And, to add icing to the cake, it meant she could avoid repeating algebra. But it also meant they had a big job to tackle. Mammi never threw anything away. Each day, Bess and Jonah tried to clean something out—a closet, a desk, a bureau. Bess felt as if she was having an opportunity to peek in on her grandparents' lives. Especially Mammi's. She cherished anything that helped explain her grandmother to her. Mammi seemed the sort who'd never really been young, yet here Bess was, finding letters and notes Mammi had written and received years and years ago.

She missed Mammi more than she could have ever imagined. She hated waking up to the shock of remembering that she was gone. Tears would come to her eyes at unexpected moments during the day, then they would disappear just as quickly. But always, like a shadow, there remained a sharp tug of loss.

Her deepest regret was that she was just starting to understand her grandmother and her unexpected ways . . . and then she was gone. Bess had never lost anyone close to her in such a sudden death. This must have been what her father felt after her mother died in that accident. Like a fresh wound that was slow to heal.

But God's ways were always best. She knew that to be true.

One evening, Jonah had already gone to bed but Bess was wide awake. She decided to brew herself a pot of chamomile tea. Once the kettle boiled, she went out into the garden, mug in hand. There would be a hard frost tonight, the first one of autumn. She drew the cold air into her lungs, and when she breathed out again, her breath hung in the air for a moment in a thin white cloud, quickly gone. The air had a touch of wood smoke in it from somebody's fire. She shivered and turned to go back inside.

Bess decided to finish cleaning one last desk drawer before going to bed. She found an unmarked large envelope and opened it. In it were yellowed newspaper clippings. That struck Bess as strange, because her grandmother didn't read anything but the Amish newspaper, *The Budget*, and these were clippings from the *Stoney Ridge Times*. She picked up the lantern and went to the kitchen table. She laid the clippings out on the table. As she realized what she was reading, she started to tremble. The articles were about the buggy accident that killed her mother. There was even a grainy but gruesome black-and-white picture. She saw the mangled buggy and the horse lying still in the background. She held it up to the light. She could hardly make it out in the background, but an ambulance had its back doors wide open. She touched the picture gently. Was that her mother on the stretcher?

There were other clippings too. Ongoing ones of the trial her father had to testify in against the driver who rammed into the buggy. It touched her deeply to see the quotes her father had made. He was just a young man, only twenty-one years old, newly widowed, with a child to raise. Yet he was quoted with such clarity and rightness. And then there were other clippings— ones that described how stunned the nation was to learn of a man who turned down an insurance settlement. There were pictures of her dad in the article. She could tell he was trying to keep his head down, away from the cameras. No wonder her father had felt the need to leave Stoney Ridge. He was such a private man.

She gathered up the clippings to slip back in the envelope. One small clipping dropped on the floor. She stooped to pick it up and held it by the light. It was a death notice, only one paragraph long, of a newborn baby that had died of sudden infant death syndrome. *Parents: Elaine O'Toole Troyer (deceased) and Simon Troyer. Surviving sibling: Lainey O'Toole.*

She read it again and again, con-fused. Lainey had never mentioned having a sister. She wondered why Mammi would have kept that clipping. Was it because it was Simon's only child? But why in this envelope? Then she noticed the date. Lainey's baby sister had died the same day as the buggy accident. She slipped the clip-ping back into the envelope. Tomor-row, she would ask Lainey about it.

13

Lainey heard the rumble of thunder in the distance and hurried outside to take the laundry down before the rain began. The air had grown thick and heavy this afternoon, signs of a storm coming. Lightning cracked again, this time much closer. So close her ears hurt. She knew this rainstorm would hit with a fury. She looked up to see Bess hopping over the fence to join her. Under Bess's arm was a large manila envelope.

"What are you doing here in this weather?" Lainey asked her, folding a stiff towel. When Bess didn't answer, she tossed the towel in the laundry basket and turned to face her.

Bess had an odd look on her face. "I was cleaning out Mammi's desk and I found this." She handed Lainey the manila envelope. "Open it."

Lainey sat down on the back steps to the kitchen and opened the envelope. She drew in a quick breath when she read the headlines on the yellowed newspaper clippings. She flipped through the clippings and stopped when she saw the obituary about Colleen. She glanced up in alarm.

Bess pointed to that clipping. "Why would my grandmother have kept that? Why . . . in that very envelope?"

Lainey's heart felt fierce with panic. It was time for Bess to know the truth, she was sure of it. Bertha Riehl had felt the same way. Jonah should have told her long ago. It was time.

But it should be Jonah telling her this truth.

She patted the seat beside her, but Bess shook her head. Lainey bowed her head and was silent for a moment, offered up a silent prayer for God to give her the right words, then she lifted her chin and met Bess with a level gaze.

"There's a story I need to tell you. It's about you and me. About Jonah and Rebecca." She told Bess everything, every detail. She kept looking up to see how Bess was taking the news. Bess stood with her arms crossed tightly against her chest, an inscrutable expression of calm on her face. Lainey rose to her feet and reached a hand out to touch her. "Bess, can you tell me what's running through your mind?"

Bess kept her gaze on the fluttering sheets, as if concentrating on how the gusts of the wind lifted them.

"Bess?" Then Lainey heard Simon shouting for her from inside the house. She tried to ignore it, but the calls grew louder and louder. She sighed. "Let me just check on Simon and I'll be right back."

She went inside to discover Simon ranting about a window left open. The wind was giving him a chill, he complained. She slammed the window shut, rolled her eyes at Simon, and went back outside to finish her conversation with Bess.

But when she went back outside, Bess was gone.

❧❧

Lainey hurried to Rose Hill Farm to tell Jonah that she had told Bess the truth: that Simon was actually Bess's father. She found him feeding hay to Frieda in the barn.

Jonah was stunned. For a long time he said nothing, seeming unable to take it in. The rain was coming down harder now and pounded the metal roof like a drum. Then, as the truth of it dawned on him, he looked bewildered. "You told her about Simon?" he asked her.

"She asked me, Jonah. She had a bundle of newspaper clippings that your mother had saved. In it was one about the death of Simon's baby. She asked me specifically if I had any idea why Bertha had saved that clipping."

His face had gone all white and taut. "But why? Why would you tell her?"

Lainey waited a heartbeat before she said, "I wasn't going to lie to her."

"You could have waited."

"For how long, Jonah? When were you ever going to tell her? You've been avoiding this conversation for months!"

"Maybe she didn't *need* to know. Maybe some things are best left alone."

He looked so anguished. She wanted to put her arm around his wide shoulders, to try to console him with her touch. But he seemed suddenly brittle, as if he might break if she were to touch him. She was desperate to give him some kind of comfort, but she didn't know how. What could she say to him in these circumstances? Every phrase that came to mind seemed inadequate.

He turned to face her. "Where did she go? She must be upset."

"I don't know where she went, but she wasn't upset," Lainey said, her voice surprisingly soft. "She really wasn't."

He glared at her. "How could she *not* be upset?"

She folded her arms against her chest. "You underestimate her, Jonah."

"Oh? You think you know Bess so

well after just a few months?" Now he was clearly livid. "Then where *is* she?"

That, Lainey couldn't answer.

"In this pouring rain, why isn't she home? Where is my daughter?" He grabbed a bridle and went to Frieda's stall, quickly slipping the bit into the horse's mouth and buckling the buckles. He led her by the reins out of the stall and toward the door. Just as he was about to leave the barn, he turned to Lainey and looked at her with anger in his eyes.

"If something happens to her, Lainey . . . if anything . . ." He shook his head as if to stop himself from saying more, then left.

❧❧

The rain hit with a fury. It was cold and sharp and falling sideways in the fierce wind. Jonah barely noticed it. When he heard what Lainey had done, he felt such panic grip his chest that for a moment he couldn't breathe. He was furious with Lainey. She had no right!

"Bess is *my* child!" he said aloud.

The words tore out of him, from some deep place, some old, long-buried hurt. He had to find Bess and explain. But where could she possibly be? He felt as if the world had become very fragile. Very dangerous.

As he rode the horse past the Lapp farm, it occurred to him that Billy might have an idea where Bess might be. The two had spent hours together this summer and it had given Jonah cause for concern. Bess was too young to be thinking seriously about boys. Then, suddenly, a well of hope bubbled up. Maybe Bess went to Billy to find comfort.

He turned the horse around and galloped toward the Lapp farmhouse.

As soon as Billy saw the frantic look on Jonah's face and heard that Bess had gone missing—that she was upset about something—he had a pretty good idea of where she would have gone.

"Give me an hour," he told Jonah. "If I'm not back in an hour—no, give me an hour and a half—then you can go looking. But there's no sense in both of us getting soaked to the skin. I think I know where she is." He grabbed a slicker and went to the barn.

Jonah followed behind him. "Then tell me and I'll go find her."

"It's too hard to find. Trust me, Jonah." Billy saddled up his pony. "You go home in case she returns there." He rode away before Jonah could object.

About a month ago, he and Bess had found an abandoned crow's nest at Blue Lake Pond, high on a ledge but protected from the rain by the branches of a sheltering tree. He knew she was there, as sure as if he could see her. When he got to the lake, he tied the pony's reins to a tree trunk. The wind was lashing through the trees, and the pony shifted its weight from foot to foot, uneasy, but the fury of the rain had eased up. Billy hiked up to the ledge, slipping a few times. There on the ledge, shivering and drenched, was Bess, hugging her knees to her chest. When he called her name, she looked up, startled, and put her fingers to her lips. She pointed to the nest. There was a black crow, staring down at both of them.

"I've been watching her land in that tree. She thinks she owns it, that it's her tree. She takes off and lands again, watching me watching her. That's what crows do. She's living her crow life," she said softly, eyes fixed on the bird.

Billy sat down next to her. "Your dad is steaming like a kettle. Said something has upset you."

"I'm not upset."

With a measured glance, he realized she was speaking the truth. She didn't seem at all upset. Wet, cold, and shivering, but she was calm. She had a look on her face that seemed peaceful. Andy always said she looked like an angel, and right now, he was right.

She turned her face to the sky, like a flower, and smiled softly. "Billy, isn't it a wonder? That the crow is here? God made nature so things can get fixed again." She turned to him. "Blue Lake Pond will have birds and fish again."

He'd been so relieved that Bess was

where he thought she'd be, he hadn't even given the appearance of the crow a second thought. "Why, you're right." He scanned the lake and heard a woodpecker somewhere, hard at work, hammering a tree. He smiled.

"God does it with people too. Makes it so that they can find their way back to him." She rested her chin on her knees. "You know what I love about looking up at the sky? It helps me to remember that I am so incredibly small and God is so immense." She lifted her face to the sky. "Behind those clouds is an ocean of stars, limitless in its infinity, so large, so large, that any of our problems, even the greatest of them, is a small thing."

Billy wasn't really sure what she was talking about, but the day was dying and they were wet and cold. He knew Jonah was out of his mind with worry. He stood and gave her his hand. "Maybe you can save your philosophizing for home, by a warm fire, in dry clothes."

Jonah had given Billy an hour, like he agreed, but now that hour was up and he was going to find his Bess. He was putting on a rainproof cloak and his black hat when he saw a pony heading up the drive with two figures on its back. He ran out the door and down the porch steps. He could see them now, Billy in front with Bess holding on to him from behind. A powerful wave of relief flooded over him, like the relief that follows the first rainstorm after a long summer drought—swift, complete, overwhelming.

The first thing Jonah did was to wrap Bess in a large towel and make her sit down by the fire.

"I'm sorry to worry you, Dad," she told him, and she saw tears prickle his eyes.

He brought her a cup of hot tea and kept fussing over her as she tried to explain how she felt. She could see he was worried sick. Billy had warned her as he left to return home.

Bess knew she should have been

shocked by what Lainey told her today, or at least terribly upset. But instead, she was filled with a strange
sense of destiny, as if God had spared
her for a reason. She told Jonah she
felt blessed, having him for a father,
and that only made his eyes water up
again.

"It's like the roses, Dad. I'm a branch
that's been grafted onto this good tree.
Your tree. An Amish tree. And the great
root of God sustains us." That thought
had come to her while she was sitting
on the ledge, and she had rolled it over
and over in her mind. She liked how it
sounded.

Her father bowed his head. She
wished she could make him understand
that it was all right. That everything
was going to be all right in the end,
just like Mammi had said it would be.

She went to him and knelt down
by his chair, putting a hand over his.
"Please don't blame Lainey, Dad. She
was only telling me the truth." There
was something else that occurred to her
on that ledge, something wondrous. A
wide smile broke over her face. "Dad,

do you realize that Lainey is my half sister?"

🍃🍃

Lainey knocked tentatively on the door to Rose Hill Farm, unsure of what kind of reception she would get from Jonah. A few hours ago, he had seemed so angry with her, and—from his point of view—she couldn't really blame him. Nor did she agree with him. But she had to know that Bess was home safely.

"Lainey," Jonah said as he opened the door. He put a hand to his forehead. "I was going to come down tonight. Bess is here. She's fine. She's safe."

Lainey exhaled with relief. "Good. I mean, I'm glad she's home." She turned to leave.

"You . . . were right. She wasn't upset. Not upset at all."

She turned and looked at him. "But you didn't believe me."

He looked uncomfortable, but he didn't dispute her. "She's upstairs, changing into dry clothes. Would you

come in and wait for her?" His eyes
were pleading.

"No. But tell her I stopped by." She
saw a hurt look cross his face, and
straightaway she wished she had not
sounded so curt. All that mattered right
now was that Bess was home.

She started to leave, but Jonah
touched her arm lightly to stop her. His
voice dropped to a whisper. "She said
that she felt as if God had a purpose
in all of that. By protecting her."

Lainey gave him a direct look. "She's
absolutely right."

Jonah took a step closer to her.
"Lainey. I'm sorry for doubting your
judgment. Your judgment is far better
than mine about these matters."

"We can talk about it tomorrow."

"I didn't want to lose Bess."

"You love your daughter." Her voice
was flat—without salience. "It's normal
to want to hold on tight to those we
love."

"Maybe there's such a thing as
holding on too tightly." He looked away.
"Tonight I wondered if God might be
testing me, the way he tested Abraham

with Isaac." He folded his arms against his chest. "As if he wants me to figure out if I trust him completely or not."

Lainey softened a little. "It's the worst place to be, half trusting, half not."

He rubbed his forehead. "That's where I've been for the last fifteen years. Stuck right in that very place. The worst place to be. I haven't really been living, I've just been tiptoeing around, trying to avert disaster."

"It doesn't work," Lainey said, quiet but firm. "You just end up missing the life you have." Through the window, she saw Bess come down the kitchen stairs and look around the room for her father. "Go. Talk to her."

Jonah reached out his hands to her. "Come in with me. Let's talk to her together."

Lainey hesitated. Doubts about Jonah had been buzzing around her all afternoon. She shook her head. "No. I'd better get back."

Jonah watched her carefully. Her words and posturing were bold, but only skin deep. As if she was on a precipice. "Lainey, please?" His question,

and the gentleness in his voice, dis-
armed her. He kept his hands extended, waiting for her to take a step
toward him. Just waiting.

A silence came between them then.
A silence she could feel, for it was
thick with words that had never been
spoken.

Jonah's face opened for an instant:
trust and hope.

She felt a sense of perspective
wash over her. This was *Jonah*. Her
Jonah. Jonah wasn't the kind of man
Robin and Ally thought him to be—
mean-spirited and controlling. Why, in
fact, she suddenly realized they were
describing a man like Simon! Jonah
wasn't like Simon, not at all. Just the
opposite. He asked her opinion about
things and really wanted to know her
thoughts. He helped her set up her pie
business. Why had she allowed Robin
and Ally to influence what she knew
to be true? How could she have let
that happen? Her friends said Amish
women had no self-esteem. If only
they had met Bertha Riehl! Bertha had
a stronger self-esteem than anyone

she'd ever known. And Bertha was Amish to the core.

Lainey's heart lifted. She knew Jonah's heart—knew it in some fundamental, important way. Yet she'd held herself back from him, not trusting this love that had come so unexpectedly, from such an unexpected source. She looked at him long and hard, tears in her eyes, then reached out and tangled her fingers with his. He tugged on her hands and drew her close. She felt his arms go round her, and they clung to each other as if it were the most natural thing in the world.

On Tuesday evening, Mrs. Stroot dropped by Lainey's cottage with an order for one hundred little six-inch pumpkin pies and seventy nine-inch pecan pies for the Stoney Ridge Veteran's Day Parade, to be delivered on Friday afternoon. Lainey was thrilled and quickly agreed when Mrs. Stroot told her about the order. She needed the money; setting up a home business had cost more than she expected, and her savings account was dwindling rapidly.

The gray light of an autumn dawn was beginning to appear at the window as Lainey sat at the kitchen table the next morning and decided she must have temporarily lost her mind. How could she possibly bake that many pies in such a short amount of time? She was still getting accustomed to a propane stove. Not every pie turned out like the one before. Even with Bess's help, she was facing a daunting task. She sat at the kitchen table, notepad in her hand, and tried to make a list of all of the ingredients she would need. Then she put the pencil down and stared at a point on the ceiling.

"I can't do it," she said to herself. "It's my own fault. I got greedy. I thought I could do it, but I can't."

"Yes, you can," Simon said.

Lainey hadn't even noticed that he had come into the kitchen for coffee and had been watching her. "My pies are too inconsistent. I would need to make double the quantity, just to make sure I have ones to sell."

Simon lifted one shoulder in a careless shrug. "I'd sooner have a slice of your worst pie than anyone else's best."

Lainey's head snapped up. She couldn't believe her ears. Was Simon actually paying her a compliment? She couldn't quite tell.

He looked away, embarrassed. "Keep writing that list. I'll head into town and get the supplies. You better get moving."

Tears came into her eyes. "Simon . . . I don't know what to say . . ."

"Don't say anything or I'll take back my offer," he groused, but he looked pleased.

There followed two of the busiest days Lainey had ever known in her life, and certainly so for Simon. The two of them, plus Bess and even Jonah, rolled out endless mounds of pastry dough, cracked open pecan shells for the nuts until their fingers were stained and blistered, stirred fillings, and sampled the results. The kitchen, in a white fog of flour, had a heavenly scent of vanilla and cloves and pumpkin and blackstrap molasses. The pies were laid out on baking racks, like little works of art. Lainey displayed a streak of perfectionism; only the best would be delivered to Mrs. Stroot. She had to keep sending Simon up to the store for ten-pound bags of sugar and another big can or two of Crisco. He went without complaint, which amazed her. He drove Jonah's horse and buggy as if he'd done it every day of his life. Boomer rode along as shotgun, just the way he had accompanied Bertha. Simon liked to gripe about Boomer, but he whistled for the big dog to come along whenever he was going anywhere.

By Friday morning, Lainey had the pies ready for delivery in pink boxes that Mrs. Stroot had provided. Jonah and Simon, with Boomer shadowing him, took the pies over to the lunch grounds for the parade. Then they came back for the pies that didn't make the cut and delivered those to grateful neighbors.

"She's been working me like a whole pack of bird dogs," Simon groused to

Caleb on Sunday afternoon. "She's aiming to put me back in the hospital and kill me for certain." Boomer lay sprawled right by Simon's side.

Lainey was used to him now and paid no attention to his tone of voice. "Don't you lie to the bishop, Simon," Lainey called out from the kitchen. She wiped her hands on her apron and leaned against the doorjamb. "But I will say you've been a big help. I couldn't have done that big order for Mrs. Stroot this week without you."

Simon turned to Caleb. "That's the gospel truth. I saved the day." He stroked Boomer's big head.

Then Simon smiled—for the first time, thought Lainey—and it was not a smile that lasted long. But still, Simon had smiled.

❧❧

Billy tossed some pebbles up at Bess's window late one evening. He cupped his hands around his mouth and whispered loudly, "Can you come down?"

Bess's heart left the ground and

sailed into the night sky. She dressed quickly and hurried downstairs. Maggie had said she was pretty sure he was courting Betsy again, but Bess didn't believe it. Would he be coming to see her now, if he were still interested in Betsy?

She opened the kitchen door as quietly as she could and met him at the bottom of the stairs. She stopped on the last step so she was eye level to him. She couldn't pretend; she was thrilled to see him. But her delight seemed to distress him. A flicker of fear came and went through her, but she dismissed it.

"Oh Bess," he said, taking her hand and holding it to his face.

Bess's intuition rang an alarm. Something was badly wrong, she felt sure, though she did not know what. She looked into his eyes. His face was working with emotion. He was struggling for words. She could almost hear him trying out different words in his head.

"I need to tell you something. I want you to hear it from me first." He swallowed hard. "It's about me. About me and Betsy. We're going to get married. Soon. Betsy doesn't want to wait."

So it was true. Bess said nothing, unable to take it in. She blinked away tears and looked down to hide her confusing emotions. Then one strong feeling broke through: disappointment that felt like a knife wound.

Billy grasped her arms and pulled her close to him. "You know, don't you? That you've meant something special to me?"

He kissed her mouth. It was a new kind of kiss, different from the one he had given her the night before her surgery. It was as if he was determined to remember the moment. She realized, with dismay, that he was thinking this would be their last kiss.

She clung to him, wanting it to go on forever, but all too soon he drew away and turned to go down the drive. Bess stared at him as he walked away, chin to chest, hands jammed in his pockets, beautiful in the moonlight. So this is what it felt like to have your heart break.

When Billy was out of sight, Bess went back to the house, up to her room, closed the door behind her, and lay down on the bed. Her body started to shake with sobs. Once she started to cry, it was hard to stop. She cried because she had lost Billy for good. She cried because life seemed so unfair sometimes. She cried because she missed Mammi. She wanted her grandmother.

⁂

Billy walked home from Rose Hill Farm that night feeling lower than any man on earth. He hated hurting Bess like that. Her face looked so trusting, so eager to please, when she first came outside to him tonight. Unfortunately, she looked particularly pretty. Her soft white skin seemed to glow, and the light blue dress she was wearing made her eyes the color of a tropical sea.

Then, after he told her about planning to marry Betsy, her face looked as pained as if he had wounded her. It tugged at his heart, and tears came to his eyes. He had to look away so that she would not see. He wished she would have yelled at him or thrown something at him. The disappointed look on her face cut him to the quick. He had dreaded telling her about him and Betsy. What he truly feared, he realized, was hurting Bess. He could bear her anger; it was her pain he could not face.

She must have heard some gossip about him and Betsy. She must have noticed how he had been unable to meet her eye the last few weeks. But she seemed shocked by his news. It shamed him, how she always believed the best in him.

Could he be in love with two different girls at the same time? And such different girls. Bess was so full of curiosity, eyes as big as saucers, and her face would light up with excitement over new things. He found himself thinking of her at the oddest moments, when he saw a soaring Cooper's hawk or found a hummingbird's nest with that delicate fir bark lining its cup. He'd never forget how thrilled she was when he brought her the newspaper clipping that the United States Supreme Court agreed to hear the case of *Wisconsin vs. Yoder*. With her face lit up with happiness, she kissed the clipping and declared she was never going to have to step into a school again as long as she lived. He thought it was ironic that she was so glad to be done with school. She was the smartest girl he knew.

But then there was Betsy. He'd been crazy about Betsy for as long as he could remember. Finally, she seemed to be equally as smitten with him. They kissed every chance they got: behind the barn at gatherings, when they met on the road, in the buggy, and—best of all—when he was at her house and her parents went off to bed and they found themselves alone. He thought about kissing her before he dropped off to sleep, and it filled his mind as soon as he woke up. He lived for those moments.

So why did he often feel a painful jumble of anxiety?

He rubbed his hands over his face,

exasperated. What was wrong with him? What kind of man was he?

He would have liked to have slowed things down with Betsy, but she seemed insistent to get baptized and married soon. Six months ago, he would've jumped at the chance to hear Betsy Mast say she would marry him. Now, it made his stomach twist up in a tight knot. In fact, it suddenly occurred to him that he hadn't actually *asked* Betsy to marry him. They were necking down by the pond and she started talking about how nice it would be to not have to stop but to wake up in each others' arms every morning. He must have murmured that he agreed because next thing he knew, they had a meeting set up with the bishop. He knew he had to talk to Bess before they spoke to Caleb Zook.

Billy loosened his collar. Lately it felt like it was cutting off his air supply.

❧❧

Jonah could see that Bess was hurting. She was quiet and pale and her eyes were swollen like she'd been crying. These were the moments when he longed for a wife. Bess needed a mother. He hoped she would talk to Lainey about whatever was bothering her, but Lainey was taking Simon to the hospital today for a checkup. Usually, that meant a long day.

When Billy came by early today to say that he needed to quit working at Rose Hill Farm, Jonah put two and two together and had a pretty good idea about what was troubling Bess. Last week, Lainey had tipped him off that she had seen Billy with a girl in his courting buggy a couple of times lately.

He found Bess in the barn, Boomer by her side, gathering up the dry petals and stuffing them into bags. They sounded like crackly tissue paper as she stuffed. His heart went out to her. Her head was down and her shoulders slumped. He saw a dried tear on her cheek.

"Bess, I need to tell you something."

She kept working, kept her head down.

"There's something I've discovered that you and I have in common." It

was never easy for him to say things
out of his heart, but there was something he needed to say. "When we
love someone, we love them with our
whole heart."

She put the bag down and bent
down to pat Boomer.

It's funny, he thought, that it's always
easier to talk about important matters
with our eyes turned away. He let his
cane slip to the floor, leaned his hip
against the table that held the rose
petals, and folded his arms against
his chest. "I've learned something this
summer. I've learned that I have a ten-
dency to make a person I love too important. They start filling the spot that
only God should hold in my life. I did it
with Rebecca, and when she passed,
I felt that great void for far too long.
I've done it with you, and when I found
out that Simon was your father, I felt
that void again." He chanced a look
at her. "The Lord has to keep teaching
me the same lesson. To hold on a little
more lightly to others and to trust him
in a deeper way."

He crossed one boot over the other.

"Lainey is a good example for us. She's always depended on God in just the right way." He was a better person for knowing her. Lainey had an ability to make him revise his stiff attitudes—like his attitude about Simon. Or about telling Bess the truth. It was an uncomfortable process, but she was so often right. And he had nearly lost her, that night. He had held himself so close and tight, so afraid to love again after Rebecca died. "When we left to go back to Ohio, Lainey was sorry and she missed us, but she wasn't devastated. She left us in God's care." He looked up at Bess. "And the Lord brought us back here, didn't he?" But he knew that things rarely turned out nice and neatly in this life.

Bess stood and picked up a handful of rose petals, letting them slip through her fingers back onto the table. "I don't think the Lord is going to bring Billy and me back together. He's marrying Betsy Mast."

So *that's* what had happened. Jonah put his large hand over Bess's. He wished he had better words, softer ones. "Then we can trust in God's plan for Billy and Betsy. And trust God has another plan for you. A good plan."

With that, Bess dove into his arms. They stood there for a while, with Jonah's chin resting on her head, until Boomer stood abruptly, hackles raised, and let out a huge bark. He tore outside and kept barking as he ran down the drive.

"Someone must be coming," Jonah said. "I'll go see who Boomer is scaring half to death." Before he turned to go, he stroked her cheek with the back of his hand. "Things have a way of turning out in the end."

She gave him a slight smile. "That's what Mammi used to say."

The taxi had dropped Lainey and Simon back at her cottage from the hospital. Lainey was so happy she felt as if she were floating. She made Simon a cup of his favorite tea and told him she would be back soon, that she had an errand. She hurried up the hill to Rose Hill Farm, practically bursting with happiness. She stopped to pet Boomer at the bottom of the hill and when she looked up, there was Jonah. She walked up to him, a smile wreathing her face.

"Simon's well, Jonah. He was given the all clear by the doctors! He still has to be tested every six months, but he can go back to living a normal life . . . whatever normal means for Simon Troyer."

Jonah put his arms around her waist and swung her in the air, laughing. "We can finally make plans!"

"What kind of plans?" she asked him boldly when he set her down. She needed to know.

He took in a deep breath. "Plans to marry, you and me," he said in a voice as dry as toast. "That is, if you're willing to have me."

When she didn't answer, his face grew worried. He suddenly looked so earnest and vulnerable and sincere that any doubts if he loved her evaporated, like steam from a cup of hot tea. In its place swept a feeling of assurance, of safety, of tenderness, and an

overwhelming love. The love she felt
for him was so strong it burned her
every breath.

The next moment she was in his arms
and they were kissing. She thought she
must be dreaming, but she felt the grip
of his strong arms around her, felt the
passion and warmth of his kiss. She
didn't need to hear him say the words
"I love you." She knew.

From the side door of the barn, Bess
watched her father with Lainey. She
couldn't hear what was being said,
but she could tell they were happy.
And in love, that was plain to see.
Her grandmother had spotted that
from the first time they laid eyes on
each other.

Boomer came charging back up the
hill to join Bess and collapsed by her
feet, panting heavily. When Bess saw
her father bend down to kiss Lainey,
she turned and closed the barn door.
She knew when to leave things be.
She smiled, though, as she went back

to work. Wouldn't Mammi have been pleased by this turn of events?

❦

Caleb Zook said no to Billy and Betsy's engagement. He explained gently that he felt they needed more time, especially after Betsy's very recent time spent running around. This time next year, if they still felt the same way, then he would be pleased to marry them. After Betsy went through instructions for baptism, of course.

Billy was visibly relieved. He even felt as if his shirt collar wasn't tightening up on him, like he'd been feeling for a few weeks now. He tried to encourage Betsy on the buggy ride home, but she was stunned silent.

When they got to her parents' home, she stayed in the buggy, her eyes on the back end of the horse, and calmly said, "We should elope."

There wasn't much Billy would refuse Betsy, but that was one thing he was firm about. "Oh no. We don't go against the bishop. I don't aim to start a marriage off on the wrong foot." He glanced at her. "To tell you the truth, I agree with Caleb. I always hoped to marry you, Betsy, but I imagined it in a few more years, after I turned twenty-one." He gently stroked her cheek. "We've got our whole lives ahead of us."

She kept her chin tucked to her chest. "My whole life starts now." She turned to him then and gave him a deep, searching look. "You're a very nice boy, Billy. But you're still just a boy." Then she hopped out of the buggy without a word and walked to her house.

He had the strangest feeling that she was saying one thing but trying to tell him something else entirely.

❦

The next week, Betsy Mast left again. Maggie hurried over to Rose Hill Farm to tell Bess the news. She found Bess in the backyard, taking down laundry from the clothesline just as the gray sky began to darken to twilight.

"Betsy's gone to stay with an aunt in Maryland."

"Oh," Bess said.

"An *aunt*," Maggie stressed, whispering in a low, conspiratorial voice.

"So you said."

"She's having a baby, Bess." Maggie's eyes were bright with the scandalous details.

Bess gasped. "You shouldn't be spreading tales, Maggie."

"I'm doing no such thing! I overheard her father talking to my dad. And my dad is the bishop, you know!"

Bess was so surprised that for a second she froze. "Billy's baby." *My Billy.*

Maggie buried her face in her hands. "No, Bess. *Not* Billy's. *Think!* That English boy at the Hay and Grain! He just used her and dumped her. He had no intention to marry her. That's why she came back. She was trying to trick our Billy into marrying her!"

But Bess knew better. "Billy might not have known all the details, but he was still willing, Maggie." She felt a little sorry for Billy. She even felt a surge of pity for Betsy. Life hadn't turned out the way Betsy had expected.

Maggie put her hands on her hips. "Are you trying to tell me that you're over Billy?"

"I guess I am." And oddly, Bess meant it.

She remembered how she had ached all over at the very thought of him. That soul-deep ache—it was less painful now.

14

Jonah walked up and down the sidewalk in Harrisburg, trying to get the nerve to walk into the Shear Delight Hair Salon. He had never been inside such a place—had never even noticed them before—and he felt a little terrified. He could see women of all ages seated in chairs with large plastic capes around them. Some were sitting under enormous metal globes. He walked past one more time, steeling himself, took a deep breath, and went inside.

The receptionist took one look at this tall, lanky Plain man with a black hat on and her mouth fell open. As she recovered herself she blurted out, "Here for a trim?"

"No!" Jonah answered, flustered. "No . . . I'm here to see, um, Robin and Ally." He pointed to them toward the back of the long room.

"They're with clients right now. Have a seat and I'll tell them you're here."

Jonah sat down next to an elderly woman with blue-ish colored hair. The woman kept staring at Jonah. He was accustomed to stares by the English, but he felt his cheeks grow warm. Or maybe it was the sour stink of the place. He had never smelled such toxic fumes before; they made his eyes start to water. He thought the smell of a hog farm was the worst smell on earth, but this hair salon was inching it out. He picked up a magazine, opened it, and quickly dropped it back on the table when he saw the contents in it. He crossed his legs, then uncrossed them, then rubbed his hands together, then tried to look out the window. The blue-haired woman continued to stare at him.

Finally, he heard Robin's voice ring out loudly from the back of the store.

"No way! An orthodox rabbi is here? For us?"

He turned his head toward Robin's station and rose to his feet as he saw her make her way toward him. He reached out a hand to shake hers, but her hands were covered with black mud.

She lifted her hands in the air. "Sorry. I'm doing a dye job on Mrs. Feinbaum."

He could tell she didn't recognize him, but Ally did. She had walked up behind Robin and peered over her shoulder.

"Jonah!" She elbowed Robin. "This is Lainey's boyfriend." She turned anxiously to Jonah. "Is Lainey all right?"

"She's fine," Jonah said. "I was hoping I could speak to you both. Just for a moment."

Ally and Robin exchanged a look. A woman in a chair with black mud covering her head was calling for Robin in a worried voice. "I gotta finish up Mrs. Feinbaum, then I can take a break," Robin said.

Jonah nodded and went back to sit down.

The blue-haired woman continued to stare. "You a Quaker?" she asked in a reedy voice.

"No," Jonah said. "Amish."

The woman frowned. "You don't pay taxes."

"Yes, I do," Jonah said patiently.

"You don't fight in the military."

"That's true. But we do serve. As conscientious objectors."

"Still. Not the same."

Jonah hoped the conversation could end with that.

"I don't understand how you can live in this country and reap all the benefits and not do your part."

Jonah sighed. The fumes in the salon were giving him a headache. He hoped this errand would turn out well. He was starting to think it was a terrible idea.

Just as the blue-haired woman opened her mouth to provide Jonah with another opinion, Ally and Robin approached. He leapt to his feet.

"I've only got ten minutes before I need to rinse Mrs. Feinbaum," Robin said.

Jonah glanced at the blue-haired woman, who was still glaring at him. "Could we go outside?"

Out on the sidewalk, Jonah explained that he and Lainey were planning to be married soon.

Robin frowned. "I figured as much."

"I came to invite you both to the wedding," Jonah said.

"Where's Lainey?" Ally asked. "Why didn't she come?"

"She doesn't know I'm here," Jonah said. "When you left . . . without saying goodbye, I think she felt a little hurt."

"Couldn't be helped," Robin said brusquely. "Your church service took too long. We had to go."

"Robin," Ally said in a coaxing tone. She was weakening, Jonah could see by her expression. She looked at him. "That's awful sweet of you, to come all this way."

"You are Lainey's family," he said. "Just because Lainey is choosing"— he emphasized that word—"to become Amish, it doesn't mean you won't continue to be an important part of her life. She . . . we . . . want you to be there.

At the wedding. And in her life. In our life."

"Aw," Ally said. Her face got all soft and tender. "You really love her, don't you?"

Robin rolled her eyes. "I gotta get back to Mrs. Feinbaum." She bit her lip. "We'll think about it." She put her hand on the door handle to the hair salon. "I think she's gonna wake up one day and regret this whole ridiculous phase she's going through. And then what?"

Ally waited until Robin went inside. "Don't mind her, Jonah. She's bitter because she just found out her boyfriend has been cheating on her. As soon as she gets over that, she'll be happier that Lainey has found true love."

"Then, you'll come to the wedding?" he asked.

"Oh ... I don't know about that. I guess it depends how long it will take Robin to get over things." She scrunched up her face. "I've found it's always best to wait until Robin's not riled up. Then I'll try talking to her."

She turned to go inside. "No promises. But . . . I'll try."

She pulled the door open wide so the blue-haired lady could leave. Jonah saw the lady aim for his direction and he decided now would be an excellent time to return to the bus station and wait for the bus to Stoney Ridge.

⁂

Jonah and Lainey decided to let Simon stay in the cottage after they married, with the understanding that he had to take good care of it and he had to start going to church.

Simon looked grieved and shook his fist. "Here it comes. I knew it! I *knew* it! It's blackmail!"

"We're not telling you to go to the Amish church," Jonah explained, "unless, of course, that's where God's leading you. But you have to go to some church. You have to worship God."

"That's out-and-out blackmail!"

But they held firm and he reluctantly agreed to the conditions.

As Lainey dressed for church one Sunday morning in mid-December, she realized that she no longer felt strange in Plain clothing. In fact, she would feel strange if she weren't wearing it. When she was in town last week, she noticed the types of clothing that young girls wore, even in winter: mini-skirts, low-cut tops. Six months ago she wouldn't have thought twice about how much skin showed. Now she felt embarrassed for them.

When Jonah and Bess came by to pick her up, she asked Simon—as she always did—if he would like to join them for church. He was seated at the kitchen table, drinking coffee.

He gave her the same answer he had given her for three or four months, "Now, why would I want to do that?"

If she had time to spare, she would try, always without success, to give him reasons why he should come. But today, this special day, she had no time to waste.

She hurried out to the buggy and

smiled when she saw Bess and Jonah. She squeezed Bess's hand. She was so glad they were sharing this day. Today, they were going to be baptized.

"I only wish Mammi were here," Bess said quietly.

"Knowing my mother," Jonah said, "she had a hunch this is how things would work out." He smiled at both of them. "Probably planned it all along."

For the last few weeks, Lainey and Bess had been attending a class of instruction, studying the Confession of Faith, with the ministers. Yesterday, they had one more opportunity to meet with the ministers and "turn back" if they so desired. The ministers, including the bishop, had emphasized that to them again and again: it was better not to make a vow than to make a vow and later break it. But Lainey and Bess had no doubts.

It was a solemn morning. Lainey and Bess wore new clothing they had made specially: black dresses, black prayer caps, long white organdy aprons, white organdy capes, black stockings, and stiff black oxfords. They filed in

and took their seats in the center section near the minister's bench. They
sat silently through the service, heads
bowed, in anticipation. When the time
came, the deacon left the service and
returned with a small pail of water
and a tin cup. Caleb turned to Lainey
and Bess. He reminded the applicants
that the vow they were about to make
would be made not to the ministers or
to the church but to God. He asked
them to kneel if it was still their desire to become members of the body
of Christ.

So Bess and Lainey knelt.

Caleb asked them a few simple
questions, which they answered. Then,
the deacon's wife untied the ribbons
from Lainey's cap and removed the
cap from her head. Caleb Zook laid
his hands upon her head, "Upon your
faith, which you have confessed before God and these many witnesses,
you are baptized in the name of the
Father, the Son, and the Holy Spirit,
Amen." The deacon poured water into
Caleb's hands, cupped above Lainey,

who was still kneeling, and it trickled down over her hair and face.

Then it was Bess's turn.

When the rite of baptism was completed, Caleb took the hand first of Bess, then Lainey, and said, "In the name of the Lord and the Church, we extend to you the hand of fellowship, rise up."

As they stood, the deacon's wife greeted them with a holy kiss and re-tied their prayer caps, one by one. Lainey searched for Jonah's face as she waited for Bess's prayer cap to be retied. Their eyes met and locked, and she was completely undone when she saw the tears streaming down his face.

❧❧

Jonah's heart felt pierced. He had prayed for this moment for fifteen years. To watch Bess, his daughter, bend at the knee, and then to have Lainey, his soon-to-be bride, do the same, felt like a perfect and holy moment. As if the heavens parted and he had a brief glimpse into the great and wondrous plans of God, weaving all things together for good. He would never, ever forget this day.

It was a powerful moment for a parent to watch his child join the church. He couldn't help thinking of the little girl Bess used to be. He wished she could have stayed a little girl, but she was growing up. Growing into a lovely, wise young woman.

He could hardly wait for Caleb to conclude the service and announce his and Lainey's wedding plans. They were going to be married on a Thursday, the week before Christmas, at Rose Hill Farm. He felt a growing impatience, eager for Caleb to wrap up.

Caleb wasn't usually long-winded, but today he seemed to be drawing out his sermon, a long admonishment to the congregation to be helpful to new members. Then he began to give instructions to Lainey and Bess to be faithful to the church and to the ministry. Jonah felt a little relieved when he concluded the sermon with Romans 6. Caleb kept making furtive glances toward the door. Jonah didn't think

anyone else noticed, but he was puzzled by it. It seemed as if Caleb was
going to preach forever today. Then
the other ministers offered their state-
ments of approval of Caleb's message,
but Caleb had run over so long that
they were mercifully brief. Finally, Caleb
rose to his feet and asked everyone to
kneel for prayer. Just as he finished
the prayer, Jonah thought he heard
the door squeak open, cautiously. He
opened his eyes and saw Caleb motion to someone with his hand.

All eyes turned to the door. It was
Simon. Bess let out a gasp, and Lainey
and Jonah exchanged a baffled look
as Simon made his way down the
aisle to the bishop, head held high.
Boomer trailed along behind him.
Caleb extended his hand to Simon, as
if he had been expecting him. Slowly,
Simon knelt, facing the church, facing
his family. Boomer settled down beside him as if he had found the perfect
spot for a winter's nap. Caleb read a
short message from the Bible, about
how the faithful shepherd didn't rest
until he found that one lost sheep.

And then it grew quiet.

In a quavering voice, Simon said, "I am that lost sheep. I have sinned against the Lord God. I confess to the sin of pride. I confess to the sin of drunkenness. Oh, and laziness too. I've got a nasty temper on me. I wasn't much of a husband to my Elaine." He glanced over at Lainey. "I might not be much of a father, neither." He looked up at the ceiling rafters. "And there might be a few other sins I'd like to keep private between just me and the Lord." He wiped tears off his face with the back of his sleeve. "But I want a fresh start. I'm ready to repent."

Caleb placed his hands on top of Simon's head. "After a sinner was brought to the Lord Jesus Christ to repent, he told the sinner, 'Go and sin no more.'" Caleb helped Simon rise to his feet. "This is our brother, Simon, home for good." He reminded the church members that Simon was now a member in good standing. "Geduh is geduh." *What is done and past cannot be called again.* His sins would not be spoken of. The Lord God had wiped them clean, he said. They were gone.

Caleb then announced the upcoming wedding of Jonah Riehl and Lainey O'Toole. As folks turned toward Jonah, he thought he probably looked like a fool, grinning from ear to ear. But he didn't care. This was quite a day.

"Let us sing our closing hymn," Caleb said, with one hand clasped on Simon's shoulder. With the other hand, he motioned to the Vorsinger.

As if the cue from Caleb was meant for him to set the key, Boomer let out a bark and, in a rare moment, the church rocked with happy laughter.

A week before Jonah and Lainey's wedding, on a gray midwinter day, Caleb Zook dropped by Rose Hill Farm, looking for Bess. He found her in the greenhouse where she was checking to see that young rose graftings were protected from the cold.

He walked around the greenhouse, examining the plants. Bess was surprised to see him and wondered briefly if she had done something wrong. In Ohio, the bishop didn't tend to call very often unless there was some unpleasant business to deal with. She could tell Caleb Zook had something on his mind and it was making her nervous. He slowly made his way to where Bess was working. She was wrapping plants in burlap and tying them with twine.

"So, Bess, have you thought about whether you're going to let Simon know that he's your real father?"

Bess froze. She hadn't expected *that*. She looked at him. "You told me that could be my decision."

"I still stand by that."

She went back to wrapping the roses. "Jonah is my real father."

Caleb took off his hat. "Yes, but—"

"I guess that's my answer," Bess interrupted. She surprised herself. Normally, she would never speak so forthrightly to an elder, much less interrupt one. But there was something about Caleb Zook that made her feel as if she could speak her mind to him. "Simon might be my actual father, but Jonah is my *real* father. Day in and day out, year after year. I just don't think Simon needs to know anything different." She gave him a direct look. "I have prayed long and hard about this, and for now, I would like to keep my secret."

Caleb looked at her for a long while, then put his wide-brimmed black felt hat back on his head. "Then that's how we'll leave things." He turned to go but stopped at the door and put his hand on the doorjamb. He looked back at her. "For what it's worth, I think you're right. For now. Maybe for a long, long time. Someday, though, I hope Simon will be told. It would be nice for him to know that his life has counted for something good in this world."

Jonah and Lainey's wedding day was sunny but bitter cold. Several friends came from Ohio for the event, including Mose and Sallie—now newlyweds—and Sallie's rambunctious twins, plus Levi Miller, the boy who liked Bess overly much. His head and body were finally growing to fit his ears, Bess had noticed, relieved, when she laid eyes on him yesterday. And his hair didn't stick straight up anymore. It usually looked like somebody had just held him under the water pump.

The furniture at Rose Hill Farm had been moved from the first floor to the second and the entire house had been cleaned. Tables were provided so that the meal would be served inside, but the barn would be where the wedding service would be held. The church wagon brought the wooden benches to fill the now bare floor. The church wagon provided dishes, glasses, and silverware, but one neighbor loaned their good dishes—with a pink rose pattern—for all of the tables. Other neighbors pooled their water glasses, pitchers for lemonade and coffee, cups and saucers, and small glass dishes for pickles and condiments.

Jonah and Lainey didn't have any frills, but Bess was allowed to order paper napkins engraved with the name of the bride, groom, and wedding date: JONAH AND LAINEY RIEHL, DECEMBER 16, 1971. The Eck, the special corner table, was the place for the bride, groom, and the witnesses, Bess and Simon. It was draped with a royal blue tablecloth and held a small two-tier wedding cake that Lainey had made and iced herself.

For the last few days, it seemed nearly every female member of the church had been at Rose Hill Farm. These experienced cooks, all red with heat and hurry, were preparing the meals to serve to 250 guests. The menu for the noon meal included roast duck and chicken, mashed potatoes and gravy, dressing, cold ham, coleslaw, corn, homemade bread, two kinds of jelly in cut-glass dishes, and a variety of cakes and cookies. A second meal would be served later. Smaller though, since most folks would have need to return home for choring.

That morning, Bess helped Lainey get ready upstairs. Lainey had made the dark blue dress herself. She tried to pin the white cap on, but she kept dropping pins on the floor.

"Look at me, Bess! My hands are trembling!"

Bess laughed. "It's an important day! You're entitled to be a little nervous."

She scooped up the pins from the floor and picked up a comb to brush Lainey's hair into a bun. It was growing longer now and could at least be gathered into a small knot, but curls were always escaping along the nape of her neck. Bess sighed. Those were just the kinds of curls she had always wished she had. She placed the cap gently over Lainey's head and pinned it into place.

They heard a car pull into the drive. Lainey went over to the window and gave a short gasp. Bess came up behind her. "Why, that's . . . that's Robin's car. Look! There they are! Robin and Ally!" She turned to Bess. "Did you . . . ?"

Bess shook her head and smiled. "Not me. It was Dad's idea. He went all the way to Harrisburg to invite them to come. Said they're like family to you and it wouldn't be a wedding day without them." She laughed. "Can you imagine Dad in a beauty salon?"

Lainey clapped her hands together.

"Oh Bess. I never dreamed that God would give me all of this. You. Jonah. Simon. I never thought I'd have a family of my own."

Bess sat on the bed. "I think Mammi knew. But then she claimed to know when anyone in this town so much as sneezed."

Lainey sat next to her. "You're right. I think somehow she did. She always seemed to know things—"

"—even before they happened," Bess finished.

They both laughed and stopped quickly when a knock came on the door.

"Bishop said it's time," someone said from the other side. "We're just waiting on the bride."

❧❧

Late that evening, after most folks had gone home, the young people piled into a couple of buggies and went down to Blue Lake Pond for a bonfire on the shore. The air was biting cold and the wind stung Bess's ears as she walked across the crunchy frosted shoreline to the huge blazing fire. The boys were still dressed in their Sunday best: black and white, with vests. The girls were trim and neat with crisply pressed white aprons under their dark capes. Before Bess sat down, she glanced behind the bonfire to the lake that unfolded before her, silvered by frost and moonlight.

Andy and Levi made a space for her between them. Exhausted but happy, Bess plopped down on the ground. She was surrounded by so many friends, new and old, all sitting in a great circle. It was peaceful here and she felt content.

The clouds that had been in front of the moon scudded past, and for a few minutes it was almost as bright as daylight. Bess noticed someone come up tentatively behind the circle, waiting, as if he wasn't sure he belonged. It was Billy Lapp. She had seen him once or twice at church but hadn't spoken to him since Betsy had left. He had been at the wedding service today, and she saw him sitting with Andy and other friends for the meals, but Bess was busy helping Lainey and her father.

A few people waved to Billy, but he held back and didn't join in. His eyes sought out Bess's before joining the circle. She smiled at him. Her welcome was real.

Somebody moved over to make space and Billy sat down in the casual way he always sat: legs apart, elbows on his knees. Andy Yoder began to sing and the others joined in. Their breath streamed out in white ribbons.

Bess's gaze returned to the fire. She listened to the voices in the dark, happy to know that Billy was a part of things, spending time with all of their friends around the fire. But she was even happier to realize he no longer gave her such a stomach-dropping feeling. It wasn't so long ago that being in such close proximity to Billy would have a physical effect on her. Her stomach would quiver, her cheeks would grow warm, her heart would pound, and her imagination would run away from her. Thoughts of Billy had filled her mind from the moment she woke until she fell asleep. She even imagined his face in the clouds, or in a fire such as this, or in the shimmering reflection off Blue Lake Pond. That was the way it had been for a very long time, ever since she had first met him.

Tonight, all she saw in the fire were flames and smoke and sparks. She looked up at the sky. Nowhere in the clouds did she see the handsome face of Billy Lapp.

Billy had been watching her. When he caught her eye, he pointed subtly toward the trees—a signal to meet him. Out of curiosity—or was it habit?—she slipped away to join him. They walked along the shoreline until they were out of view of the others.

Billy stopped and turned to her. He swallowed hard. "Bess, would you let me take you home afterward?"

Bess looked at him, her eyes went all around the face that she had loved so much, every line, every crease of the skin so dear to her.

If she agreed to go home with him tonight, it would be so easy. They would be back to where they had been before. In time, Betsy Mast would be forgotten.

But Bess would always wonder. What would happen if Betsy came back again? Or if she had never left? It was too much to ask. Bess didn't want to wonder and doubt and worry anymore.

"No, Billy." Her voice was gentle and polite and sincere. "But thank you anyway."

His face was surprised and sad. More sad than surprised.

He began to say something.

"Bess, I do care for you . . ." Then he stopped.

Bess waited quietly. His words drifted on the still night air.

"I never meant to . . ." He stopped again.

"It's all right, Billy," Bess said. "Really." It *was* all right. "Mammi used to tell me: 'Gut Ding will Weile haben.'" *Good things take time.* She used to think Mammi meant food—like not rushing the making of a pie crust—but now Bess realized she meant other good things too. Like love. And the mending of a broken heart.

Maybe someday, when the time was

right, Bess and Billy would find their way to each other. But maybe not. That time would be far off in the invisible future. And if there was one thing Bess had learned she couldn't see at the age of fifteen, it was ahead.

She thought she saw tears in Billy's eyes and looked away quickly. Then she walked quietly past him to go back to the fire to join her friends.

Discussion Questions

1. Conflict and reconciliation are central themes in *The Search*. Discuss the ways in which the characters come to peace with their past.

2. What kind of a woman was Bertha Riehl? As you were reading, what was your reaction to her? Did your opinion change over time?

3. As Jonah puts Bess on the bus to go to Stoney Ridge, he tells her, "Be careful because—"

   Bess teased him that each time he said goodbye to her, even as she hopped on the school bus, he would add the caution, "Be careful, because . . ." *Because . . . I won't be there to protect you. Because . . . accidents happen.*

What is Jonah really afraid of? How does he finally come to terms with that fear?

4. In one scene with her two visiting friends, Lainey defends her decision not to go to culinary school, as she had planned. "I've learned more about cooking in the last few months here than I ever could in a formal school. Here, food means more than nourishing a body. Sharing a meal nourishes a community." What did she mean by that? In what ways is the Amish relationship to food and meals different from mainstream society's?

5. Simon spent a lifetime trying to be "significant." What finally spoke to his heart? Do you think his change was permanent?

6. What kind of future do you see for Bess and Billy? Do you think they will end up together? Or do you think Bess has outgrown Billy?

7. Do you think Bess will ever tell Simon that he is her biological father? Do you want her to tell him? Why or why not?

8. What did you learn about Amish life in reading this novel?

Acknowledgments

I'd like to express my deep appreciation to my family, near and far. To my sister, Wendy, and daughter, Lindsey, and good friend, Nyna Dolby, who generously shared their insights and also read an early draft of this manuscript. A heartfelt thanks for reading this manuscript with tough and loving eyes, offering candor and guidance. As always, enormous gratitude to my agent, Joyce Hart, for being so wise, warm, and steadfast. I'm very grateful to all the people at Revell, especially my editors, Andrea Doering and Barb Barnes, who make my books so much better.

And above all, abiding gratitude goes to the Lord God, for his wisdom on matters seen and unseen.